Looking for
PRZYBYLSKI

Looking for

PRZYBYLSKI

K.C. Frederick

THE PERMANENT PRESS
Sag Harbor, NY 11963

For information, address:
    The Permanent Press
    4170 Noyac Road
    Sag Harbor, NY 11963
    www.thepermanentpress.com

Library of Congress Cataloging-in-Publication Data

Frederick, K. C. –
    Looking for Przybylski / K.C. Frederick.
        p. cm.
    ISBN 978-1-57962-273-2
        1. Self-realization—Fiction. 2. Life change events—Fiction.
    3. Detroit (Mich.)—Fiction. 4. Road fiction. I. Title.

PS3556.R3755L66 2012
813'.54—dc23   2012016406

Printed in the United States of America.

For Toni, of course.

But also for my sister Fran Clancy, in recognition of the
help she's given to all of my books,
and in memory of my brothers Tim and Mike.

CHAPTER ONE
꧁꧂

When Ziggy Czarnecki walks into Rok's funeral parlor for Eddie Figlak's wake he isn't thinking about his old nemesis Przybylski, he certainly isn't thinking about going to California; all he's hoping for is to get this unpleasant business over with as quickly as possible.

Eddie's drawn a pretty good crowd, Ziggy can see right away. But then, he always was something of a crowd-pleaser when he was alive. At a certain time of the night he was likely to launch into a long, complicated story that went in circles and lost itself, about how he could have been this or that—a doctor, a lawyer, an airline pilot: whatever was the last thing he saw on TV before his meter clicked off—and sooner or later he'd forget himself and start all over, the story becoming even more complicated the next time around. Then he'd get sad, and cry, maybe, and likely toward the end he'd start screaming about Stella, his wife, asking God what sin he'd committed that could possibly justify his being hooked up with her. Really, when he got going like that you could listen to him all night; he should have been a priest.

Ziggy's put off coming to the funeral parlor as long as he could. A lot of people like wakes, he knows, but he isn't one of them. For one thing, when you get to be his age, you can't help feeling that when you walk in everybody figures you for the preview of coming attractions. So he just signs the book at the entrance to the chapel where Eddie's laid out, puts his head down and makes a beeline through the dim voices straight for the casket. He drops to his knees at the kneeler and buries his face in his hands as if he were praying. Only then, when he's ready at last, does he look at Eddie Figlak.

Man and boy he knew Eddie for almost sixty years, through the long bad times and the sweet short (so they seem now, anyway) good times of the numbers; but when he looks at his dead friend tonight, the first thing he feels is disappointment. There he is, lying in the silk-lined casket with the plaster face of some old pope and the comfortable paunch nowhere to be seen, hands folded on his chest with a purple-beaded rosary; and he's wearing the most god-awful shit-colored double-breasted suit that makes him look like a Yugoslav just off the plane. Eddie, whatever his faults, was a sharp dresser, and when Ziggy sees that $29.95 Goodwill special he can't help thinking it's got to be Stella, who's having her last laugh, dressing him up this way; unless it's the work of old Sam Rok, the undertaker, who's charging high and buying cut-rate clothes for his customers' going-away outfits.

Ziggy's still thinking about that awful shirt his friend is wearing when he has to blink because he could swear he saw Eddie's hand move. And what was that? Who the hell could be belching like that here in Rok's parlor. His first thought is that it had to be Mike Skowron, who pops onions into his mouth the way most people eat peanuts—but isn't Mike supposed to be laid up at home with a bad back? He looks at Eddie again, keeping his eyes away from his friend's face this time. Who gets the rosary after the funeral? Of course, they'll tell you they bury it with the body, but you can't just believe that. Sam Rok probably strips . . . There, out of the corner of his eye, he sees it once more and he almost jumps from the kneeler: it's Eddie's head that moves this time, it actually jerks up an inch or so from the silk pillow where it's been resting. Jesus Christ. Ziggy looks away, and for a couple of seconds he's embarrassed for his friend, though nobody else in the room seems to have noticed. Then he realizes what he's just told himself: that Eddie's corpse has actually moved.

He closes his eyes and hides his face in his hands. This time he really is praying: God—whoever—let me be dreaming. All at once he realizes that he's scared shitless. Maybe he's going crazy; if he can only get the hell out of here quietly before anyone notices that he's flipped. At the moment, though, he doesn't trust his knees to hold him up and he takes a deep breath, inhaling the thick sweet smell of the lilies, praying that when he looks again he'll find out he only needs a new pair of glasses.

But after a couple of seconds it's clear that peace isn't going to come to Ziggy just with the closing of his eyes, because even in the darkness he's becoming aware of the commotion going on around him. The background murmur of Rok's parlor has suddenly quieted and Ziggy feels like a fisherman who just knows, having turned his back in order to dig out a new worm from the bait can, that the lake has frozen solid around him, July or no July. There's a sudden total silence, as if a giant plug has been yanked out of the room's floor, then a low gasp, excited voices, a long moan and something that sounds like the beginning of a religious song in Polish. "*O Boze*"—Oh, God, a woman shrieks and Ziggy knows now that nothing can make him open his eyes. Whatever's going on he wants no part of, and he's trying to recall the exact layout of the chapel so that he can ease his way out of here with his eyes still shut; when suddenly he hears another belch, loud as cannon-fire, and he knows it can only be coming from the casket. Before he realizes it he's looking at Eddie: there he is, dead pope's face and all, eyelids shut tight, hands crossed on the chest of his double-breasted Yugoslav suit, and he's sitting upright in the casket.

Ziggy, drenched with sweat, hears metal chairs tumbling in the background as a strange unpleasant smell reaches him and suddenly, with a quickness he thought his sixty-five-year-old body had forgotten decades ago, he's on his feet—shouldering his way past white-faced women who are holding on to chairs as if they're walkers, openmouthed men hurriedly crossing themselves, dashing past the new monsignor who looks like an altar boy; and with all the grace of a bowling ball clattering down the stairs, he's soon just outside the door of Rok's funeral home, looking into the cold wet street, his breath frosting on the damp air, and he's hearing the distant comforting sound of a siren on its way to something perfectly normal, like a murder. Behind him people are shouting and he recognizes the voice of Eddie's ancient mother wailing, "It's a sign from God."

As the thin aluminum storm door closes behind him, Ziggy stands there in the street for a few seconds, his head filled with the excited cries of the people in that room. He wishes God would just stick to his own business and worry about heaven—things are spooky enough in Detroit these days without signs from the Almighty dropped without warning into Polack funeral parlors. What he needs just now isn't any sign from heaven; he needs a stiff drink, something to stop the tremors that make his jumpy hands feel as if they aren't connected to the rest of him; and the sudden hard pounding of his heart, the breath snatched away from him, like what you'd feel seconds after a close call on the highway.

Not that, at this distance from what caused it, that rush of his blood is totally unpleasant, any more than the feeling that you just survived some awful danger—he's alive and alert, he can probably see more acutely than normal. But the feeling sure as hell needs a drink to go along with it.

The crowd at Connie's is still fairly small, but Ziggy knows that throughout the evening people will be coming in from Rok's parlor talking about Eddie Figlak. Some of them will keep repeating the scientific explanation he's heard a dozen times before he finally left the place, about gases trapped in the body that the embalmer hadn't been able to get out. "It's worse with juicers like Eddie," someone will be sure to say; and others will shake their heads muttering "I don't know, I don't know," their eyes gone glassy—those are the ones who'll be headed for the confessionals like a thrashing school of smelt on its annual spawning run as soon as St. Connie's opens tomorrow. And, before a day has passed, the number of those who'll claim to have seen Eddie Figlak's last performance will add up to a fair-sized Saturday afternoon crowd at Tiger Stadium.

Ziggy's been lucky to get his drink before they've really started coming in, and he's been able to belt down the lovely rasping shot that makes his eyes sting without having been dragged into a conversation. "Ah," he says to himself alone, feeling the alcohol rush to distant parts of his body. He's comfortable for the first time all day. He holds the glass with the beer chaser and lets himself sink into the dark brown cave of Connie's with its heavy airless smell, its rows of shiny bottles arranged in front of the long mirror, its beer ads dangling above the bar: huge clocks on plastic chains, revolving disks and illuminated labels. He brings the beer to his lips, takes a sip and puts it back on the cool bar, never letting go of the glass.

"Christ, that Sophie was something . . ." It's little Jimmie Bork talking to Walter Romanski, a pair of old guys like himself. "Every time, like when it was summer and you could see those arms—I never saw such arms. Some women have tits . . . Holy Jesus, she could punch her way through that wall, I swear—I'd bet on it."

"I could never figure how a skinny guy like Gabby married her."

"She wasn't always that big, they say."

"She used to really throw him down the stairs?"

"Once in a while, yeah." Jimmie's quiet for a few seconds. "Christ, I think about those arms. She'd be sitting right here, where you're sitting. And those arms: each one as big as a ham—only red, because she'd get sunburned."

"It's hard to believe she's gone."

"Yeah. And Gabby too."

Ziggy nurses his beer. This is what you have to expect all night, he knows. That's what he hates about wakes and funerals: not just the caskets and the black, the priest droning and the smell of incense, the shovelsful of dirt; but this: the way everybody's going to be talking about the old times, all night long, tomorrow, the next few days.

"That Gabby was a great guy . . ." And there'll be that too. Gabby Sendlik, who never did a day's work in his life, who mooched drinks and lived off his 230-pound wife Sophie, the numbers runner, who even occasionally stole money from his own kids—hell, they used to say he'd sell both of them for a bottle of Seagram's—now he's being remembered as a great guy. Gabby was a smart guy, maybe: he knew a deal when he had one. But a great guy?

Ziggy allows himself a grunt as he feels the old ache in the left shoulder—all his aches and pains: the knee, the shoulder, the ear—seem to collect on the left side. He tries to concentrate. Really, he wants to try to remember what it looked like when Eddie Figlak popped up in his casket—it happened so fast that it rushed by him—and the conversation is distracting.

"Remember when old Gabby climbed the telephone pole and cut the wires so the cops wouldn't hear the number come in?"

"He was a hell of a guy."

Well, that's true enough: you have to give Gabby credit for that. The one time he did something out of the ordinary was the day of the raid when he cut those wires. Ziggy still remembers the befuddled look on the lieutenant's face when his flunky with the buck teeth was standing before him in Ziggy's front hall, holding the phone as if it were a used rubber john, saying. "I'm getting nothing. It's dead." The cops didn't need any evidence that might come over the phone, there was plenty in the house. Still, it was good to see them frustrated.

Ziggy laughs to himself. He rewarded Gabby then, gave him a bottle of booze and a turkey, invited him out to the Fourth of July stag party on the island where Gabby got drunk and fell asleep in the sun and got burned like a lobster. Ziggy holds the glass to his mouth, his lips touching the thin foamy head of the lukewarm beer; and he remembers the island: the sun beating down on the blue-green water, the warm smell of the creosoted wood on the dock, the drone of the powerboats on the St. Clair river, Ace Stepaniak crunching up the gravel drive in his white battleship of a Continental, the trunk full of fireworks bought in Toledo, the green willows with the long hanging branches that touched the quiet water of the canal.

He puts the glass down. Remember Rule Number One. When he lost it all in the fifties and, after a rough decade or so, he decided he'd just as soon keep on breathing anyway, he established Rule Number One: don't ever look back. He turns when a noise from the door signals the entrance of about a half-dozen people just as Jimmie and Walter move off to the pool table.

Come to think of it, there never was a Rule Number Two.

It's stupid, he knows, to think you can keep people out of Connie's—there's no way he can have the place to himself tonight, no matter how much he might want it. Hell, he couldn't even have managed that in the old days when he owned Connie's. But there he goes, breaking the rule again. All because of Eddie Figlak.

And it looks like he's going to have to continue to pay too. The crowd that's just come in, Rabbit Baranek and his gang of beer-drunks, is only a couple of years out of St. Connie's High, the kind that like to call him "old-timer." (Not that he isn't, but you can mean a lot of different things with that expression.) Ziggy signals Turk, the bartender, for another quick one. Turk doesn't go back as far as he does, but at least he isn't a young punk and Ziggy holds him there for a minute like a hostage, to make sure Rabbit and his twerps keep their distance. Turk doesn't seem to mind.

"Was it like they said, Ziggy? I mean, did Eddie Figlak really sit up in the casket?"

"Yeah." He hopes that's enough on the subject.

Turk laughs. "That's more than he could have done here a lot of nights. What's Rok doing? Embalming them with a do-it-yourself kit?"

"Sam Rok's a cheap bastard. He'll cut any corner he can find."

"I guess that's one thing you can say about old Przybylski," Turk sighs. "He knew how to put them away in style."

"Przybylski wasn't that great." Ziggy hasn't thought for a long time about the man who used to be the parish's other undertaker and that's all right as far as he's concerned. He remembers the large smooth face, like wax fruit, the gold-rimmed glasses, thin blond hair, mustache and soft purring voice. "I never liked that guy," Ziggy says, though this is hardly news. "Remember the way he used to sit there and sip Vernors—did anyone ever see him drink real stuff? He'd sit there as if he was watching everybody and waiting for us all to kick off, like he was mentally taking measurements for our caskets."

Turk frowns and looks toward the group that's just taken a table. "What I heard, he sure was measuring yours—" The bartender stops all at once as if he's just slapped himself and his eyes are suddenly restless. "Hey, I've got to run now," he says, flicking his head toward the TV, where President Ford is shown coming down the steps of Air Force One. "Some guy wants me to switch channels."

For a moment as Turk moves toward the TV, Ziggy doesn't know why he feels confused and irritated. Something's up, but what? When he realizes he hasn't downed his second shot he makes up for it in a hurry. The whiskey steadies him: it's like when your car shimmies at a certain speed and you can either slow down or go faster to keep the front end from jolting. With the shot he's going faster and his head is now clear, he knows what it is that's focused his attention. It's Turk's comment about Przybylski. Was Turk really saying what he seemed to be saying? That the silky undertaker who left the city ten years ago, his caskets full of money, that he had something to do with the police bust back in '52 that was the start of the finish of the numbers house and transformed Ziggy from the numbers kingpin to just another Polack? The shimmy is gone and the car is flying along the highway, tires buzzing and wind rushing in through the vents: for the first time in a long while Ziggy lets the car speed on, he's allowing himself to be curious, there's something out there that he really wants to find out.

He swallows some beer. He always had his suspicions about Przybylski: from the time he and the undertaker donated money for the electronic scoreboard in the St. Connie's gym and he was told that Przybylski resented having his name on the device alongside a "cheap crook's." "Do you think I like to see my name alongside some bodysnatcher's?" Ziggy answered anyone who told him that. But though it was true that Przybylski looked sneaky enough for anything, Ziggy never had any real proof that he'd been involved in the bust; and the fact is, there were a lot of people by then who might have wanted to bring him down. But does Turk know something definite? And how can he know?

Ziggy looks up from the bar and sees his reflection in the mirror: the white, close-cropped hair, the bespectacled pop-eyes and the sagging face, the figure, even seated, somehow smaller than he expected it to be—it's always a surprise at first, and makes him feel the way he did when he came back into a room where he'd been watching TV and Maggie had switched the channel: for a moment he'd wonder why the cop show had so many wisecracks until he realized he was watching a comedy; once he made the adjustment, everything was clear.

Looking away from the mirror, he lifts the beer glass and takes another sip. He made the adjustment long ago: the thing to do now is to lift his foot from the pedal and slow that engine down. What the hell does it matter after all, what Przybylski did or didn't do twenty years ago? Ziggy has a furnace that's been acting up, it's always running out of water, and he has to look into that. The winter is already over, thank God, but he has to get the thing checked out before the next season of cold weather, and that's going to be a little harder to manage now that he isn't even getting those paychecks from the city—maybe somebody he knows has a brother-in-law who can do the job cheap. Still, just as he's bringing himself back to everyday problems, the gas pedal goes down again and the engine roars: was it that bastard Przybylski after all? He raps the bar with his fingers: Rule Number One.

He's actually glad when Father Bruno comes in. Paunchy and genial, a little bit of everybody's uncle as he was in the old days, the priest makes his way through the greetings and takes a seat beside Ziggy at the bar. It isn't the first time Ziggy's noticed the priest's resemblance to Frenchy, a cop he used to pay off back when the numbers were going good. Old Frenchy killed himself and his girlfriend, finally, almost ten years ago—some kind of triangle, as Ziggy remembers. Somebody was cheating on somebody. The usual.

"And how are you?" The priest wheezes between sentences. "You're looking good. Just a ginger ale for me, Turk."

"So are you, Father." Actually, when he sat down, he seemed to have sunk into himself like a collapsing black tent. He had large fleshy pouches under his eyes and his face had thickened so that it looked as if it were meant to be seen on a wide screen. "The suburbs seem to be treating you well. Did you come in to see Eddie?"

"I did. He wasn't laid out, though. I heard about the problem."

Ziggy's feeling more comfortable now. The priest's familiar bulk is like his furnace: it keeps things in the present. "How do you find the old neighborhood?" he asks Father Bruno.

He half-lifts himself when he answers. "It's changed," he sighs. "Nobody can deny that. And so many people our age are dying . . ."

Ziggy doesn't need this kind of gloomy talk. "Did you see the new monsignor? He looks like an altar boy."

Father Bruno shakes his head. "The church has had its problems," he wheezes, "with vocations." He pauses for a moment as if he's heard for the first time what Ziggy has said and he laughs suddenly. "Maybe recruiting altar boys wouldn't be such a bad idea . . ." His words trail off and all at once he looks like a drunk who's wondering how he's managed to get to the place where he finds himself. Ziggy's sure the priest isn't planning to stay long. "Say," Father Bruno says at last, his eyes alert once more, "you'll never guess who I heard from last Christmas."

Ziggy looks at him inquiringly.

"Father Teddy, Teddy Krawek. I got a card and the poor guy sounded pretty lonely."

"How long has it been?" Ziggy asked, not particularly interested.

"It's fifteen years since he left the priesthood."

Ziggy says nothing.

"Teddy's in California now. God knows what he's doing— he doesn't say in the card. He gave me an address and he sounded like he was interested in getting in touch with people from the old days."

Ziggy shakes his head. "How do you figure that? Leaving the priesthood." Ziggy figures it means Teddy is pretty dumb to have given up a pretty cushy situation.

"Oh, we priests know all about spiritual problems," Father Bruno says. Looking at his beefy face, you can hardly bring yourself to accuse him of anything spiritual, unless you could think of power steering that way. "Well, I can give you his address," the priest says, reaching into his black jacket and extracting a gold pen.

"I don't know," Ziggy waves it away. No, why try to bring back the past? "Hey," he gets up. "Excuse me for a minute, padre."

He leaves the priest abruptly, as though he's just heard the unsettling growl of a Doberman. Christ, something is still bothering him as he makes his way down the steps to the men's room in the basement. The pleasantly comfortable stench, a mixture of sweet disinfectant soap and vague acrid odors that have accumulated over a half-century, the faded octagonal tiles on the ancient floor that somehow give the cramped room the look of a hidden recess in the church across the street—all these familiar details, he probably hoped as he'd bolted from the priest, would help to keep his mind free of some shapeless, bothersome concern that's been flitting on the edges of his consciousness. It even occurs to him that, since the men's room is in the basement, it ought to remind him of problems he can handle, like the furnace. Only it doesn't. He's thinking about Przybylski and he knows it.

He's alone in the men's room. It's cool here. The sounds from the bar come to him hollow and distant. Water glistens on the pipes, he reads the name of the plumbing company, long since gone out of business, on the porcelain tank. After the raid everybody was busted and most of them had to do time. Ziggy was lucky to have had the Irishman for a lawyer—he kept him out of prison; but then one thing after another happened—the booze, the IRS, the loss of his liquor license—and his days as a big-time numbers man were over as surely as if he'd gone to Jackson with Big Al and J.J. If he'd have known in his forties what the next twenty years would be like—working at two-bit jobs for the city, battling the bottle, driving a nine-year-old Fairlane that probably needed a valve job, and watching the neighborhood and the whole goddamned city deteriorate around him—he probably would have said there was no way he could deal with it; but when he came out of the fog some years back, he decided that he'd played his hand and got beat and that was that. There was no use crying over spilt milk.

He smells the sweet soap. But, Jesus, he wants to know before they stick him in the casket and shovel him under, he wants to know: did that bastard Przybylski really pull something like that? He wants to know and, damn it, he's going to find out. As he climbs the stairs to the bar he feels better for having come to that realization. After all, you itch, you scratch.

Where's Przybylski now? he wonders. Somewhere out in California is all he knows.

At the top of the stairs with his hand on the metal rail, he catches Turk by the cigarette machine and asks him for a match. "Say," Ziggy says, "you canceling your order with Sam Rok yet?"

"Me, I'm getting cremated."

"All these undertakers are bloodsuckers." Ziggy feels himself groping in the dark, his hands touching the reassuring surface of a wall as he moves toward some unknown place. He can see that Turk wants to get away, but he can't just come out and ask him what he wants to know—still, he has to get there quick. "Like that asshole Przybylski. He used to lay them out in one suit and bury them in another—that's what I heard." He doesn't really know if this is true, but it sounds good. "You knew," he throws in casually, his hands leaving the wall now, "that in the old days he was in cahoots with the cops? You knew that, didn't you?" In the background they hear the click of balls on the pool table.

Turk hesitates a moment, looking at Ziggy the whole time; then he nods.

"Ah, that's old stuff," Ziggy says, exhaling. "Who told you about it?"

"Allie," he answers, looking away. "Just before he died."

"Sure," Ziggy snorts, "I figured. Thanks." He gives him back the book of matches and starts for the bar. So Allie was in on it too. Of course, that made sense, you don't have to search for reasons. At one time or another Ziggy has mentally put the finger on just about everybody. Except that this is different, this time it isn't a guess. It's true, then, what Przybylski did, and not just one more idea he's had his hunches about. Christ! For the first time tonight Ziggy is really angry. So many times he wanted to punch out that big, still face of the undertaker and he didn't have any good reason; and now, when he has a reason at last—but Przybylski was smarter than the rest of the Polacks, he saw what was coming and when he pulled out of the neighborhood in the sixties it was already going to hell in a handbasket with the rest of the city; and even as he left he probably knew that in ten years it would be shabbier still, with everyone under fifty in suburbs like Warren, the old frame houses now occupied by blacks, run down, with windows punched out and porches sagging, or—often you couldn't tell the difference—vacant, then torn down finally if you were lucky so that you weren't living next door to a potential bonfire. Now the neighborhood is full of empty spaces like the gap-toothed mouths of a lot of the old-timers who still live here and it's hardly fit for living, and Yugoslavs, wild animals whose women fight in the middle of Chene Street, are the only whites who are still moving in.

Ziggy stands there a minute. Someone has played a record on the jukebox—"Detroit City." The hillbilly crooner is howling his familiar complaint while the guitar twangs in the background and, strangely, it seems as if, through the dim haze of cigarette smoke, everything in Connie's is shining. Ziggy feels—what? It isn't just anger, he realizes: his heart is beating strongly, his blood pounding—he's excited, he's hungry to do things. The motor is racing again.

Damn it, like the old days. Yeah, he feels he has something to do.

Father Bruno's glass is empty and Ziggy can see that the big priest is ready to get up and leave. Obviously he's paid all the dues to the old neighborhood he's felt were necessary and he's eager to get into his Toronado and wheel down the expressway to Warren where, safe and comfy in his modern rectory, he'll have plenty of time for a late night snack.

"Another, padre?"

"No, thanks." Father Bruno is beginning to lift himself— it's a little like one of those zeppelin launches from before the war that Ziggy has seen on old newsreels. But this zeppelin never gets off the ground. Ziggy sees himself laying a hand on the priest's white wrist, and when he's made contact he looks directly into Father Bruno's pale blue and suddenly confused eyes.

"Another?" Ziggy suggests again in a voice with a certain amount of weight behind it. He remembers the times when not only Father Bruno but his boss Monsignor Baran used to come to him asking favors. "You'll have just one more," he says. It isn't a question.

He sees the large black zeppelin sink back onto the barstool. The priest's heavy-lidded eyes have glazed over with the old look of someone who's accustomed to taking orders and Ziggy feels good. He removes his hand from Father Bruno's wrist, knowing he has him now for a while anyway. He isn't certain how long he can hold him, though—in fact he isn't even sure exactly what he wants from the priest; but he's following his instincts and he's determined not to lose this opportunity to get whatever help he can on the subject that's been occupying his attention.

"Ever hear from Przybylski, Father?" he asks after he's allowed him to sip his ginger ale.

Father Bruno shakes his head. "No," he laughs. "Smart man, to get out when he could." He glances up at the clock above the bar. Ziggy wonders whether he remembers it's ten minutes fast.

"Where'd he go? Do you know?"

The priest shrugs. "Somewhere in California. Los Angeles, I think. Yes, somewhere in the Los Angeles area, I heard."

Ziggy has downed his third shot and his head isn't as clear as it might be. All at once, as if he's turned a corner and bumped into himself, he wonders what the hell difference it would make if he did manage to find out where Przybylski lived. Is he planning to send him anonymous threats?

Come to think of it, that's not such a bad idea. Przybylski. Ziggy pronounces the name under his breath and the syllables seem to slither along the floor, over spilled potato chips, around table legs, past the bright bulky shape of the jukebox, under the pool table and toward the steps that lead down to the men's room. Ziggy pulls himself erect. More than ever, he's sure the priest has something he can use, something that might help him.

He can see, though, that Father Bruno is getting antsy, he wants to slip away from here. He's downed his ginger ale and now he faces Ziggy impatiently. But Ziggy's determined to keep him here a few more minutes.

"Think Teddy's in touch with Przybylski?" he asks.

The big priest laughs. "Sometimes I wonder if Teddy's in touch with himself." His eyes go blank for a moment, then he smiles. "No, on second thought I think it's likely he is in touch with himself." He winks at Ziggy to make sure he catches the reference to "touching yourself," the formula they use in the confessional for masturbation.

"I hope he's got something," Ziggy says, just to kill time. What's the thought shaping itself on the edge of his mind, like a drop of water gradually getting bigger? He hears himself saying, "My son Charlie's in California, you know."

"The dentist? I didn't know that. When did he go?"

"Four years ago. Royal Oak wasn't good enough for him."

The priest looks sad. "Seems like everybody from Detroit's winding up in California. Say, maybe he could get in touch with Teddy."

"You kidding? That one's another Przybylski. Once he left this neighborhood he never came back."

"Where is he?" the priest asks abstractly.

"Burbank. Where the Johnny Carson show comes from. Do you know if that's anywhere near where Teddy is?"

"Geez, I don't know," Father Bruno says. "I've never been out there." And all at once Ziggy sees that the priest is old, that for all his fat and jolly look there's a kind of paleness about him, as though he's been dusted with flour; the skin around his eyes is dry and pinched like a crumpled paper bag and he winces a little when he moves. This is the same priest who, at the stag parties on the island, dressed in his black trousers and sleeveless undershirt, would lift the tree trunk that the strongest numbers men couldn't budge. Sweat pouring down his face, a beer bottle in his hand, he'd acknowledge the congratulations with a little joke about washing his hands in holy water before he'd attempted the feat.

"I'm glad Charlie's doing well," the priest says quietly. He picks up his glass and seems surprised to find it empty.

"Who do you think put him through about a hundred years of school?" Ziggy says, suddenly angry again, though he's not sure what he's angry about. "And what does he do? Pretends he isn't even a Polack. Him and that Gloria of his. She's the one that convinced him to move . . ."

The priest looks at him, without reacting. He's already lost to Ziggy and will be gone in a few minutes at the most. But like a prisoner who knows he's being visited by the only person he knows in the outside world, Ziggy's determined to hold him as long as he can.

"What did you say Teddy's address was?"

"Oh, sure." Father Bruno snaps out of his daydream. "Here, let me see."

He pulls out a little black address book and the gold pen that Ziggy's seen before, a gift from his parishioners, no doubt. The priesthood is the game to get into, all right. Except for the sex thing, they have it made. And the sex can always be arranged. Ziggy knows of enough cases like Father Andy from St. Casimir's. No, he could never understand why, once you got into it and had been there for a while like Teddy, you'd ever want to leave.

"Here it is: 605 Oceanside Lane, Venice, California 90291. It'll do him a lot of good to hear from some of the old gang."

Ziggy takes the sheet with the address. He makes a note to play 605 in the lottery. "Oceanside Lane. Sounds pretty nice."

"I hope for his sake it is. Like I said, I've never been out there. Two weeks a year in Florida is the best I can manage."

"They say Florida's changed a lot," Ziggy says.

"Oh, yeah, it has. It's all condominiums now."

"That's too bad," he answers distractedly. He's bored with Father Bruno now and is glad to see that the priest is slowly rising from his seat.

"It's been too long," Father Bruno wheezes, "too long. We'll have to get together again sometime soon. Under pleasanter circumstances. I'm sure Teddy would be glad to hear from you."

Ziggy's grateful when he's gone at last. The priest had come to be a distraction and he wants to keep his attention on this feeling he has, that he's on the verge of doing something—though he doesn't know yet what it is that he's going to do. The buzz of talk in the bar is like the noise from some unseen machine that's causing everything to vibrate in front of him, as though the things on the bar itself—glasses, bottles, ashtray and cigarette pack—have begun to slide crazily for the edges while Ziggy has to try, with the only two hands he has, to keep them from going over the side. Because in his mind everything is sliding: California, Przybylski, Father Teddy, Florida, Father Bruno, Charlie, California . . . He has to keep reaching for these objects, has to try to put them in their proper places.

Somebody has played the "Helen Polka" on the jukebox. There must always have been a record of the "Helen Polka" in Connie's jukebox, whether the bartender was Turk or Fajka or Boom-Boom. The clarinets tootle, the accordion sighs and the drummer bangs. Przybylski would be in that corner leaning over his glass of Vernors, smiling but showing no teeth. He seemed to be able to drink without opening his mouth.

Ziggy looks at the Schlitz ad, a sailboat leaning almost on its side. *Florida.* Palm trees. There were dog tracks and jai alai, grown men in white suits, Panama hats. The DC-3. It's probably changed a lot, as Father Bruno had said. All condominiums. He'd been one of the first to come to the stag parties and one of the last to leave—he knew how to enjoy himself in those days. Not like Father Teddy, who'd sit on the sidelines and smile a bashful smile. What the hell could have caused him to leave the priesthood? Was it a woman, maybe? A man?

Suddenly he sees Eddie Figlak sit up in the casket and he's chilled to the bone. Christ, that wasn't Eddie, that solemn old man with the dusty clay-colored face and no beer belly. Ziggy grabs his glass and swallows what beer is left. California— that's where Przybylski has run to. The numbers went down the tube, the place on the island is gone, all those years working for the city in the job the monsignor got him— Christ, that fucking bastard of a Przybylski had no reason to do whatever he did to try to cut the numbers down. After all, they didn't poach on his territory, nobody was writing up tickets for stiffs. The goddamned fucking bastard Przybylski.

"You Polacks are too easy. You should do like the big boys: you should use a little muscle when somebody crosses you."

"Hell, no, you play rough, I figure the rough stuff can come right back at you sooner or later."

He met Little Mickey Fingers once on a boat off Miami. "You ever get into a little trouble, call on us. We can handle it for you." The big white boat was rocking in the water, there was music, booze and broads. Even as he nodded back at Mickey, Ziggy knew he wasn't ever going to push that button because once you let those gorillas work for you, pretty soon you found yourself working for them. Full time.

"I mean it," Mickey had said, touching Ziggy's jacket. "Any time. Give us a call."

Listen, Mickey, I do have a little problem. There's this undertaker.

Hey, sure. Give the details to Jimbo there.

Where did Mickey Fingers wind up? Was it Lake Erie or Lake Huron? And he needed a hell of a lot more than a life jacket.

"Hi, buddy, how you doing?" It's Stan Kowal. He must be forty and he's still living with his mother. Somebody said he's working again, driving a laundry truck.

"I'm OK, I'm OK."

"They say you were there when Eddie Figlak exploded in the casket."

Ziggy looks at Stan's horseface. He's all set for a good laugh. "Eddie Figlak did not explode," Ziggy says patiently. "It's all scientific. It was the gases that built up." He stabs at the bar for emphasis and just barely catches the edge.

"Well, explanations, gas leaks, whatever . . . ." Stan's disappointed, you can see.

"People can be so dumb sometimes," Ziggy rasps. "It's all scientific."

Stan looks away. "Christ, I wish I'd have seen it anyway. Did his . . . Did he really have a hard-on like they say?"

Ziggy tries to ignore the question. He feels something in his hand and unfolds the paper: "Teddy K., 605 Oceanside Lane, Venice CA 90291." He's going to play those numbers.

"Did he?'

Ziggy waves it away.

"Maybe he was in heaven already," Stan giggles. "Jesus, if that's what it's like there I'm going to confession tomorrow."

Ziggy gets up and stands there a second in order to get his bearings.

"Hey, where you going?" Stan calls. "The confessionals don't open till tomorrow."

Though he answers too quietly for anyone to hear him Ziggy knows at last what he's going to do. "I'm going to California," he says under his breath.

CHAPTER TWO

A̲ll through the following week Ziggy experiences flashbacks from that night: the shock of seeing his dead friend's face turned into the solemn, monumental visage of a medieval pope, the horror of Eddie's sudden popping up in the casket, the breathless hush that fell over Rok's parlor all at once, the air sucked out of the room for a long moment, followed by the quick shuffle of feet and clang of colliding chairs, people bumping into each other as they struggled to get up, to get away, to get out of there as fast as they could—the gasps and white faces, the panic everybody felt.

Judging from the shock so many of the mourners carried with them into Connie's, a stranger might have thought a UFO had appeared out of nowhere and hovered over the casket, thrumming like some giant eyeless insect, one light blinking ominously while the monsignor waved a crucifix in its general direction for a couple of seconds before fleeing in terror. It was at Connie's, amid the manic roar of people desperate to believe that the dead stayed dead, that Turk told him about Przybylski; and even now he remembers the way that bit of news hit him, turning the familiar scene into something strange, so that even the sight of big Father Bruno wheezing as he set his Vernors down on the bar was somehow touched by the uncanny.

He remembers the smell of the men's room in the basement where he'd fled to get some privacy and peace. Only it wasn't peace he found, was it? Because before that night was over something had got hold of him, like the cold, bony hands of a movie ghoul around his neck, the sudden, surprising conviction that he was going to California and see Przybylski.

Christ, what had he been drinking?

It's like the kind of stories the nuns used to tell: a colossal ray of light from heaven knocks the Christian-persecuting Saul off his horse and blinds him, but even before he hits the ground he's changed completely, he's already on his way to becoming the person who'd later be revered as St. Paul. Well, Ziggy lives in the real world. He isn't St. Paul, and he isn't Saul either.

He remembers, though, that there in the basement of the bar as he breathed in the familiar smells of Connie's men's room, the idea of traveling across the continent all the way to California and tracking down the sleazy undertaker had given him a charge, no doubt about it. But a charge is a charge, isn't it? A charge comes and it goes. Except that this one seems to have legs and, days later, Ziggy still can't completely shake it off, for all he recognizes that he's a citizen of the real world.

Here he is, walking down Joseph Campau on his way back to the beat-up Fairlane with a couple of pounds of Richie Zielinski's best kielbasa, for which he'd driven into Hamtramck, since Richie's prices are worth the drive. The streets around him are dingy—hell, Hamtramck didn't used to be dingy, but so much has turned to shit since the good times: nobody cleans the streets anymore, people are scared, there are iron grates on the storefronts and nowadays everybody makes sure they're inside by nightfall, just like in the old vampire movies. God's punishment, his mother would say if she were alive. But punishment for what? She firmly believed the Second World War was caused by women wearing slacks.

So here Ziggy is, trudging through what the world has come to, an old Polack who's come to Hamtramck to save a couple of pennies on kielbasa, something he does every week, something he's likely to be doing for as long as he's able to. Not exactly the way he pictured it when he was on top. On the other hand, if you consider the alternative—and who at his age doesn't?—it isn't all that bad. He's been through some pretty rough times and come out alive, after all, and there are worse fates than driving to Hamtramck every week to get some good kielbasa.

Still, he can't deny feeling that charge. Was what Turk told him really true? He'd sure like to know.

It's your life, after all, your one shot. You only get one chance to live it and, Jesus, a whole lot of it you can't fathom at all; but if you do get a chance to understand a little better some part of it, especially something important that changed your life, why wouldn't you want to find out what really happened? That isn't asking too much, is it? It isn't as if he's trying to change history, as if he's begging God to give him back everything he's lost. No, he just wants to know certain things. What's wrong with that? Something's stirring in him, for sure. Here on the dingy streets of Hamtramck the thought of smooth Przybylski living out there among the palm trees is bothering him, he has to admit, it's a hair across his ass. He can see Przybylski with that thin smile of his. In California he'd be wearing sunglasses, making him look even more sinister.

It's not as if I want to punch him out, Ziggy thinks. I just want to ask him a question.

He feels his stomach drop. Here on the street, with the smell of kielbasa wafting up from the shopping bag, it's as if in the time it takes him to cover a stride, he's experienced the full mysterious arc of his life, taking him from that desperate skinny young guy he'd been—with two kids and another on the way—wondering how he was going to be able to support his growing family making Chrysler Airflows until a lucky break got him into the numbers, changing everything, carrying him to the flush years during the war and just after when he had the bar and the cottage and the building on Medbury, all the way to that day in '52 when the cops cracked down on the Polacks; though when it happened nobody guessed at its full impact, and by nightfall of that day they all thought they'd dodged a bullet.

That was the funny thing: the slide was already beginning even as he and Big Al were in Connie's celebrating their release from a few hours in jail and swapping their lawyers' rosy predictions about how things would turn out, already sliding toward his lawyer's fateful decision to separate Ziggy's trial from that of the others, who were eventually sent up the river by a judge who wanted to set an example, leaving Ziggy free but baffled and guilty, drifting into booze and the hard years after that, leading all the way to the present, where he's just another Polack shopping for kielbasa. He was on top maybe a dozen years; he's been on the bottom now for, what, two dozen? Who could have predicted it? Not his old man, who didn't try to hide his disapproval when Ziggy quit the factory for the numbers, never really accepting his son's success; not his mother who attributed all worldly fortune to God's doings—hell, neither of them gave Ziggy any credit; though his father, if he were still alive, would certainly have pinned the blame for his fall on the son who wasn't smart enough to stick with a good thing and spend the rest of his life making Chryslers.

Well, as the nuns used to say, only God knows. Though it's hard to believe even God could have foreseen that particular turn of events.

The smell of kielbasa is replaced by the gassy fetor of exhaust from passing cars. Who'd have predicted it for Detroit, either? During the war when all the auto plants ran three shifts making bombers and jeeps and all kinds of weapons, and you'd sometimes have to wait and wait at the railroad crossing while brand new tanks on flat cars lumbered by, squat, menacing, prehistoric, shaking the earth as they passed, their numbers endless, who could have thought the city—the Arsenal of Democracy, they called it then—would fall so low? Who'd have believed the race riot of '43 was more of an omen than all those tanks?

Christ, he's getting philosophical or something. But what got him started has nothing to do with God or the fall of cities or with any of those things that have happened in the big world around him. What he's feeling, what he's been feeling since the night of Eddie Figlak's wake, is an itch, and it's an itch that needs scratching.

"What's bothering you, Ziggy?" Maggie asks him at breakfast about a week after the wake.

"What do you mean?" he counters suspiciously, looking up from the paper that he hasn't been reading.

"I mean," she says, "you're walking around like a zombie these days. I know you're not sleeping. Half the time I'm talking to you and I might as well be talking to myself. Something's bothering you and you're not letting me in on it." She shakes her head. "Look, it's not like I expect you to be Cary Grant or somebody like that, but this isn't the way I want to spend my golden years, trying to talk to a doorknob."

"It's nothing," he says, trying for some force. "You're imagining things."

She turns a look on him and holds him with her eyes. What that look tells him is that there's no way he's going to get anything past her, not after all these years.

He shifts uneasily. "I don't know," he concedes, figuring he can wriggle off the hook by telling her a bit of the truth. "Seeing Eddie dead, I guess . . . You get to thinking about, you know, how much longer you might have yourself."

It seems a plausible explanation, but Maggie continues looking at him skeptically. Having listened to hundreds of his lies and evasions on every subject over the years, she can probably gauge the exact amount of truth behind every one of his utterances.

"Oh, hell," he blurts out at last, "it's that goddamned Przybylski."

"What about him?" she says, looking puzzled. "It's no secret that the two of you never sent each other Valentines. Why are you even thinking about him now? Didn't that feud end a long time ago when he left?"

Ziggy steams silently for a while. "It's more than that," he says, "more than just the way he used to act back in the old days." She stands there across from him in their kitchen, waiting for his explanation. "I heard something the other night." His voice is tentative, quiet, as if he were some squirming teenager in the confessional trying to find the least incriminating way of telling the priest how often he's masturbated. "I heard Przybylski was the one who fingered me back when we got busted."

Maggie sighs and looks into her cup. "Ziggy," she says mildly, "all that's water under the bridge." She thinks for a moment before going on, "And besides, it was that Lieutenant Nolan of the Rackets Squad who was the bad guy. I thought he got the order from above to bust the Polacks and he was determined to do it one way or another. You said it then, everybody said it. It was a big deal, that raid. It didn't happen just because of what one Polack undertaker might have said to a cop."

Ziggy's silent. That raid certainly was a big deal. He remembers the headlines in the *Times*: "$13 Million Gambling Ring Smashed." As Maggie noted, even if Przybylski had cooperated with the cops, his contribution would have been a small part of the whole operation.

"Still," Ziggy says. "Still. He was never man enough to admit it."

Maggie sighs and sits down across from him. "Ziggy," she says, "I know you had your rough times but, all things considered, you got through them more or less in one piece. All that's over, though. You know what they say: there's no point in opening up closed rooms."

Then he finally says it out loud, what's been taking shape in his mind ever since the night of Eddie Figlak's wake. "I want to see him. I want to ask him to his face about it."

There's silence as Maggie moves her cup along the Formica table. Ziggy's ready for whatever objections she's going to throw at him, but all she says is, "Isn't he in California? You want to go out there?"

"Well, yeah," Ziggy answers, a little miffed. "If that's where he is, then that's where I want to go. Unless you can think of some way to kidnap him and bring him to Detroit." He's uneasily aware that they're actually discussing this thing now. He has to say it over again to believe himself. "Yeah, I was thinking about going to California."

She doesn't gasp, doesn't throw up her hands. "How do you plan to get there?" she asks, as if this were something reasonable, like a trip to Pontiac or Port Huron.

"I haven't worked out the details," he says, "I'm not sure, but . . ." His voice trails off. How did they get on to this subject in the first place?

"And you think," Maggie asks quietly, "that if you go out there and ask him something, that's going to settle things?"

"Yeah," he answers, then quickly corrects himself. "Oh, I don't know, but I know I want to do this. Christ," he says, suddenly furious at nobody in particular, "I've been behaving myself, haven't I? I've been driving in low gear for a while now. I was going to work every day till the city laid me off, and then I start that other job the monsignor has lined up for me next month." (In his head he says that other shit job, but he knows it's wise to be outwardly grateful.) "Hell, Maggie," he says, and just lets it go with a sigh.

Minutes seem to pass before she says, "Why don't you visit Charlie then?"

He looks at her. "Are you serious?"

"Why not?" she says. "You have some time before you start your job with the DSR."

"Christ," he says, "Charlie doesn't want to see me. And Gloria wants to see me even less." The idea that he'd actually choose to spend time voluntarily with Big-Time Charlie and his family is beyond belief. But she's right: it would be a way of getting a foot in the door in California.

Maggie's smile is oddly mischievous. "They could hardly refuse you if you asked, could they?"

All at once Ziggy's alert. He looks at her narrowly. What's she up to?

At last she says, "Look, Ziggy, I know you. Sometimes when you get a bee in your bonnet, you're hard to live with. Me, all I want is to get through my time the best I can, cutting the aches and pains to a minimum. I'm satisfied if I have a roof over my head, a bed to lay in and food in the refrigerator. I don't need to go on any crusades." She shakes her head. "But you're different. There are things you need that I can't do anything about. So I say, don't just keep talking about it. Do something about it if you can."

Ziggy feels a chill. He swallows hard, then takes a sip of cold coffee because he has no response to that. Maggie, who'd been thin, pretty and shy when he married her forty years ago, had only dreamed of raising a family, having a house of her own, maybe going to an occasional movie or picnic on Belle Isle. She hadn't bargained for the roller coaster of the numbers, never really enjoyed the parties, the fur coats, the trips on Big Al's boat. She'd been happier just staying home, she'd loved the place on Harsens Island best when just she and the kids were there, not when all the numbers people showed up for a shindig. And she certainly couldn't have been happy about all those trips to Buffalo and Cleveland where she could guess about what went on. Not to mention the business with Helen Nadolnik.

Ziggy knows he owes her big time. When he went into his fog after all his buddies wound up in prison, she did her best to keep the numbers going; but she never had a chance and people who owed her money just walked away. She shouldn't have had to go through that, and many a woman would have cracked under the pressure. The experience toughened her, though. With Ziggy becoming increasingly undependable, she learned to drive, she took a part-time job at a nearby nursing home and soon became indispensable there. Ziggy's absolutely certain that if he were to die, she'd manage. Maybe that's a blow to his old self-image as her protector and provider, but he can't help being proud of what she's managed to accomplish.

But sending him off to California to see Charlie? Is she thinking of that as a rehearsal for the time when he's gone for good?

"Well?" she pushes now. "Do you think you could bring yourself to visit Charlie and Gloria if that's what it took to get you your meeting with Przybylski?"

"I . . ." Ziggy wants to protest something, though he's unsure what it is. Because suddenly he's gripped with fear, an arctic chill that goes all the way to his toes. And just when he's sure he's going to freeze solid, the fear leaves him and he's in some place where everything is clear and peaceful, as if he's accomplished something big, the entire sequence of his feelings mirroring what he experienced as a teenager once when, on a dare, he managed to convince himself to dive—drop, really—off the high board at the Y. Somewhere in the course of that stomach-tightening plunge, in the grip of gravity, all his fear had left him and he yelled at the top of his lungs as he hit the water, swallowing a mouth- and noseful of chlorinated liquid. It stung, but nothing had tasted so delicious. "Well," he says now, "maybe."

In his mind, though, maybe has already mutated into yes. He can do it, all right. Already he's calculating—God, he's excited. After years of keeping his head down, trying to be a good boy, here's a chance he doesn't want to miss. He's going on a trip, all the way to California. He's never been to the coast before. Even in the palmy days, he only got as far west as Las Vegas. Out there, on the far edge of the continent, he's going to track down Przybylski, he's going to look him in the eye and ask him a yes or no question: did you work with the cops against me? His answer won't change anything—it certainly won't bring back the plush years, it won't bring back the place on the island, the big parties where even Mayor Van Antwerp was likely to show up. But it will be something, it will be something. Once again Ziggy feels a shiver. It's as if, at least for a while, he'll be able to touch his own past, to shake hands with the Ziggy who came before him, and something of the fear he felt moments ago returns. But he's going to do it.

He gets up and walks over to Maggie, pulls her to her feet and gives her a hug. "Whoosh," she says, catching her breath. "I hope you're feeling this good when you come back."

CHAPTER THREE

Ziggy's in Chicago. Under the roaring El whose steel girders enclose the street like a cage, he lights a cigarette: the match's sulphur and the burning tobacco blend deliciously with the smell of pizza and frying onions coming from somewhere down the block. When was the last time he was in the Windy City? Probably for one of those bowling tournaments with the numbers guys when he was in his thirties. God, that was so long ago. He remembers the bunch of them, sharp dressers except for Morty Krause, already gathered at the back of the car with their suitcases as the train pulled into the station, little kids impatient for Santa's arrival. The memory warms him, though the pleasure of recalling those days is, as always, muted by a tinge of regret, even guilt. Well, everybody's paid in their own way. He exhales a thin cloud of smoke and watches it dissipate in the street. Gone, like all those years.

He hasn't come all this way just to stand around and mope, though. It will do him good to walk a little. He's grateful for the opportunity to move his old bones and joints after being cramped in the bus through the first leg of his trip from Detroit. Then too, he just needs to be doing something because his blood is pumping, the way it did in the old days. The funny thing is, this surge he feels has nothing to do with his mission, if you want to call it that, nothing to do with his having taken the first steps toward hunting down Przybylski, and clearing up the mystery of the undertaker's role in his fall—hell, Ziggy hasn't thought of Przybylski at all. No, it's just that he's on the road, on his own, feeling free for the first time in God knows how long. He breathes in the gritty aroma of the street: cars' exhaust, cigarettes and chewing gum—the smell of people in motion. Chicago has always excited him, and he remembers the wild times they had when they came here for those bowling tournaments. They actually managed to get in some bowling—Ziggy himself had been pretty good in his day—but it sure wasn't bowling alleys they'd come here to see.

A train thunders by overhead, car horns squawk, wide-assed buses belch exhaust into the street and pedestrians with something to do rush by—he's in a live city for a change, where people aren't afraid to come out after dark. Why did Chicago turn out to be lucky, he wonders, escaping what happened to Detroit? Sure, it's a lot bigger and it's always been more important: every school kid knows that most of the big rail lines in the country converge in Chicago, because of the stockyards, wasn't it? Of course, there's the lake—Detroit only has the river—and you can't deny there's a lot more to do here. Hell, even the museums are interesting, and Ziggy, who isn't much of a guy for educational tourism, remembers being more than impressed when he went down under the earth to the coal mine in the Museum of Science and Industry. So, OK, Chicago's got more to see and do. Still, there was a time when you could get off the train from Detroit at Union Station and expect to be treated as if you came from some place that mattered, because it did matter, and nobody could say otherwise.

Now, it's like two different worlds and there's no question which city, given the choice, anyone would want to live in. Who wouldn't want to be part of this noisy hustle? For a couple of heartbeats he lets himself entertain the fantasy of just staying here. Forget about that long trek in a bus across the country. He could get a pretty good bang for his buck here in Chicago before he ran out of money, couldn't he? He tosses away the cigarette. Well, there were times in his life when he just wanted to disappear somewhere, but those days have come and gone.

It feels good, though, to be carrying a bit of cash for a change. He has to hand it to Maggie, who worked up quite a package for this venture, pooling some of the stash she's accumulated for a rainy day with a bit of his own money, then hitting up Steve and Alice for what amounted to a humor-your-old-man tax, so that in the end he has a few hundred bucks in his pocket—well, not in his pocket exactly, since the money is dispersed into a number of safe places. The fact is, he has plenty for the kind of low-budget trip he's planning. The bus is cheap and it isn't going to cost anything to sleep there. As for food, he certainly has no plans to dine in five-star restaurants along the way. Once he gets to the coast, Maggie kept telling him, he'll have free room and board at Charlie's; but he and Charlie have never really hit it off, and the prospect of spending an extended amount of time with his daughter-in-law makes his skin crawl. Fortunately, Ziggy has already come up with some ideas of his own. First thing, he's going to look up Father Teddy; there's more than an even chance he can coax some free lodgings out of the ex-priest. He's done his homework and found out that Venice isn't all that far from Burbank on the map, so he might be able to spend a couple of days there. He's given himself no more than two weeks for this trip. Hell, if he gets lucky, he might even get the business with Przybylski done without having to stay more than a day or two with Charlie and Gloria.

"Spare some change?" The sharp croak comes across as a challenge. When he looks up he sees a short, dark guy in ratty jeans and a denim jacket, his head topped by a cowboy hat adorned with a dirty, broken feather. The man, who could be anywhere between forty and sixty, is staring darts at him, as if he's convinced Ziggy's the one who stole all his money, ran off with his wife and poisoned his dog.

"Yeah, you," the man snarls. "I'm talking to you." An Indian, Ziggy sees now. A bum, but an Indian.

"Sorry, buddy," he answers, irked. "I've got nothing to spare."

The Indian's mouth twists into a sour smile. "You're breaking my heart, Roscoe," he snaps. "You trying to tell me that after you took all the land from my people and broke all your solemn treaties and slaughtered all the buffalo and screwed us out of our mineral resources for trinkets and dime-store jewelry, you got nothing to spare." He shakes his head. "And you people call yourself civilized. Hah!"

Ziggy tries to get past him but the man blocks his way. This Indian has already made himself a major pain in the ass but, more than that, Ziggy can't figure him out. Is Chief Wahoo here for real or is this some kind of act? He looks around for help, but the people nearby are all hurrying past him without paying attention, as if they're part of some biblical parable.

When the Indian leans closer Ziggy can smell the beer on his breath. "You're telling me you can't even spare a nickel," he laughs maliciously, "a nickel with the red man's face on it. Not even a nickel. That's the trouble with you white people: you're all constipated, you hold everything in. You walk across the land and never feel it under your feet. Do you ever listen to water flowing, ever hear the wind?"

Ziggy's curiosity holds him here. Any second now the guy is going to crack a smile, isn't he, and reveal that all this is nothing but a put-on? Ziggy studies the man's dark face—could it be makeup? But he does seem to have the cheekbones of an Indian, all right. Throughout his tirade his features have remained for the most part expressionless; still, there's no hint of anything but genuine hate in his eyes.

"Shit," he says, "I don't need your stinking money, white man," and pivots sharply, as if to leave. He stops a moment, though, and when he speaks again there's a distance in his gaze, as if he's looking at a butte on the far horizon. "You're going to pay, my friend," he says, "you and all your white buddies. Nature is going to take its revenge on you with fire and flood." He cocks his head. "You think you chased away the spirits, but they're still out there waiting for you."

In a flash he's gone, melted into the crowd, and Ziggy's heart is pounding. I didn't kill any goddamned buffalo, he wants to protest, I never bought any land with dime-store jewelry. He's glad, though, that the man is gone. "Hah," he laughs out loud; but he has to admit that the encounter has shaken him up just a little.

Soon he's back at the bus station, cheered unreasonably by the echoing sound of place names coming from the public address system. There's not an Indian in sight; he can resume his journey in peace now. He appreciates the break he's just had, though the trip from Detroit wasn't that bad. After the last few years of being a hamster running on a wheel, he felt a sense of expansiveness as he left the dingy streets of Detroit behind him and was carried westward past Ann Arbor, where the leafy spring landscape became gently rolling. It reminded him of the Irish Hills, where he and Big Al had gone a couple of times when they'd decided they were going to be golfers. It didn't take them long to realize they should have stuck to bowling, though it had been satisfying just to be on the course with all those snooty types who obviously hated their guts.

Passing through Jackson, though, he couldn't keep from thinking about Big Al and J.J. doing time in the prison there. Ziggy's friendship with them never survived that. "You have to remember," his expensive attorney Edward P. Fitzgerald kept telling him, "your responsibility is to protect yourself and your family. You have to separate your trial from that of your associates. Believe me, they'd do the same thing if they were in your shoes." In the end there was no doubt the lawyer was right: doing time in Jackson was nothing Ziggy missed. He was glad when they were past there, heading toward Battle Creek and Kalamazoo, all those places he'd learned about as a kid in Sister Gendura's geography class; and he could visualize a line moving westward over the mitten shape of the lower peninsula toward Lake Michigan.

He wasn't alone, of course. Most of the trip he spent listening to a little bald guy in his fifties who sat beside him. He was on his way to Kalamazoo but he lived in Pittsburgh, and he spent the whole time talking about the factory where he worked making golf balls, which was soon going to shut down and move its operations to Virginia. He was the union secretary at the plant, so he felt pretty secure in the face of the coming layoffs and the relocation of the factory, or so he said. But he kept telling Ziggy he'd put in just over twenty-eight years with the company—you could see he knew that figure down to the day, and he was sweating that last year and some months before his pension started kicking in.

Listening, Ziggy couldn't help remembering his own time at Chrysler, when he was in his twenties. God, he'd gotten pretty desperate toward the end. He hated coming to work, haunted as he was by the sense that he was going nowhere, he was doomed to grow old in the factory and eventually turn into his own father, which was a truly frightening prospect. "You think you're Mister Big Shot," the old man would bellow at him, "but you're not going to amount to shit." If little Billy Pelz hadn't shown up that day looking for Moose Kubek, who was sick, Ziggy would never have gotten into the numbers and there's no knowing how things would have turned out.

Whatever happened to him later, Ziggy never regretted having got himself out of that damned factory.

The guy who made golf balls was trying to put the best face on his situation, but he didn't really seem to believe in what he was saying. From what Ziggy could see, he might have had himself a bigger problem than getting laid off. "I got a bad bronchial," he kept explaining whenever he had to stop talking because of his cough. It was probably the fumes from his work, he guessed. He hoped things would be better in Virginia, though the new plant there wasn't going to be unionized. "My union's going to be down there working day and night to unionize it," he said, but he didn't seem to feel they could do much. Even if they succeeded, he confessed, it would still take them years before they could achieve all the benefits they had in Pittsburgh. Ziggy wished him luck, but it didn't take much imagination to see that story ending badly.

You had to give the guy one thing, though: he was really interested in his work, describing for Ziggy in great detail how golf balls were made: they froze the center and then wrapped rubber thread around it—that was about all Ziggy remembered. That and the fact that some of the girls who made the golf balls were very nice. "I like to treat them like a gentleman," the guy said. "You don't find a lot of that these days." It certainly sounded as if he had a crush on one of them. He wasn't sure how many of them were going to Virginia, he admitted, shaking his head sadly.

At last it's time for Ziggy to re-board the bus. He'd eaten a hot dog earlier but he bought a candy bar for the trip. The walk had done him good. He even had a chance to use the rest room in the station, which was much preferable to the cramped one on the bus. Getting back on, he returns to the window seat he saved near the back and is getting pretty comfortable as the departure time approaches, thinking that the place beside him will be free on the next leg of his journey. A couple of minutes before the scheduled start, though, he hears a commotion in the front of the bus and soon a short, bespectacled man is making his way clumsily toward the back, burdened by a duffel bag slung over his shoulder that gives him the look of a hunchback with an unbalanced hump—and Ziggy just knows the stranger is going to sit beside him.

"I'm sorry. Sorry. Excuse me," the man keeps saying in a kind of whiny voice as he bangs against the seats, approaching ever closer.

Ziggy's still trying to remember how much free space there is behind him when the man pulls up beside his seat.

"Do you mind?" he asks with a guilty smile.

Ziggy shrugs. What can he say? It isn't his bus.

The newcomer fusses as he stuffs his bag under the seat and at last sits down beside Ziggy. He pushes back his horn-rimmed glasses, then runs his hand nervously through his hair. "Whew," he sighs and settles into his seat, though he pops erect an instant later, his eyes ranging nervously around the bus. He fiddles with the leg rest and turns toward Ziggy with a look of vague appeal. "I'm Lennie Kurzweil," he says with a tentative smile. His nostrils twitch. "Do you smell gas?" he asks with quiet alarm. "You think there might be a leak?"

Ziggy shakes his head. The rest room isn't far away and there are various other kinds of unpleasant smells all too likely to make themselves evident on a long trip, but at the moment he doesn't smell any gas. He closes his eyes, hoping the stranger might just be going a short distance.

"Ever been to LA?" Lennie asks, and Ziggy opens his eyes.

The man beside him is probably in his thirties, pale and fidgety. His gray windbreaker is zipped all the way to his neck and his restless insect-like eyes dart from one object to the next; his hands move abruptly to his face, then drop to his lap, he keeps shifting in his seat. Every now and then he checks, either with his feet or with a look, to assure himself his duffel bag is still there.

This Lennie, Ziggy can see right away, is a talker. Without even waiting for Ziggy's answer about LA, he informs him that he's on his way there, where he's going to try to make it as a stand-up comic. "After that, who knows, right?" And on he goes, recounting how he'd taken a bus from New York to Chicago, where he'd stayed with his sister Cynthia, who was married to the world's shortest dentist. "I swear," Lennie says, "when I got my first look at him I said to her, 'Cynthia, he'd better have insurance. Aren't you afraid he might drown in a root canal?' But my sister would have done anything to get out of the house and there was no stopping her. Of course, if you knew our mother, you wouldn't blame her . . ."

His manic patter makes Ziggy appreciate the man who made golf balls. He might put you to sleep with his loving descriptions of how the dimpled white spheres were made; this guy talks at least twice as fast, in a high-pitched voice that keeps jumping to the edge of panic, and he's likely to make sudden transitions without any warning.

"I can't believe I'm really going to be crossing the plains," he says as the door closes with a hiss, the driver shifts gears and the bus begins backing heavily out of the bay. "I feel like a pioneer." Seconds later, his voice drops. "This is the first time I've been this far west and, well, Chicago's at least a real city; but when you think of what we're going to have to pass through to get to the coast, it can send a shiver up your spine, don't you think?"

Ziggy has already got into the habit of nodding amiably. Lennie was pleased to learn he came from Detroit. "Well, then you know what it's like to live in a city," he said. "I guess the idea of all those empty spaces scares me a little." He laughs nervously. "You know, it's pretty spooky to think we'll be traveling through John Wayne country."

"I doubt that we'll run into Geronimo out there," Ziggy says. Pronouncing the name, he remembers the Indian he encountered on the street in Chicago.

Lennie lowers his voice. "It's the cowboys I'm worried about."

The guy isn't putting on an act, Ziggy has already decided. It sure looks as if his seat-mate is genuinely terrified to be traveling through the empty middle of the country to the coast. Why didn't he fly then and avoid all the hazard of the wild west? Probably for the same reason Ziggy is on this bus, why everyone else here is riding the 'hound: because he doesn't have the money. Well, they have that in common anyway.

"Jeez," Lennie says, leaning closer to whisper, "did you see that soldier who's sitting right behind the driver? The look he gave me . . . I know exactly what he was thinking:

this piece of scum burns American flags and laughs about it. I wouldn't want to be in a foxhole with G.I. Joe, I tell you. He and the driver seemed to be whispering something together when I got on, and they just clammed up when they saw me." His restless eyes search the bus. "Well, I survived the trip from New York even though there were at least a couple of potential serial killers aboard. I mean, judging from their sweet faces and icy stares. And a pair of really grim missionary types in white shirts got on looking like they were part of the Mormon Tabernacle Firing Squad. I don't know, though, the little old lady who kept coughing into her handkerchief could have been the most dangerous of all of them. I'm sure she had the Black Plague, if not something worse."

Ziggy half-listens to all this. It's apparently enough for Lennie, who seems to feel he'd found a confidant. Jesus, Ziggy thinks, and he's going all the way to California.

A little more than an hour into the trip, though, Lennie suddenly interrupts himself and declares, "I'm beat. I haven't had any sleep for the last three nights," and in seconds he's snoring, his head slumped to one side, actually looking at peace for the first time. Ziggy's more than ready for some peace of his own, now that he can give himself over to the luxury of just looking out the window, not having to respond, not having to pay even minimal attention; and for a time he lets himself be lulled into a pleasant state between sleep and wakefulness during which he moves through space and time without taking either into account. He's on the island watching Big Al's white boat nose its way to the dock, there's some kind of celebration at Connie's and he's in the center of it; he's on the phone with the monsignor, who wants him to be head of the East Side Homeowners' Association . . .

Now he's at the Museum of Science and Industry, on an elevator that's lowering him and others to the coal mine beneath the streets of Chicago and, amid the chatter and laughter of his fellow tourists, his breath suddenly comes fast, his heart pounds in his chest. This is a museum, he keeps telling himself, everything's under control; but his head is filled with all those stories his mother used to tell him about her life in Scranton before her family moved to Detroit: the uncles who were trapped in cave-ins, the one who died and the one who was crazy by the time they'd brought him back to the surface; about the underground fires that burned for years, the dirt that never came off the miners' skin, the fear that was always there. Take it easy, he tells himself, breathing deeply. Everything's under control.

All at once he's jolted awake and for a moment he has no idea where he is. Bathed in panic, he gradually orients himself—he's on a bus moving west, that much he remembers; but, as he looks at the man sleeping beside him, he's aware that he hasn't been able to shake off the chill that he's brought with him from his dream. He turns to the window and stares at the unfamiliar surroundings. It's near sunset but the sun is nowhere to be seen. They're well out of the city by now, even the near suburbs are behind them; and the shape of the land—flat, immense, seemingly endless— has begun to assert itself, making the scattered houses look like pieces from a Monopoly game. The landscape they're passing through is presided over by brooding skies where enormous pyramids of cloud loom over the flimsy dwellings of humans that emit pinpricks of light. They're out on the real prairie now, aren't they, just like the pioneers, as Lennie said. It suddenly occurs to Ziggy that he's here with a bunch of strangers, headed across the country, on a bus that will carry him through unknown territories—and all at once he's scared. Why the hell has he put himself into this situation?

You're going to pay, that Indian said. Nature is going to take its revenge on him, even though as far as he knows he's never been within a mile of a buffalo. The guy was certifiable.

Outside, the huge purple clouds that look like celestial bruises are poised above a landscape that's incredibly flat and as boundless as the ocean; he finds himself missing the tidy rolling hills around Ann Arbor, he even thinks fondly of Jackson with its prison where his friends did hard time. All those places to which he had at least some connection are sliding into the east behind him, farther away with every second. At the same time, something warm and unpleasant is twisting slowly upward in his chest. Possibly it's the result of the hot dog with sauerkraut he ate in Chicago, but even that digestive discomfort seems to carry a spiritual ache. As Lennie's snores punctuate the indistinct murmur of other strangers, Ziggy is stabbed by a sudden sharp intimation of his own mortality—don't they always say heart attacks are sometimes confused with indigestion? What if he were to die somewhere out on this prairie, far from the neighborhood, from the church, from Connie's, from all those familiar streets he'd left behind?

You made this bed, he tells himself; you're going to have to lie in it.

To the old Polacks, everything that happened to you was the result of something out there bigger than you. Call it God, call it luck, whatever. To his mother, he knows very well, a glass of milk couldn't get knocked over on the table without portending some kind of doom, and God forbid if you should find a dead bird in your house. But, after all, why wouldn't they think that way after their experiences in the old country, where most of the men spent their days looking up the smelly ass of some old plow horse, hardly daring to take an occasional furtive peek at the sky that could dump a hailstorm on their pitiful half-acre and wipe out their whole crop; or, if God or the Devil happened to be in another mood, withhold its rain, killing more slowly but just as surely the potatoes or beets or whatever the hell it was they were trying to grow? Then when they came to this country his family wound up in Pennsylvania, spending their best hours in narrow tunnels picking away at coal hundreds of feet under the earth until a lot of them must have been willing to give up their firstborns for a glimpse of the sky every now and then. How could they have done that, spent the day in those damp, cramped spaces under the earth, breathing air that might be poisonous, or combustible, their lungs getting blacker all the while; finally after their backbreaking hours down in the mines, being carried up on the elevator to the surface, where they stumbled home exhausted to eat a meal they probably couldn't taste; how could they, waking up the next day, get themselves ready to go down again into those places where they all knew so many people who'd never come back?

It's true, they didn't call the shots. Even in America, they didn't call the shots. But in America you could move if you decided to, you could leave the coal mines for the car factories of Michigan and it might even turn out that, in one of those factories, you got a chance to do something else, something it turned out that you were good at, and you made things happen for yourself and your family; so that after a while you owned a couple of buildings in the neighborhood, you had the place on Harsens Island, you had cars, you could buy nice clothes for your wife and kids, and if you wanted to, you could get a block of tickets to a Tigers game and treat your friends—you could spread out a little and not live the cramped life to which you might have thought you were destined.

Sometimes in those days you felt as if you could breathe it all in. Stepping into Dubois Street on a summer morning in your favorite cream-colored jacket and freshly pressed pants, lighting a cigarette as you faced the high brick wall of St. Connie's across the street, you wanted to take it all into your lungs: the tobacco, the street, the neighborhood, the city itself. Because even as you were wishing it could all go on forever, in your heart you already suspected that it wouldn't.

Still, even if it should turn out that in the end you lost it all, that the cops raided your house, your friends went to prison and wouldn't talk to you anymore because you escaped their fate, that your response to getting off relatively lightly was to turn into a boozer who couldn't keep track of your own money, let alone what you were supposed to be handling in the numbers, since you were too busy running from the bears in your closet that only you could see; and then later you were preoccupied with making ashtrays at the rehab place and finally, when all of it was gone and you were more or less sober again and working at crummy jobs the monsignor got for you—the monsignor, who used to get so oily and complimentary when he needed a donation from "one of the parish's most distinguished members"—when all that happened to you, the old babas could be counted on to cluck away about how all this was God's punishment, it had all been foreseen and there was nothing anyone could have done about it. But Ziggy knows that's nowhere near the whole story: he's made choices, good ones and bad ones. Sure, there was luck of both sorts, but he had some say in the matter.

And now he's going to California because he wants to find out what really happened all those years ago. That isn't asking for much, is it?

CHAPTER FOUR

Sleep isn't easy to come by on the bus: hunched to one side, his shoulder jammed against the window, Ziggy squirms and wriggles, trying for a comfortable position, but nothing is right for his neck, his back, his knees. Well, what did he expect after all? The good news is that it'll only be a couple of days of this. Still. He breathes deeply, trying to empty his mind. It's not going to help to think, to remember. Eyes closed, he surrenders to the steady, hypnotic buzz of the engine until he could be anywhere, nowhere.

He must have fallen asleep because he comes awake sharply with a cramp in his leg. With great care he eases the still painful limb to a more comfortable angle and leans forward to rub his calf. Outside it's raining, a deluge in fact, now that he's had a better chance to get his bearings. Thick drops slap the window and even from inside he can tell that the rain is being driven by a ferocious wind. Meanwhile, along-side him, Lennie is sleeping, apparently along with everyone else in the bus. It's pitch black outside and Ziggy has no idea where they are on the map, somewhere in Illinois presum-ably, headed toward St. Louis. In the long corridor of the bus, people have turned off their lights and all he can make out as he peers over the seat-backs is a dim, churchly quiet. Is it possible that he and the driver are the only ones awake to the drenching fury of the storm they're passing through? In a few moments the sounds coming from outside change: a clattering drumbeat against the window signals that it's started to hail, and hard. The bus continues to hurtle through the wet, black night like a spaceship bound for some distant star, and Ziggy's glad he doesn't have to be at the wheel, driving through this stuff. But shouldn't the guy at least slow down?

He's still listening to the hailstones popping against the window when, abruptly, he feels the bus go weightless under him, taking his stomach with it. Jesus, he realizes, his breath snatched away from him, we've gone into a skid. Instinctively, he shuts his eyes for a beat or two but when he opens them, hoping to escape from a bad dream, he's back where he was, the bus fishtailing beneath him, struggling to recover stability. Everything is happening too fast; at the same time, things seem to be moving in slow-motion. By now the passengers have been jerked out of their sleep and startled cries punctuate the rattle of plastic bottles, the thud of duffels and the bang of countless other items violently released from confinement. Ziggy's hanging on to the arm of the seat, his mouth forming soundless words as, after long breathless seconds, the big vehicle finally regains traction and, to his immense relief, is moving forward once more, at a slower pace now.

"What's happening?" Lennie asks. "What's going on?"

Ziggy shakes his head, a cigarette already in his hand even before he's decided he needs one. "Don't know," he says. "But we're in a hell of a storm. Must have been hail on the road." That skid—it came out of nowhere, they could have been killed. When they brought the news to Maggie, he'd want to let her know somehow that he was sorry, he shouldn't ever have left on this harebrained mission. He glances outside, where hailstones fly like comets through the stormy air and skeletal streaks of lightning dance on the horizon, illuminating an empty plain.

"We had ourselves a little unexpected adventure," the driver's voice comes over the public address system. "But everything's under control now."

"Do you think everything's really OK?" Lennie asks, looking around the bus, where lights have been turned back on. "I mean, shouldn't we stop and wait for this to be over?"

Ziggy takes a deep drag, pulling the hot smoke down so far that when he exhales, his hand is trembling. "I guess the driver's a trained professional," he says. "He'll know how to handle this." To be truthful, he's not so sure Greyhound's standards are very demanding. What do they pay these guys anyway?

Lennie peers out. "Wow," he says, "it's pretty intense out there." And it's true: there's been no letup to the pounding on the window, and Ziggy's hope is that nothing this strong can last very long; but the fact is, they might be heading right into the center of this storm and who knows how much territory it covers? What he does know is that there's a lot of country out there. In the past few minutes the lightning outside has become more or less continuous, though the hail has receded, replaced by fierce pellets of rain that sizzle against the window.

Everybody's talking at once, but in a moment of relative quiet Ziggy hears the word "tornado." "What's that guy saying?" he leans over to ask the person in the seat in front of him.

The heavy man has a deep voice, a bit of a drawl. "Guy up ahead's got a radio. Says there are tornado warnings."

Ziggy tries to put things into perspective. "I guess they must get a lot of tornado warnings around here."

"Yeah," the man agrees with a snort. "That's because they get a lot of tornados."

Ziggy leans back. Beside him, Lennie is staring into the blackness outside.

"At least I gave it a try," he's muttering to himself. "I could have stayed back east. It would have been a pretty good life, I guess. But I never would have known, would I?"

"Hey," Ziggy tries to reassure him, "if there's a tornado we're in the safest place we could be. Maybe the wind can pick up a cow, or maybe even a car, and move it, but did you ever hear of one that picked up a bus?" He doesn't know whether he believes this but it sounds convincing to him. In *The Wizard of Oz*, he remembers, there was a house flying around in the storm. But that was a movie.

"I don't know," Lennie says. "Think of all those windows, all that glass. In a tornado it would be like hundreds of knives flying around in here."

Thanks, Ziggy thinks. And I've got the window seat. But to his relief, the bus has slowed to a crawl. At least the driver's being careful.

Still, what the hell have I got myself into, Ziggy can't help wondering, and did I really have to do it?

You're going to see Przybylski.

Yeah, and when I find him, what's supposed to happen?

You can ask him if he really fingered you back in the fifties.

And that's going to change what?

Look, you decided all this already. You'll find out what it all means when it happens.

There are times when thinking about things is no comfort at all.

The bus continues moving at a reduced speed for almost a half hour and the storm outside shows no signs of abating, but now there's an unmistakable stir among the passengers in the front of the bus.

"Do you know what's going on?" Ziggy asks the big man who told him about tornado warnings.

"There's trouble ahead," the man answers gravely. "Seems like there are flash floods. I guess there's talk of a bridge being out."

Jesus, this really is a storm. "What would that mean for our schedule?" Ziggy asks. "I mean, do you think we're going to be late getting into St. Louis?"

"You can't always meet your schedule," the man says. "I know that from experience. I'm a bus driver myself. I drive tour buses back east in New Jersey." He laughs quietly. "I know,

I'm taking a busman's holiday. So I don't have any timetable to meet. That's more than I can say for our driver."

His tone suggests that he knows something. "What do you mean?" Ziggy asks.

"I talked to the guy, though I wouldn't exactly call him sociable. He's on a tight schedule, and he's got his own reasons for that. He's divorced and he's trying to see his daughter before she leaves for school. After that, she goes to live with her mother. That's why he took on this route, he told me."

From what he's seen of their driver, Ziggy isn't surprised by this information. The thin, balding man in his forties who looks like a ferret that's suffering from permanent heartburn struck him as someone in a hurry. "You think there's any real chance we might not be able to keep up with our schedule?"

The other man snorts. "Hell, if this bus lasts the year it would surprise me. The company I work for wouldn't let a piece of junk like this on the road. Have you heard how it strains through the gears? If this were a horse, it would already be in the glue factory."

Ziggy looks at him disbelievingly.

"Maybe you're wondering why I'm riding this bus at all," he says. "Sometimes I wonder myself. Call it professional curiosity. And then," he chuckles, "I do get a substantial discount." It's dark and the man's face is half-turned so that Ziggy can't get much of a look at him; but somehow he has the feeling that this guy's enjoying a private joke, only it seems to be a joke that isn't very funny.

"I heard what that guy said," Lennie tells Ziggy when he settles back into his seat. "I knew it. I had a bad feeling when I got on board." He shakes his head. "This is exactly like some movie I saw as a kid."

"Don't worry," Ziggy says. "This isn't a movie. Things are going to be fine." What else is he supposed to say? "Take the plane," Maggie had urged him. "You'll be there in a flash." But no, for some reason he'd insisted on doing it this way, as if it was a penance a priest had assigned him in the confessional. Trying to sleep in his seat has been penance enough, but he figured that was going to be a short-term pain in the ass. He certainly never counted on weather delays. He looks outside. It's hard to gauge their progress, but it's clear they're going nowhere near the speed limit. There's no way they'll get to St. Louis on time unless the driver really stands on the pedal later on. It's not going to help to think about things you can't do anything about, though.

"Are you really going to be working as a comedian?" Ziggy asks Lennie. "You mean like Red Skelton or Milton Berle?"

"Well, no," Lennie says, "not exactly." His nose wrinkles as if Ziggy's called him a name. "Those guys are, like, from vaudeville days. I'd say my stuff is more like Mort Sahl's or, say, Bob Newhart's."

Ziggy nods at the last name, which he vaguely recognizes, though in truth he hasn't kept up with the comics on TV. What's so bad about Uncle Miltie anyway?

"Do you know Robert Klein?" Lennie asks and Ziggy shakes his head. Lennie sighs. "Really, you know, it's such a long shot even to think of making it like those guys." He's silent for a while. "I have an agent there who's going to look for gigs for me."

Ziggy's never understood exactly what an agent's supposed to do. "That should be a help," he says nevertheless. "Does this agent have anything lined up for you once you get there?"

Lennie shrugs. "Like real jobs?" he says with a frown. "No, he figures that's going to take a while. But he promised to set me up with some kind of work I can do while I'm looking for opportunities and getting around, going to comedy clubs, doing some improv, making connections."

The bus by now has slowed to the pace of a funeral cortege and the once-sleeping passengers are all astir, energized by the storm. The man on a busman's holiday introduces himself as Royall K. Spears ("Plain Roy'll do, though.") and offers a silver flask to Ziggy and Lennie. Ziggy takes a gulp: some kind of bourbon, anything but velvety as it goes down, but appreciated. Lennie hesitates a moment before taking a modest sip and returning the flask, his eyes glistening. In the midst of this unexpected distraction, a general camaraderie seems to be sweeping the bus. The strumming of a guitar coming from the front is interrupted by someone's shout: "Can you play 'Nearer, my God, to Thee?' " which produces a burst of laughter from some, though it seems clear that not everybody's taking the situation so lightly. Ziggy thinks of the bus driver, trying to squeeze in a visit to his daughter as he slowly pilots his vehicle through sheets of rain while whips of lightning slash across the black sky. There may be floods ahead, bridges may be out, and he's driving a run-down jalopy of a bus. Ziggy can imagine the man's grim and desperate determination, grimly pushing on while half his passengers are partying and the other half are praying.

At the moment, though, Ziggy's feeling surprisingly good. Maybe it's just that swallow of booze, but he realizes that he's glad to be part of all this. True, he'd already have landed in California by now if he'd have taken a plane, but unless the plane crashed, the trip couldn't be anything like the adventure he's experiencing.

"You don't sound like you come from New Jersey," he says to Royall Spears when he's passed on the latest bit of news. "If I may say so."

"I guess that's not hard to figure out," the man says. "I'm from Texas originally but, hey, you go where the money is."

"You headed back to Texas?" Ziggy asks. "On your vacation?"

The man shakes his head. "I'm visiting my son," he says, his eyes going suddenly dark. "He's at Fort Sill, Oklahoma." After a moment, he asks, "You ever serve in the armed forces?"

Ziggy shakes his head. "I had a deferment during the war," he explains. "I had a family." It's not a subject he's comfortable with, since the war was a boom time for the numbers and Ziggy really raked it in during those years, while so many others from the neighborhood served and some were even killed, like his friend Vince Nadolnik. He was going to set up Vince in the numbers when he got back. Get into something safe, he kept telling him, like the quartermasters corps, don't be a dummy and put yourself somewhere they're going to be shooting at you. But Vince was stubborn, he wound up in the infantry at Anzio, where he was first declared missing and finally dead—a hero, his commanding officer had written to Vince's widow, Helen. Ziggy had a hard time connecting that word to the fun-loving horse-faced Vince he'd known before his friend had enlisted, the kid who'd pulled the fire alarm at school so that they didn't have to spend the pleasant spring day inside. The word "hero" turned him into someone else, someone Ziggy didn't know.

"Hey," Big Al used to say, "we're performing a service with the numbers by keeping up morale. Think people are just going to spend all their time building tanks and planes? We brighten up their lives, give them a little sizzle, a little hope. FDR ought to give us medals."

Yeah, and Ziggy sure was brightening up Helen Nadolnik's life when he went to see her after they'd heard about Vince, bringing her little gifts like ham and butter that were hard to get in those days; and talking with her about Vince and how unbelievable it was that he was gone and the empty way it made you feel, until . . . well, they were consoling each other, he kept telling himself.

Ziggy doesn't want to think about any of that, least of all how he had to abruptly break off the affair when things got too complicated. It was one of the worst times of his life. There's no way of knowing how much Maggie knew about Helen, but Maggie's not dumb. In the end, he wound up hurting both of them. And why? He still doesn't understand why some things happened. The numbers brought him a lot of good things, sure, but there was a lot of grief along the way too.

Christ, though, this is something he hadn't counted on: with all the time to himself on this trip, the memories keep being dredged up. He thought he'd got all that under control long ago.

He's grateful that Spears has passed back a photo of a young guy in an army uniform. The G.I. in the picture looks like a million other soldiers, but Ziggy says, "Nice looking kid. He have any brothers and sisters?"

The man hesitates before answering. "No," he says at last. "Tyler's all the family I have." He clears his throat. "Lou, my wife, died five years ago."

"Sorry to hear that," Ziggy says, and the man falls silent, no doubt caught up in sad memories. What the hell must it be like, after all, to be a widower? For five years too. You drive a bus for a living, and when you have some time off you get on another bus and travel a couple thousand miles to an army base to see your kid. He sure hopes father and son get along better than he and Charlie do.

It's quieted around them now and Ziggy's attention turns again to the outside, where there's been no letup in the storm. The rain keeps pounding the bus and he can hear the whistling of the wind on the other side of the window. Lennie is quiet, looking straight ahead. Even in the darkness, he seems to have turned paler.

Ziggy settles back in his seat and closes his eyes. It's not just his trip anymore: this bus may be carrying him toward a showdown with Przybylski, but it's also taking Lennie either to some kind of recognition or to obscurity; it's taking their bus driver to a visit to a daughter he probably fears he's lost in the breakup of his marriage; and it's taking the transplanted Texan to a meeting with his son that seems more than just casual—this is a bus-ful of stories. And that's not even counting the storm they're driving through that's battering the plains. Whatever he'd been expecting, this sure isn't what Ziggy bargained for.

When they approach the outskirts of a town, marked by the familiar shopping strip, he comes alert. The department stores, supermarkets, fast food joints, pet shops, beauty parlors and auto supply stores are shut down at this time of the night, but the flashing lights of police cars and tow trucks are reflected in the plate glass windows.

"What's up?" Lennie asks as the bus slows down to make a wide turn into a residential street.

"Looks like they're sending us on a detour," Ziggy tells him. For a few blocks the big vehicle lumbers slowly past deep-porched houses set behind generous lawns. From the time he was a kid the briefest glimpse of places like that made him wonder what it would have been like to grow up in a small town. How would his life have been different? Would he have become a different person? At last, they leave this street of houses and emerge on another road, presumably on the other end of town. As the bus executes this maneuver, word gets around among the passengers that a portion of the highway they were supposed to travel on has been closed because of a tornado that apparently touched down somewhere near here. So we're close to this thing now, Ziggy thinks, following in its tracks. Even here, in a seemingly safe area, limbs ripped from trees lie in driveways. Further along he becomes aware of more damage from the big wind: a marquee that's been torn from its supports dangles in front of the entrance to a bank, a utility pole leans drunkenly, sparks from a nearby wire crackle on the wet pavement. Everywhere lights flash, men in slickers are gesturing, and through the bus window he can faintly hear the sounds coming from a bullhorn. What was it that the Indian in Chicago said about nature taking its revenge? If I start believing he had anything to do with this, Ziggy thinks, I'll really have gone off the deep end.

The driver has already announced that their next scheduled stop has been delayed. Sitting beside Ziggy, Lennie looks on forlornly, as if this scene of devastation is pretty much what he'd expected when he'd signed on for this trip.

"We'll stop somewhere," the driver says after a while, making no effort to hide the frustration in his voice, "only I don't know where." And on they continue.

Ziggy comes awake suddenly and realizes that the bus has pulled to a halt. Where are they? A check of his watch tells him it's well past midnight. When he looks out the window, he can see that they're in the wet parking lot of an all-night restaurant and the driver is announcing a twenty-minute stop. Because of the hour, some people who are trying to sleep choose to stay on the bus, but Ziggy is among those who get off, and Lennie's decided to join him.

"Smell the air," he says when they're on the pavement. It's cool outside but the rain has stopped. "I think I can still smell the electricity from the storm."

Ziggy sniffs. It's a change from the bus, though he can't tell if it's electricity that's filling his nostrils or the bus's exhaust.

Inside the restaurant, he has Lennie order him a coffee while he steps over to the adjoining convenience store where he buys some cigarettes and Twinkies.

"Looks like you've had some pretty rough weather around here," he says to the big, tired-looking woman about his own age at the cash register.

"We've been lucky here," she tells him. "A couple of twisters touched down in the next county. Lots of damage. My sister-in-law Renee lives down there. She says there's been roads closed and a bridge near her is down because of the flooding. Hope that's not where you folks are headed."

"I don't exactly know," he tells her. "I think we might have to change the original route. All I know is that eventually we're supposed to get to California."

The woman's face softens. "Don't I wish I were headed that way," she sighs and looks away. "I always figured I'd get out there while I was young enough to enjoy it." She turns down the corners of her mouth. "Something always seemed to get in the way. Now, all I want to do is to get out there and see the place." Turning back to him, she gives him a wink. "Well, I can dream, can't I?"

Ziggy remembers the song with that title. Wasn't it the Andrews Sisters who sang it? He and this woman were both a lot younger then. He takes his change. "I hope you make it to California, and soon," he says. He wonders why he's feeling so good until he remembers that in the woman's eyes he's one of the lucky ones, headed as he is to the Golden State.

"Aren't we supposed to be getting back on the bus pretty soon?" Lennie asks when he rejoins him at the counter.

Ziggy looks at the clock. "We have a few more minutes yet. The driver is still on the phone. We can't leave without him."

"That's the problem," Lennie says. "He's been in that booth the whole time we've been here. I don't think he's even been to the john."

"He's probably getting directions from Greyhound for an alternate route," Ziggy guesses. "I mean, they'd know more than he does about the weather conditions ahead, wouldn't they?"

"I always heard that weather moves from west to east," Lennie says. "Maybe the bad stuff's over."

"Could be," Ziggy shrugs.

But Lennie no longer seems to be interested in meteorological speculations. "What's with that driver?" he asks. "Did you see what happened? He left the phone booth and I was sure he was going to be heading back toward the bus, but he only got more change from the counter to make another call. I've got this funny feeling we're going to wind up staying here a lot longer than twenty minutes."

"I guess he figures he can make it up once we get back on the road," Ziggy tries to reassure him.

"I don't know," Lennie says. "He's got this weird look. Something's going on with him."

"Well," says Ziggy," at least we can stretch our legs a little longer." He does so, enjoying the luxury of the extra space.

"I don't like it," Lennie says. "There's something fishy going on."

Does the guy ever calm down, Ziggy wonders, other than when he's asleep? No, he figures: his dreams are probably frantic too.

By the time they get back on the bus after a stop of more than a half hour, though, Ziggy's begun to think Lennie may be on to something. When the driver finally finished his phone calls he looked not only upset—he looked like someone who wasn't quite sure what he was going to do next. Whatever his thoughts might be, though, he keeps them to himself. When he starts the bus up again, he makes no explanation for the delay, nor does he offer any illumination about what he might have learned from his phone calls; he just settles back into driving. If he's determined to make up for lost time, though, the road conditions are working against him, since the bus seems to be following the precise path of the windstorms, and every couple of miles, there are delays and detours that slow their pace. When Ziggy is able to get a glimpse of any of the towns they're passing through, he sees more evidence of the storm's force: power lines sag, utility poles are down and stoplights don't work, broken glass litters the road. Police are directing traffic and power company trucks are in the streets. Lights flash, sirens wail and chain saws whine.

It's obvious they've been thrown way off of their schedule and when they arrive in St. Louis they're hours late. At least, though, they're off the open prairie with its small towns scattered across empty spaces. This is a city with a downtown and tall buildings, and it might just be the sheer concentration of people, but whatever it is, Ziggy feels more at home here. There's a confused clamor in the big bus station. Buses are late, buses are cancelled, schedules are being changed. Names of places echo dimly from the public address system while would-be passengers are sleeping on benches, waiting for things to clear up. The storms may have passed, but they've left their mark on people's plans.

"This is a spooky place," Lennie says, flicking his head in the direction of a couple of shady characters in hooded sweatshirts hanging around the fringes of the station. "I'm staying close to my bag."

"Watch mine too, for a second, will you?" Ziggy says. He has to use the rest room and makes his way downstairs where, in contrast to the bustle above, he's entered a zone of eerie quiet. Closing the door to his stall, he's just about convinced himself he's alone down here when he hears a low, protracted moaning coming from somewhere nearby. He strains to hear the words but nothing comes clear, at least nothing that resembles English—it's just sound, primitive, prolonged, indecipherable. He can't even tell whether the man making that sound is experiencing pleasure or pain. It's creepy listening in on something so intimate, Ziggy doesn't want to be here. He's hoping someone else comes into the men's room, which would at least provide a distraction and maybe even convince the moaner to stop. It doesn't happen, though, and Ziggy quickly finishes his business, the sound continuing all the while, barely audibly now. He hasn't a clue to what it might mean or what he should do about it. Is somebody in trouble, maybe having a heart attack, or is it some guy jacking off, is there more than one? He knows he has to get out of here, though. He pumps a dab of liquid soap into his palm, splashes on some water and rubs his hands quickly, running them across his gritty face. Out of the men's room at last, he catches sight of a scrawny old white guy in rumpled clothes with hollow eyes and a look of general aimlessness about him, like some wino who lives on the street. God, he thinks, what a loser, just before he realizes that it's himself he's seeing, his reflection in a full-length mirror, and the recognition rattles him. He makes his way quickly up the steps, fleeing the apparition, and in seconds he's back in the lobby. The worst thing about that guy, he realizes, was that he seemed barely visible, like a ghost or even a smudge that could be removed with a shot of Windex.

He's grateful for the company when he rejoins Lennie and Roy Spears in a booth at the station restaurant. "St. Louis," Lennie is saying excitedly. "The gateway to the West. Who'd have thought I'd make it this far?" Jesus, Ziggy is thinking, was that really me I saw? A smudge? He remembers the moaning in that john under the station, like the lament of some lost traveler who was never going to be able to get back on his bus.

Spears laughs at Lennie's exclamation. "Gateway maybe," he says. "But, shoot, we're nowhere near the real west yet. This was a big city even in the nineteenth century, full of bankers and merchants. You want to find the real west, you have to get a few hundred miles beyond here. By the way," he says, dropping his voice, "did you fellows see the lady who's joining us for the next leg of the trip?"

"No." Ziggy's pleased to have some distraction.

"Young," Spears says, "a real pretty face. She's a little heavy, got some meat on her bones, but she has a pleasant personality. I'd say she's no more than twenty. Says her boyfriend ran out on her in North Carolina and she's on her way to see her mother in California, but I'd say she doesn't seem very brokenhearted. She's traveling with her own pool cue, case and all, and I think she's having a ball seeing a little of the country."

Ziggy smiles. "Sounds like the talkative type if you know all that about her already."

Spears nods. "That she is, all right. But I can tell that she's a goodhearted kid, and I'd hate to see her taken advantage of by some of these sharks you always find on buses."

"Sounds like you're appointing yourself her guardian," Ziggy says. "Maybe guardian angel."

"Well," Spears admits, "there may be a bit of truth in that. The fact is, she might very well be able to take care of herself, but yeah, I intend to keep an eye on the young lady."

"Has anybody been keeping an eye on our driver?" Lennie asks, looking at the clock. Their departure is already late. "I mean, shouldn't someone have seen him by now?"

"Well, now," says Spears, "you're right about that. I wonder if he might have taken sick all of a sudden. He did look kind of upset, didn't he?"

"He didn't look sick to me," Lennie offers. "I'm thinking something else. Do you guys think it's possible that he might have just decided to skip out on us?"

Spears frowns. "That would be pretty radical."

"But you said he was in a hurry to get someplace, didn't you?" Lennie says. "It sure looks as if we're hopelessly behind schedule now. Maybe he decided to ditch the bus and take a plane."

Spears frowns. "I don't know . . ." He ponders the possibility a moment. "Hell, I've never heard of a driver just abandoning his bus like that."

"Isn't that like a captain deserting his ship at sea?" Lennie asks. "I mean, could he be court-martialed or something?"

Spears shakes his head. "That's a little melodramatic, but you're right, a driver sure as hell isn't supposed to walk away from his bus. Damn," he says," I wonder if you could be right."

"How would we find out?" Ziggy asks.

"I'm going to the information counter," Spears says. "I'm going to have him paged. We'll find out something that way."

"You know his name?" Ziggy asks.

"Sure. Bob Cormier. It's on his uniform."

When Ziggy and Lennie return to the bay where people are waiting to re-board the bus, Lennie pulls back sharply. "Let's keep back here," he whispers. "There's someone I want to avoid." He indicates a woman, probably in her fifties, whose gray hair is pulled back in a bun. "She's a librarian whose hobby is visiting the graves of presidents. If she corners you she'll never let you go. 'People have been unkind to Mr. Hoover,' he mimics a schoolteacherly singsong. 'History will remember him as one of our greatest leaders.' Old Herbie is buried in Iowa, by the way."

"What's the matter," Ziggy kids him, "don't you like history?"

"I don't want to get to the point," Lennie says, "where the two of us are bent over her collection of pictures of Millard Fillmore's grave."

Before long it's become clear that the bus is nowhere near ready to leave and the crowd starts to get restless. Soon the story that the driver might have abandoned them begins to circulate and people begin spilling back into the station, looking for answers.

Ziggy has a chance to meet the tall, long-haired woman Spears mentioned, who's wearing jeans and a denim jacket. "Are you the one who's traveling with her own pool cue?" he asks, pointing to the skinny case she's carrying. "If so, that's a pretty short stick."

She gives him a naughty smile. "It comes in two parts," she says. "Don't worry, when I screw it together, it's plenty long enough."

Ziggy's already seen enough to conclude that this woman doesn't need any guardian angel to protect her. She may only be about twenty, as Spears said, but she seems as if she can handle herself.

"Hi," she says, extending a hand to Lennie. "I'm Sharlene, that's with an S. Hey, you're kind of cute. Do you shoot pool?"

"Sorry." Lennie's hand goes to his glasses.

"I could teach you," she suggests, "at one of our stops. I'll bet you'd pick it up pretty quick."

Lennie is agitated. "Do you realize our driver might have abandoned us?" he asks her.

Sharlene smiles broadly. "Well, funny things happen, don't they? Who knows? Maybe it was meant to turn out that way. I always say, don't make too many plans. You've got to be ready to make the most of whatever comes your way."

Lennie throws up his hands. "I'm sorry," he says, "I find all this pretty disturbing. I mean, how are we supposed to feel when the guy who's supposed to be leading us just decides to bug out?" He looks around the station as if he thinks he might be able to catch a glimpse of Bob Cormier before he skulks off, and maybe get him to change his mind. "I'm going to see if I can find Roy," he says to Ziggy. "I'll find out what I can."

When he's gone Sharlene turns to Ziggy. "You're not his dad, are you?" Ziggy shakes his head. "I was just funning with him. Though I do have a fondness for short men." She tilts her head. "Well, usually not intellectuals like him, though, but he's a lively little feller, isn't he? Jumps around like a Mexican jumping bean."

"I didn't know Lennie was an intellectual," Ziggy says.

"I guess I meant the glasses." She squints, as though trying to remember what he looked like. "The thing is, you can never tell about some of those deep thinkers. They can surprise you."

When Spears and Lennie return, it's to confirm that the driver has indeed jumped ship. "Nobody in authority can get in touch with him, so they've decided he's gone. He must have figured there was no chance he'd get to see his daughter at this rate," Lennie opines. "This is incredible," he says.

Ziggy looks at Spears. "You ready to take over?" he asks. "We're lucky to have a replacement riding with us, aren't we?"

"Real funny," Spears says. "Actually, Greyhound says they'll have another driver," he tells them. "They say within the hour, but I wouldn't hold my breath."

Lennie shakes his head. "I still can't wrap my mind around this. What a disaster. We're late already. How much longer are we going to have to wait?" He sighs. "I've had a bad feeling about this trip from the beginning, and now I'm wondering, how do we know we're even going to make it to California?"

"Look at the bright side," Sharlene gives him a big smile. "I guess we'll all have a chance to get to know each other a little better."

They all return to the restaurant, where they're joined by a wiry little guy named Wayne who Sharlene has managed to pick up in the last couple of minutes. Wayne, who works on river barges, is going to be a fellow passenger for the next segment of the trip. "I'm not going far," he tells the others. "Just to the other side of the state." His words are accompanied by the sly smile of someone who seems to know more than he's letting on, and he keeps stroking his chin when he's not talking. He's just worked thirty-eight straight days, he tells the others, and now he's going back to Pitt Corners where he has a little house. "I'm going to call ahead when we're about a hundred miles away," he says. "There's a lady who looks after my place. I'm going to have her turn the heat on." Once more he looks at the others and strokes his chin. "Been all over the world," he declares, "but there's no place like Pitt Corners." His eyes are on Sharlene. "My, that's pretty," he says, admiring the roses embroidered on her denim shirt.

"I did that myself," she says.

"You're a very talented lady, I can see," he says. He strokes his chin and smiles to himself. "You know," he says, "you really ought to see my place. I've got a real nice pool table in the basement."

Spears glowers darkly as she answers, "Actually, my plans are pretty loose. Going to get to Ventura eventually. But I don't have any timetables."

"Hey," Lennie says, "they just called our number."

"I'm not sure our new driver is an improvement," Lennie says a few miles into the next leg of their trip. "I'm already beginning to miss grim Bob Cormier."

"I don't know," Ziggy counters. "Maybe you could pick up some tips from him. He obviously thinks he's pretty funny." The driver, whose broad, amiable face and athletic build give him a vague resemblance to President Ford, has kept up a constant stream of chatter since they left St. Louis.

"Ever wonder why they call Missouri the Show-Me state?" he asks breezily, then answers his own question: "Because so many people who live there keep asking, 'Can you show me the way out of here?'" He pauses a couple of beats before a quick shift in tone, "Just kidding, all you fine folks who come from Missouri. It's a wonderful state, really." This is followed by a naughty chuckle. "I hear that up there in the capital, Jefferson City, they have at least a dozen people who can read and write." Again, the husky sincerity. "Just a little joke, folks. Just trying to make your trip a little more pleasant."

Lennie makes a sour face. "This guy's got himself some real problems: first, he needs to get someone else to write his material; then he's got to do some major work on his delivery."

It's a sunny morning and they're traveling through a rolling, thickly wooded area of the Ozarks. Ziggy is surprised to see such lush vegetation—of course, they're pretty far south by now, he reminds himself. He doesn't know what he was expecting from Missouri. He remembers a little book J.J. gave him during the war that was full of dirty jokes about hillbillies, with illustrations of skinny guys with long black beards who wore overalls and tall black hats. One of them was likely to be sitting high-kneed and sleepy-eyed on the rickety porch of a falling-down shack, a jug of moonshine by his side. The picture might include a floppy-eared mule or a pig that looked as if it had just guessed its ultimate fate, and in the distance would be a teetering outhouse with a half-moon on the door. The jokes were mostly about outhouses, moonshine and sex. He remembers one cartoon showing a naked woman who's just come out of a swimming hole. Seeing a hillbilly guy looking at her from behind a bush, she's frantically covered her front with a metal tub. You see her from behind, as Ziggy remembers, just her back and shoulders, her hands gripping the rim of the tub. Even though you can't see her expression, you can imagine the look on her face as the grinning hillbilly says to her, "I bet you think that thar tub's got a bottom to it." That kind of stuff. The Ozarks. Could have been Missouri, or maybe Arkansas.

Ziggy hadn't thought of that book until just now and yet it's all come back, the way the pages smelled as he flipped through them at the Chene-Trombley Bar, the radio in the background carrying war news. He and J.J. and Zeke the bartender were laughing. Nobody knew how anything was going to turn out.

The bus driver is talking again. "Don't want to scare you people, but they say these woods we're passing are full of fugitives, scads of folks on the run from the law: you know, army deserters, exes who are tired of paying alimony, boyfriends who have angry fathers chasing after them. Shoot, you know that fella they've been trying to catch for the last couple of years, the one they call the Missouri Slasher? There's a good chance he could be looking at us from behind one of those trees as we're driving by. Mm, mm—scares you to think of that, doesn't it? Then too, there's all those caves in this state. Heck, who knows who or what you'd find in them? Back in the days of the old west, the James gang used to use 'em as hideouts." He laughs to himself. "All I know is, I'm not picking up any hitchhikers around here."

Lennie rolls his eyes and gives a thumbs-down sign.

Later, as they're passing through a small town made up of a handful of plain frame houses set on grassless plots, each dwelling with a propane tank at its side, the driver points out a gray structure made of cinder block that houses Miss Eloise's College of Beauty. "I don't know," he says, "as many times as I've passed through this town, I can't say I've actually seen one of Miss Eloise's graduates." He waits a couple of seconds. "I'm pretty sure I've seen some people who flunked out, though." The ripple of laughter encourages him. "Thank you," he says. "Thank you, kindly."

Lennie groans. "Put a gun to my head. This is torture."

"You're just jealous," Ziggy says. "The guy's got a captive audience."

The bus makes a brief stop at the army base at Fort Leonard Wood, and the sight of all the soldiers walking around nearby clearly excites Sharlene, who's sitting a couple of rows ahead of Ziggy. She waves at the G.I.'s from the window and calls to them, though they can't hear her. "Look at all those cute army men," she says to nobody in particular. "Do you think they'd let me get off here for a while? I'll bet they have some nice pool tables there. I could get on the next bus." She turns pleadingly to Roy, though it's hard to tell how serious she is about her query.

"No, no," Roy says, "they don't let private citizens off here." Ziggy figures this can't be true. What about the people who work at the base? But it seems to be enough for Sharlene, who sinks back into her seat with a comic pout and contents herself with watching the soldiers from her window. Beside her, Wayne looks grateful.

A few miles beyond the base they stop at a roadside convenience store, where they pick up a new passenger. She's a busty woman well past her first youth who seems to have watched too many Mae West movies. Above her miniskirt, fishnet stockings and high heels, she's wearing a short jacket that seems to be made of the fur of a domestic cat, and the flowered cloth bag she's carrying could hold a litter of them. Her hair may or may not be real—the color, a vaguely metallic shade suggesting caramel corn, certainly isn't—but there's a lot of it. Getting on the bus, she moves, with much jangling of jewelry, as if she's trying to wriggle out of a tight girdle and is enjoying the process.

"My God," Lennie reports to Ziggy, "our driver actually got up and helped her in. I think he's smitten." Sure enough, once she's on board, the newcomer takes the seat behind the driver; and when the bus is underway again she begins a tête-à-tête punctuated by her frequent hearty laughs, which, much to Lennie's delight, has the effect of severely cutting down his public pronouncements.

"It's amazing," Lennie says to Ziggy after a while. "A real live floozie. Up until today I thought they only existed in books. But there's nothing else you can call someone like that. Her name is probably Moll or Doll, Nell or Belle, and I'll bet she's got a flask of whiskey in that big bag of hers. It won't be long before she's offering our driver a nip. But at least she's keeping him quiet." Raising his eyes, he says, "Thank you, God—or whatever."

At the next rest stop, when Wayne goes off to phone the woman to turn the heat on in his house, Roy says, "I know what that little weasel has in mind."

"We all do," Ziggy says. "Including Sharlene. But Wayne doesn't look too hopeful to me. I think she's already turned him down."

Roy waves away Ziggy's guess. "When he gets off that phone he's going to try to make his big move. He's getting pretty desperate."

Ziggy shakes his head. "She's just enjoying herself. I'd say it's pretty flattering to have little Wayne working so hard to please her. I'll put my money on her."

Roy says, "I'm not going to take any chances."

"Is that why you bought those Snickers bars?" Ziggy asks. Sharlene has already told them that she's partial to Snickers.

Roy laughs. "All's fair in love and war, as they say." Then he frowns. "I just don't like Wayne, don't trust him. From the first time I laid eyes on that little bugger I didn't like him. And if it's the last thing I do, he's not going to take her to that place of his."

"You, sir," Ziggy says, "are a knight in shining armor."

"So be it then," Roy says, moving with the Snickers bars in his hand toward the booth where Sharlene is waiting for Wayne to finish his phone call.

In a few minutes, Lennie joins Ziggy. He's agitated once more. "Whew," he says, "I just got away. Miss Lathrop cornered me. You know, that librarian who's visiting the graves of the presidents. 'You wouldn't believe this,' she told me, 'but I spent a whole summer visiting my sister in Indianapolis when she was sick, and it was only when I got back that I realized that Benjamin Harrison was buried there. Imagine, being so close to the grave of our twenty-third president.' She still hasn't seen it, she told me. I should have told her that's what gives life its little sizzle: unfulfilled dreams."

"I think she's sweet on you," Ziggy says. "Or maybe she's looking for some protection from that Missouri Slasher."

"I don't know," Lennie says, trying to ignore Ziggy, "she seemed awfully eager for us to get started again. I wanted to tell her not to worry, since dead presidents aren't likely to go anywhere. I mean, if there's one hobby that I wouldn't associate with impatience, it's got to be hers." He knits his brow. "Do you think our driver was making that up? About the Missouri Slasher? Has anyone seen a local paper? I never heard of this guy, of course. If he's for real, he could be on our bus for all we know. I've got a couple of candidates picked out already."

"No," Ziggy says. "Didn't you hear what the driver said? He's hiding in the woods."

"Who's hiding in the woods?" Roy asks when he comes back.

"Did you have your little talk with Sharlene?" Ziggy asks. "I can't help noticing that you don't have your candy bars with you."

"I had my five minutes with her," Roy says. "It's that little weasel's turn now. Look at him grinning. I wish he was the one who was hiding in the woods."

"Calm down, boy," Ziggy says. "You're turning purple."

As if she senses that they're talking about her, Sharlene looks over from the booth and waves to them. "There," Ziggy says, "she knows Daddy's watching. And I'd say it's a good sign she's eating that Snickers bar."

Roy smiles sourly. "I've got faith in that girl," he says.

When they start up again, Roy seems to go quiet. Something is bothering him, Ziggy guesses, and he's not sure it's just the Sharlene business. As the bus labors up a hill, Roy turns toward Ziggy and tells him, "I still don't like the way that engine sounds. They sure as hell didn't do much to this bus in St. Louis besides clean it out, and they didn't do a very good job of that." Ziggy waits for more but that seems to be all Roy has to say for the moment, and the further west they travel, the deeper his silence becomes. It's true that they're getting closer to Wayne's place, but Ziggy can't help thinking that Roy may be brooding about his visit to his son.

For some reason Ziggy remembers Al Kozak, who was beaten to death last winter, one more reminder of how the old neighborhood had gone to hell. Is it possible, he wonders, that Detroit will make a comeback some day? Not likely in my lifetime, he's thinking when he hears Roy's voice again. "Why do you suppose we're pulling off the main road here?" he says. "Can't say I'm aware of any weather detour this time."

Ziggy looks out the window: this steep, twisting two-lane blacktop can't be part of the bus's regular route. "Yeah," he says, "I see what you're saying."

Lennie leans in. "Hey, you don't suppose our bus driver could be the Slasher, could he? Maybe he's taking us into the woods to kill us all." He gives them a nervous laugh but neither of them responds.

After a few minutes, though, another passenger is apparently concerned enough about their traveling the back roads of Missouri to approach the driver and ask him about it, because after the passenger has returned to his seat the driver makes an announcement. "Some of you sharp-eyed people may have noticed we left the main highway a couple of minutes ago. Guess I should explain that I'm doing a favor for a lady who's got to get to work. I know we've got a lot of working people aboard and I'm sure you don't mind a very short detour that's kind of an act of kindness, do you? We can make up the time once we're back on the highway."

"The floozie," Lennie exclaims. "I can't believe it." Sure enough, after at least fifteen minutes' travel across the back roads, the bus enters the outskirts of a doggy town and pulls into the parking lot next to a low cinder block building whose neon sign announces the place as Cal's Cave. A string of Christmas tree lights above the door spells out "Welcome." Ziggy wonders who the hell comes to a place in the boondocks like this to drink. He wouldn't be surprised to see one of those leaning outhouses from the little book J.J. gave him.

"Suppose she tends bar there?" Lennie speculates. "Or does she own the place? I hope our driver at least got her phone number." The bus comes to a stop and the woman gets out of her seat and slings her bag over her shoulder. When the door opens with a hiss, the driver accompanies her out and walks her to the door of the building, where he decorously bows and kisses her hand. There's a spring in his step as he returns to the bus and excitement in his voice when he announces, "Once a Boy Scout, always a Boy Scout. That's my good deed for the day." A couple of people actually applaud but it doesn't seem as if that's the majority sentiment.

The bus does indeed pick up speed once they're back on the highway, though it's not a sure thing that they'll make up the lost time. They're still behind schedule when they arrive at the town where Wayne is getting off, and Ziggy watches him as he grimly gathers his things and says goodbye to Sharlene, who smiles brightly and gives him a peck on the cheek but is clearly not going to accompany him. When the bus pulls away at last, leaving Wayne behind, Ziggy leans over and whispers to Roy, "Looks like you guessed right about old Wayne striking out."

The other man smiles. "Oh, I always had faith in Sharlene's judgment," he says, "but I don't like to leave things to chance. When I had those few minutes alone with her at the last rest stop, I told her I was proud of the way she was making Wayne feel good—given what he'd told me about the terrible social disease he had."

"You're a pretty wily old dog, aren't you?"

"I never claimed I was dense, did I?" He frowns. "I told you, I just didn't like that guy. There was no way she was leaving with him."

Well, Ziggy thinks, if she didn't leave with Wayne it was because she didn't want to. When she decides to go, though, even Roy won't be able to stop her.

"I like Sharlene," Roy says, apropos of nothing. "She's got a lot of spunk. It's just that when you're that way, sometimes you need somebody else to be careful for you."

A few miles into Oklahoma, Roy leans back once again. "Listen to that," he says, his face wrinkled with concentration. He holds up a finger and Ziggy turns his attention to the sound of the bus's engine. Even he can tell now that there's something wrong. For the last couple of miles the bus has been traveling more slowly, and even to Ziggy's untrained ear, the engine's power seems to come and go in fitful spurts, like a balky plumbing system. He's grateful to see that they're on the outskirts of a town.

"What's that smell?" Lennie asks as the bus labors along the town's main street. "Isn't that smoke outside your window?"

He's right: Ziggy isn't the only one to see the black plume, and a mournful ululation ripples through the bus. There are shouts and cries of alarm. Within seconds, a few people have bolted upright in their seats, two or three have scrambled into the aisle. Frantically, the driver appeals for calm. "Everything is under control," he yells, jerking the bus off the road. Through the smoke Ziggy can see that the crippled vehicle has pulled into a large open area on the edge of a used car lot. "Seems we've got a little problem," the driver announces with a failed attempt to sound in control when he's turned off the engine. "Let me get a look at what's wrong. Meanwhile, if you good folks would just stay where you are, I'll report back to you right away."

It's immediately clear, though, that not many people relish the idea of staying on a bus that may be on fire, and he's quickly followed out the door by those who are sitting in the front seats, which precipitates a rush of the rest of the passengers. Before long, they're all gathered around the bus in the warm Oklahoma air that's slightly acrid with the smell of smoke, though the plume itself has pretty much dissipated and there seem to be no lingering flames. Not far away, colorful pennants flutter above shiny cars that carry signs reading, "A Steal," "Like New," and "Easy Terms."

"OK, OK," the driver tells the group with a harried air, "I'm going to have to check this out." He wipes his brow with a handkerchief. All traces of his former high spirits have vanished. "I'm going to call the company and see what they can do," he says. "Meanwhile, I guess we're likely to be here for a while." He looks at his watch. "Why not take a look around town and check back here in, say, an hour?" There's a collective groan punctuated by curses and angry muttering.

Gradually the passengers begin to disperse, and Ziggy looks from the smoke-stained bus to his new surroundings, a cluster of commercial properties not far from the center of town. Certainly Roy can't say they're not in the real west now. Ziggy's already noticed a number of people on the street who are dressed in cowboy clothes. Oddly, some of them seem to be wearing cowboy clothes from another time—a bearded man who looks like a gambler from *Maverick* with his flat-topped hat and flowered vest is standing in front of a booth in the used car lot looking at the bus, a toothpick moving in his mouth. And it's begun to dawn on Ziggy that an awful lot of men seem to be wearing beards. Has the bus driven through a time warp, he wonders.

"Look," Lennie points to a sign above the street that says, "Frontier Days." Carnival music comes to them distantly from what looks like the town center a couple of blocks away. A crowd is gathered there and it's clear some kind of celebration is going on.

"Well," Roy says, "if we had to make an unannounced stop, it looks like we got lucky and landed in a pretty interesting place." He sniffs at the air. "Ah, that's the real west," he says. "You can smell the dryness."

So that's what it is, Ziggy thinks. He hadn't been able to put his finger on it.

The three of them have moved about a block or two from the abandoned bus. Nearby is a bar that's been decorated to look like a saloon from the Wild West. "Territory Days Prices," reads a sign above the door.

"Hey, I guess I can deal with that," Roy says. "Let me buy you one."

"Sure thing," Ziggy nods. He can taste the dryness in his mouth, smell the dust on the windy air. "What about you, Lennie?"

"I don't know," he says. "I thought I'd take a look at what's happening down the block."

"We'll join you after a drink," Roy says. "How about you, Sharlene?"

She's already picked up with a pair of local cowboys. "These nice gentlemen have offered to show me around," she says.

Roy frowns. "You boys be awful sure you take good care of that little lady," he says, and the bearded cowboys acknowledge this with a touch of their hats. When they leave, he shakes his head. "I bet she'd be able to find a man in one of those harems."

"She's young," Ziggy says. "She wants to have a little fun. Besides, how far can they go here?"

They're met by a blast of air-conditioning when they enter the bar but, after a short passageway, they encounter a set of swinging doors like the ones in the saloons of old westerns. The floor is covered with sawdust and behind the bar there's a large gilt-edged mirror and a painting of Custer's Last Stand.

The furniture looks like the kind that gets routinely broken on the bodies of brawling Hollywood cowboys. Roy orders a couple of draughts of beer from the mustachioed bartender whose slick hair is parted in the middle.

"I'll be back in a minute," Ziggy says when he sees the sign for the men's room.

The tinkling sounds of "Buffalo Gals, Won't You Come Out Tonight" from an old-fashioned player piano follow him down the corridor, fading as the men's room door closes behind him, but still distantly audible. He could be at a Saturday afternoon western at the Ritz Theatre back on Chene Street, and the thought pulls him into an abstracted state. The men's room itself is clean and modern. A sweet soapy smell is a welcome relief to his dry nose, and a few feet away, across the tiled floor, there's a sink with shiny chrome fixtures. He moves toward the gleaming porcelain bowl, still dimly aware of the music, which is now caught up in a dim roar, like the sound inside a seashell, coming in waves. He's very tired, it hits him all at once, overwhelmingly weary from all this traveling— and he's a bit woozy as well. He catches a brief glimpse of himself in the mirror and suddenly everything around him seems a hundred miles away, as if he's dreaming all this; and then he's on the floor, his cheek pressed against the cool tile. Hearing the loud beating of his heart, he wonders, what just happened? Did he actually faint? For a moment he's not sure where he is, then, moment by moment, he orients himself. He blinks the world into darkness and then back to light. He moves his fingers, tentatively pushes out a foot—thank God he's not paralyzed. He remembers feeling lightheaded just before everything went blank. Now, on the floor, he knows he has to get up but he isn't ready yet. His heart races. What is it? All that sitting on the bus? Should he have been drinking more water? Is it his heart? Has he just had a stroke?

Carefully he brings himself to his knees and rests there for a few seconds until with a grunt he's ready to pull himself back into a standing position. Fortunately, no one else has come into the room. Most of the other passengers must have gone to see what was happening down the street. When he gets to his feet at last he leans on the sink, he waits for his head to clear and examines himself in the mirror. No cuts or bruises—he was lucky when he fell, he must have just crumpled. He turns the faucet and the water hisses, he splashes some on his face. But what the hell was that about? Looking down at his old man's trembling hands, he realizes how scared he is. Is he sick? Is it possible that he's going to die on this trip? *Christ, I'm sixty-five years old. It could all be over for me in the blink of an eye.* He feels a jolt of pure terror and stands there, leaning against the sink, letting the feeling pass through him.

"You were in there a while," Roy says when he returns. A good portion of his beer is already drunk.

Ziggy tries for a smile, then settles carefully into his seat at the bar. "I think I prefer johns on dry land over that cramped little cabinet we have at the back of the bus," he says.

Roy nods, distracted, then sighs. "This trip is like some kind of bad dream for me. The closer we get to the finish, the slower things become." There's a note in his voice that Ziggy's picked up on before, and he's convinced that this is just an introduction, that Roy has something important to tell him. He re-experiences a brief twinge of the terror that visited him in the men's room, but he takes a deep drag on his cigarette, holds in the tobacco smoke for a while before exhaling, and things are better. Not great, but better. "You eager to see your kid?" he asks.

Roy takes a long drink and sighs, then shakes his head. "Not really," he says. "No, not really at all." There's a pause before he goes on. "I don't expect this to be an easy visit but it's something I've got to do."

Ziggy takes a quick drink of his beer. "You and your kid don't get along?" he asks.

Roy sighs again. "Tyler is only part of the story," he says. "You see . . ." He takes another swallow of beer before going on. When he resumes he has the resigned air of a suspect who's decided to confess at last after a punishing round of questioning. "The fact is, for a long time I was a lousy husband and father." He looks into his glass. "Lou and I had two kids, Martha and Tyler." He pauses as if to allow Ziggy to digest this information. Still avoiding Ziggy's eyes, he goes on. "The fact is, I had a rough time back in Texas." He lifts a hand an inch or two from the table and lets it drop. "I basically got run out of town for my misbehavior, but the straw that broke my marriage was when my daughter ran away." Once again he pauses before going on. "She was fifteen when she just took off one day in the middle of the week and left a note saying that she just couldn't stand it anymore, all the fighting at home." He stops as though pausing for breath.

"You said your wife died five years ago?" Ziggy asks after a while.

Roy leans forward heavily. "That's right," he says. "Only what I didn't tell you is that she wasn't my wife anymore by that time. She left me as soon as it was clear Martha wasn't coming back." He shakes his head slowly. "We drove her away, she said, and she was right. I suppose what she was really saying was that I drove her away, and I'll accept that." He runs his fingers abstractedly along the sides of his glass. "I was too busy with other things, I guess. You see, my father was a preacher and I'd had a pretty deprived time of it when I was growing up, and as soon as I got free of him I told myself I was going to enjoy life. Well, enjoying life meant drinking, gambling and partying." When he stops it's clear he's remembering specific scenes. "I never noticed," he goes on, "that time was passing real quick and my kids were growing up. Pretty soon my little daughter was a teenager, she needed more from me. And my son too, for that matter . . ." He drifts off.

The piano continues playing music from the old west, and the two of them turn when a pair of gray-bearded men who could be car salesmen enter the saloon, bringing with them a brief wash of sound from the outside. "Yee-haw, I've got me a real thirst," one of them shouts. "Ditto for me," the other echoes, and they belly up to the other end of the bar.

When things settle down Roy resumes his story, his voice firmer now. "OK, why I'm on this trip. Lately I've had reason to believe that Tyler has been in contact with his sister—no proof, really, but some interesting indications." He nods to himself. "That's what I'm going there to see him about. Now the problem is, he and I don't get along very well, we don't communicate much: he doesn't write, he won't answer my calls. The only way I'll ever get him to talk about his sister is if I go to see him."

He pulls himself erect for a moment. "Will he tell me anything? Does he know anything? I have no idea, really. But it would mean an awful lot to me if I could believe at least that Martha's still alive somewhere, that, whatever else I did to her, I didn't cause her death." His voice breaks on the last phrase and he clears his throat. "If my son will talk to me," he continues, "and that's a big 'if,' I want to try to do right by my kids, finally. I intend to tell him I'm not making any demands on either of them, I just want to know if Martha's all right. I don't have to know where she's living, if she's married or not, any of that. If she needs anything, I'll be glad to help and I'll do it through him if she doesn't want anything to do with me. I just want to find out."

Well, Ziggy thinks, some busman's holiday. "Boy," he says, "I can sympathize with you. I've done a few things myself I wish I could take back. I sure hope things go well for you and your kid."

Roy nods. "Thanks," he says, "I appreciate that."

"You must be getting nervous as we get closer to that army base. I know I would."

"Yeah," Roy says. "Nervous and scared. But I have to try this. At any rate, I'll know pretty soon how all this turns out."

"Well," Ziggy says, "we'll be getting another bus sooner or later. It can't be that far to Oklahoma City."

"No, it isn't." Roy is silent for a long while. "Thanks again," he says. Then he brightens. "So why don't we enjoy ourselves while we're here and find out what these Frontier Days are all about?" They've learned from the bartender that the town is celebrating its seventy-fifth anniversary.

Out in the street they immediately encounter a pair of bearded cowboys engaged in a serious conversation. "Probably a couple of bankers discussing mortgages," Roy observes. He looks around. "I wonder where the Indians have gone?"

Ziggy and Roy make their way in the direction of all the activity a few blocks away, the music becoming louder all the while, occasionally punctuated by the popping of gunfire, presumably blanks. Soon they're smelling sawdust and cotton candy as they enter the area of carnival booths and rides set up in the street. Near the merry-go-round a sign in old-fashioned lettering informs readers that all mature males have been ordered to wear beards for the celebration, and the failure to do so is only one of the violations against the "western spirit" that can send the offender to the "hoosegow," which the bartender had explained was a mock jailhouse on an elevated platform across from the city hall.

A couple of minutes after reading the proclamation about facial hair, Ziggy and Roy are challenged by a sharp-nosed red-faced man wearing a huge Stetson hat and boots that look to be made of rattlesnake skin. A badge identifies him as a deputy and, of course, he's bearded, though his facial hair is thin. "Excuse me," he says. "I couldn't help noticing that you two gents have bare chins."

"We're strangers here, just passing through" Roy declares, entering into the spirit of the game. "We've got the papers to prove it."

The deputy looks them over with mock care before waving away Roy's offer. "Shoot, fellas," he says. "Enjoy yourselves."

"How are you boys doing?" Sharlene waves to them from under the umbrella of one of the outdoor tables where she's having a beer with her cowboy friends. "Did you hear what happened to Lennie? He managed to get himself arrested." She smiles. "It's just for fun, though."

Just like Lennie, Ziggy thinks. "Where is he?" he asks.

"One of those deputies arrested him and said he was taking him to that jail over there. Actually, Lennie was pretty upset. He didn't want to go but that deputy was a big guy."

"Let's have a look," says Roy.

Carnival music swirls around them and children shriek at the popping of more fake gunfire. The two of them make their way toward the city hall and it isn't long before they have a clear view of the cage elevated above the street, a backward "S" on the HOOSEGOW sign over the door. It looks to be about fifteen by fifteen and, sure enough, there, behind bars, is Lennie, a picture of despair as he slumps, head in hands, in the chair that's the only piece of furniture in the cramped space. When the prisoner looks up and sees them, he springs abruptly to his feet and runs to the bars, where he yells, "Get me out of this place. Please."

Ziggy's first impulse is to think Lennie's overreacting, as usual. After all, this isn't a real jail cell. But as he clutches the bars a gang of bearded young drunks at a nearby table sends up a loud, nasty "boo." "Go back to where you came from, city slicker," one voice booms. "We're real Americans," another shouts at Lennie, "and we don't need your kind out here."

"God, guns and guts," a third one chimes in. "That's what made the west great."

This could get ugly, Ziggy thinks, and Lennie shouldn't have to put up with this. "Who's in charge here?" he asks.

"That would be me."

Ziggy turns to see a bearded man in jeans and a Stetson who looks like an ex-linebacker gone to seed. His eyes are the color of dirty water and the deputy badge pinned to his Western shirt a couple of inches above his swelling paunch identifies him as Dewey Rawlins.

Roy steps forward. "How can we get our friend out of there?" he asks mildly.

The man cocks his head and looks at Roy, his mouth curled into a sneer. "Oh," he drawls in all seriousness, "he's got to serve his full sentence of an hour. He's only been here ten minutes so far."

This guy's one mean son-of-a-bitch, Ziggy can see. His blood is boiling. "Look, mister," he says, pushing ahead of Roy, "we don't live in this town, we're just passing through. You don't have any jurisdiction over this man. Let him out of there or I'll call a real cop, if there is such a thing in this town."

Dewey Rawlins' mouth moves sideways for a few seconds before he speaks, and out of the blue it comes to Ziggy that this pretend deputy looks like a man who'd buy a dog just so he could kick it around. "That little fella there insulted the western way of life," Rawlins says levelly. "He made remarks to some of our leading citizens that weren't very friendly." His mouth finally twists upward into a strained smile though his eyes remain cold and steely. "Hey, this is all in fun. Can't you fellows take a joke?" The last question sounds like a threat.

"How do we get him out?" Ziggy persists, stepping close enough to him so that the cowboy can surely smell the beer on his breath.

The deputy retreats a half step, as if he needs more room to launch a kick, all the while keeping Ziggy locked in his gaze, but Ziggy has no intention of backing down. "The fine is five dollars," Rawlins says at last, throwing in, "it goes toward the building of a new town library."

"Here," Ziggy fumbles with his wallet and pulls out a wrinkled bill. "Maybe you can buy yourself a book with this. As for us, we've got a bus to catch."

The man looks at the money for a few seconds as if there's a chance he might refuse it, but he takes it at last, slowly smoothing it in his hand before pocketing it. He lifts an oversized set of keys from a table near the jail and takes his own sweet time before opening the cell door, muttering something to Lennie as he exits. Lennie hurries past without looking back, though Dewey Rawlins has enough time to hiss something else to him before he's out of earshot. The prisoner's release is accompanied by a smattering of "boos" from nearby. The three of them leave the area of the jail as gunshots pop around them.

"I'm going to look in on Sharlene," Roy tells the other two when they near her table.

"Sure thing," Ziggy says, and he and the silent Lennie walk back in the direction of the saloon.

"What did that guy say to you back there?" Ziggy asks after a while.

Lennie snorts. "He said, 'You're lucky your friends came for you, you little shit. The snake was next.'"

"The snake?"

"Yeah, he said with some of their so-called prisoners they put a rattlesnake into the jail cell with them. It's horseshit, of course, but that guy's a sadist who wanted to see me sweat. I wouldn't be surprised if he'd actually found some big harmless old snake and would have stuck it in with me just to watch me cringe." When he takes off his glasses for a moment, he looks different—stronger, more determined. Underneath the outer layer, Ziggy can see, there's a toughness to this would-be comic.

"What did you say to him that would piss him off so much?" he asks.

Lennie shakes his head. "From the second that asshole and his friends saw me, they started needling me. One of them said, 'A nose like that you can only get in New York.' I mean, those guys have probably seen three Jews in their lives, but that was apparently enough for them. I'm sure old Dewey's got a swastika in his bedroom. I guess he and his buddies just wanted to put a little scare in me." Lennie lets out a long breath. "Well, I'll tell you, I'm tired of being scared. I told him I'd read somewhere that in the Indian language Oklahoma means 'Shit-hole.' That's when Dewey really started to throw his weight around." Lennie snickers. "I guess some people just can't take a little joke."

"Good for you," Ziggy says. "That guy needs some lessons in manners. And the same goes for his buddies."

When they're seated in the saloon, Lennie runs his hands through his hair and says, "I'll tell you, I had some doubts about California, but after this, I can't wait to get there. I mean, anything would be an upgrade over this place."

"Amen to that," Ziggy says, and lifts his glass. Remembering the hard, cold eyes of the fake deputy, he realizes how much he needs this drink. Jesus, he thinks, there's a lot more work involved in traveling than I expected.

Across from him, Lennie raises his glass and downs his whiskey in a swallow. "Whew!" he says. His eyes are glassy and he shakes his head like a dog who's just had a bath. Then a kind of peace descends on him, or at least such peace as Lennie Kurzweil is able to manage, accompanied by a dopey smile.

"What's the joke?" Ziggy asks.

"If Leah could see me now," Lennie says. "She wouldn't believe it."

And soon he's telling Ziggy about his long sad romance with Leah Pritzker. "She's a librarian in Brooklyn. I've known her since grammar school." He smiles to himself. "Leah's sexy in a sneaky way. To me, her glasses were erotic objects. I mean, she was always reading and when her eyes were tired she'd take off her glasses and put them down—looking at those smudged lenses, the elegant curve where the glasses fit behind her ears, it would make my . . . my heart jump, if you know what I mean. She's got this lush black hair that would fall like heavy drapery when she let it down—I can smell that hair when I close my eyes." Now he does just that for a few seconds, savoring the memory. He and Leah would have stimulating discussions about books, politics, movies, he says. "No," he corrects himself. "Not stimulating, incandescent." He shakes his head. "Leah is one smart woman."

He's silent for a while. When he resumes, the light in his eyes is colder. "The problem was, Leah was impatient to get married and start a family—to start her life, really. She didn't like the uncertainty of my life, the dubiousness of my prospects, you might say." He takes a deep breath, as if getting ready for what he has to say next, and he sighs. "Finally she gave me an ultimatum and then not only did she break up with me but she started dating my cousin Morris." He glowers. "This is a guy in every way unlike me, a loudmouth who was on the rise in his father's glove factory, the kind of guy who's always said to have excellent prospects."

He gives Ziggy a look of disgust. "I mean, it's transparent, isn't it? He's so different from me that the only reason she started going out with him had nothing to do with liking or not liking him; it was just her way of shocking me into getting regular work." Lennie looks into his empty glass, picks it up and puts it to his mouth again. "In all truth," he says, "I was wavering. I mean, was this ever going to work out, this dream of mine of being a comic? I didn't know. But when she brought Morris to the restaurant where I was working as a waiter and in spite of all my protests I had to wait on them, it was the last straw."

He's silent for a while, as if he's deciding whether or not to continue. When he does, the words come quickly. "I mean, the guy was so pompous that I couldn't help myself: I just flipped and poured a dish of lasagna into his lap." He brings the empty glass to his lips once more and slams it to the bar. "I was fired, of course, I was through with Leah, I knew, but I felt strangely liberated by that act and it was then and there that I decided on this LA venture."

He looks down at the bar for a few seconds; then his head shoots up. "Listen," he says with a sudden urgency, "I should have thought of this before, but it came to me in that jail: you never can tell what's going to happen when you're traveling. Let me give you an address in case I have some kind of emergency."

"Hey," Ziggy protests, "we'll be out of this town pretty soon, and if we're lucky we'll never see it again."

Lennie nods. "I know," he says, "But still . . . Anything can happen out here, can't it?" Ziggy remembers the episode in the men's room and tries to push back the memory. Meanwhile, Lennie reaches into his pocket and pulls out a little notebook. Is this where he writes down jokes? Ziggy wonders. With a ballpoint pen he quickly scribbles something onto one of the pages and tears it out. "What about you?" he asks. "You got any address for me in case something should happen to you?" He tears the sheet in two and hands the part without writing to Ziggy.

To Ziggy's surprise, this solemn moment is a bit upsetting. His hand is shaking as he writes his own address and phone number in Detroit and exchanges papers with Lennie. He's also surprised when he looks at what Lennie's written. He'd expected to see Leah's name.

"Sam's my agent," Lennie explains. "He'll know how to get hold of the important people."

"Sure thing," Ziggy says, pocketing the paper.

The two of them are silent for a long time while phantom fingers strike the keys of the player piano and Ziggy thinks of how different this bar is from Connie's back in the neighborhood. He remembers the place on the night of Eddie Figlak's wake, the people, the noise, the "Helen Polka." Odd, he thinks, the way time works. It seems months since he was last in Detroit.

When a replacement bus eventually arrives from Oklahoma City, the passengers are told that they'll be leaving in twenty minutes—without their previous driver—who's been instructed to stay with the old vehicle. Though a number of people seem to want to prolong this carnival interlude to the last possible moment, Ziggy notices Miss Lathrop, the woman who's visiting the graves of presidents, is already in her seat. Lennie's right: she certainly is eager to resume her hobby.

"Ziggy," an excited Lennie is suddenly at his side. "I need your help. We have just enough time too."

"For what?" Ziggy asks.

"You'll never believe what I discovered," Lennie says, and he leads him to an alley near the bar where they had a drink. "See that black pickup?"

"Sure," Ziggy says.

"Look at that license plate." Ziggy can see that it reads "DU-EE." "That's his, our deputy's, I'm sure," says Lennie. "It's about his level of ingenuity."

Ziggy isn't too keen about going along with this escapade, but he can't deny that Lennie deserves his shot at revenge. So he agrees to stand watch at the head of the alley while Lennie deflates two of the truck's tires. "Come on, come on," Ziggy urges. "Two is enough."

At last Lennie scurries out. "Let's get on that bus now," he says. "And I hope it leaves right away."

A few minutes later they're rolling westward. "Good riddance to Dodge City," Lennie says as they leave town. He chuckles to himself and sings, "I fought the law and *I* won." He holds up a hand. "I know it was petty, beneath me, really, but sometimes if pettiness is all that's available, you might as well be petty. Anyway, it sure felt good." At that moment, Lennie seems happier than at any other time during the trip.

At the same time, as the dry, empty landscape moves past, Ziggy's spirits are sinking. Without the distractions of their last stop, he's haunted once more by that fainting spell in the men's room. It could happen to anyone, he keeps telling himself, it could mean nothing at all. Dehydration— aren't they always talking about that? Then again, who knows what else it could mean?

"Hey, you're being pretty quiet," Lennie observes.

"I'm having fond memories of Frontier Days," he answers.

One thing that's contributing to his mood is that Roy is leaving them in Oklahoma City, just a few miles away. He hadn't realized until now how big a part of this trip the tour bus driver from New Jersey has been, especially since his revelation in the saloon. I'm never going to know how that story comes out, he thinks.

When they get to Oklahoma City at last, everybody gets off the bus and collects their luggage. They have a longer layover here because they're changing buses.

"Well, pardners," Roy says as he takes leave of Ziggy and Lennie, "I hope you both find what you want in LA." All three of them are standing beside their bags.

"You too," Ziggy says. "I hope things go well with your kid."

"Thanks." He lowers his voice. "You'll look after Sharlene, won't you?" Back in the town where Lennie'd been briefly imprisoned, Roy had been able to drive off her two cowboy admirers and have a heart-to-heart talk, he told Ziggy.

"Sure thing."

"Well . . ." Roy begins, though he never finishes the sentence. Instead, he picks up his bag and turns away.

Before he has a chance to disappear into the crowd, though, Sharlene herself races across the bus station to him and wraps her arms around him, almost knocking him over in the process. She squeezes him hard and for a while it looks as if she isn't going to let him go. When she does at last, her eyes are wet. "*Vaya con dios*," Roy manages to mutter.

"Bye, my Snickers man," Sharlene says before walking away quickly without looking back.

When the bus resumes its journey westward, Ziggy sits there vacantly looking out at the dusty landscape. He's tired, his bones ache, and a savage homesickness has gripped him. Everything's so bare here, it's so different from Michigan with all its lakes and woods. On Mort Neff's *Michigan Outdoors* TV show, they're always going to some place like Houghton Lake up north and catching lots of lunkers. Houghton Lake: it was so strange that J.J. went up there to live after he got out of prison, J.J. who always talked about moving to Florida. That was a sad story. Ziggy isn't sure how their friendship would have fared if it hadn't been for J.J.'s wife. After his sentencing

Ziggy went to visit her in their big place in Indian Village, but she wouldn't let him in the door, she called him a Judas. They weren't going to be able to stay there, she told Ziggy, as if everything was his fault. She convinced J.J. to move up north when he got out, and Ziggy'd pretty much accepted that he'd never hear from his old friend again, when out of the blue J.J. called him last year to tell him he was dying of cancer. It was an odd conversation, real short, over too quickly. Ziggy wished he'd had a chance to get ready for it. J.J. said he didn't really like it up north.

"They call this God's country," he said, "but that's only if you're a bear." It was the old J.J. When Ziggy asked him about prison, he said it wasn't so bad, as long as you were careful. Ziggy wanted to hear more about it but J.J. just cut him short and said, "Look, all this stuff between us was bullshit. I don't blame you for what you did, I'd have done the same thing myself." Why did things happen the way they did? He didn't know, he said, but when you were dying you saw that it was stupid to hold grudges. Then he said, "We had some times, didn't we?" He actually sounded happy. "Remember Niagara Falls," he said, "remember the party on the island after the raid? You and me," he said, "we did better than our fathers did, you have to say that. We had something, didn't we?"

When Ziggy asked J.J. if he could come to see him, though, he said it wouldn't be such a good idea. "Marie's taking all this stuff hard," he said. "I think it's easier for her if there are good guys and bad guys."

"Hey," he said, "if they've got numbers down where I'm going, I'll try to save a spot for you." It was amazing, Ziggy thought, that he kept his sense of humor under the circumstances.

"Oh, my God." Ziggy's reverie is interrupted by Lennie's exclamation.

"What?" he asks.

"I just figured it out," Lennie says. "The Missouri Slasher. It's Wayne."

Ziggy looks at him. Does this guy's mind ever stop spinning out fantasies?

"Think of it," Lennie says, "that house he keeps coming back to. His basement could be filled with bodies." He's quiet for a while. "Well," he says at last, "we'll never know, will we?"

That's right, Ziggy thinks, there's a lot I'm never going to know.

Some distance west of Oklahoma City, the bus is moving through a particularly desolate stretch of landscape when the new driver announces that they're going to make an unscheduled stop in the next town but that nobody will be allowed to leave the bus.

"What's going on?" Lennie asks. "Don't tell me this bus is going to break down too. I don't think I can take any more of this. Or are we going to change drivers again? And why won't they let us get off?"

Speculation mounts among the passengers until the bus reaches the next town and is directed to pull over by a state trooper standing near the flashing lights of his car in the parking lot of a diner. There's another state police car parked nearby, and when the driver follows the signals and brings the bus to a stop, the doors hiss open and a pair of grim-looking officers step aboard.

"Will Amelie Lathrop please identify herself?" one of them calls. After a certain amount of nervous shuffling, the woman who's visiting the graves of presidents brings herself to her feet and calmly answers, "I'm Amelie Lathrop." The policeman summons her to come forward but when she reaches down, presumably to pick up her bag, the man takes a step forward and shouts, "Keep your hands at your sides, ma'am, keep your hands at your sides." Ziggy's squirming to get a view. Even from this distance it's clear that the cop is nervous, ready to draw his weapon at the slightest suspicious move. "We'll get your things for you, ma'am," he adds hastily, keeping a careful eye on her as he indicates with his hand that he wants her to come forward. "Easy now," he says, "easy now." When she reaches the front of the bus the cop deftly cuffs her and is about to lead her out the door, when she suddenly resists and turns toward her fellow passengers, shouting something at them before she's hustled off the bus.

"What did she say?" Lennie asks while the other passengers all ask their own version of that question. "Do you think she could be the Missouri Slasher after all?"

While they watch Miss Lathrop, no longer resisting arrest, being led into one of the police cars, word bubbles back that the woman's parting comment was, "You're all a bunch of suckers." As the car with the captive speeds off, another trooper gives the bus driver permission to resume the trip. Once on the road, the driver informs his passengers that their former traveling companion is charged with allegedly running off with the funds from the bank in Illinois where she works.

"That lady was quite an actress," Lennie says after a while. "Think of all the trouble she had to go through to create that whole librarian persona and learn all that stuff about the graves of presidents as a cover story, because, you know what? I'll bet my last dollar that all those little facts she mentioned about the presidents' graves are true. Think of the discipline. I should have paid more attention to her. I'll bet I could have learned a thing or two from her about show business."

Clearly he's still thinking about the unlikely thief for a while afterwards, smiling to himself. At last he says, "In a way, though, I think it would have been a better story if she'd really been a librarian and robbed all that money, because then we'd all be asking ourselves why she'd have needed so much dough, and the logical conclusion would have to be that she had to have it to feed her habit of visiting presidential graves. Pretty soon people would be nodding their heads sagely and saying, it starts out innocently enough with a sneaky visit to Grant's Tomb, and before you know it you're knocking over a gas station to bankroll a trip to Herbert Hoover's grave."

Ziggy smiles. "I think I'm beginning to get a better idea of the way your mind works."

CHAPTER FIVE

≈≈

Staring through the dirty window at some flat, dusty stretch of Oklahoma (unless they've already passed into Texas and he hadn't noticed), Ziggy's awash with exhaustion. Jesus, he thinks, I couldn't move a muscle right now, even if there was a rattlesnake down on the floor next to my shoe. He feels as if he weighs a ton, like one of those TV astronauts climbing into space at the top of a shuddering metal cylinder, his face gone rubbery under the punishing force of the thrusting rocket, blood, bones and organs turned to stone. The image is scary, and Ziggy has a brief flash of his uncle Stanley, a white-faced mummy with a crooked, lipless mouth, slumped in his wheelchair, a plaid blanket over his legs even in the stifling heat of a Detroit summer. His mother wouldn't listen to any of Ziggy's pleas or excuses. "He's your uncle, he always used to give you a nickel when he came over. It'll make him feel good to see you." You sure couldn't tell that from the slack face and empty eyes, though. What those eyes were seeing Ziggy, who couldn't wait to get back outside, didn't want to think about.

That's not me, he insists as the southwestern landscape rolls by, I'm not that old. He jerks up suddenly in his seat, pushing through the bleary stupor with a grunt.

"Hey, what's up?" Lennie asks.

"Nothing," Ziggy says. "A cramp, that's all."

Lennie nods. "It's been a long trip. A lot of sitting."

"Yeah." Ziggy takes a deep breath. If it were only something as simple as that. Of course there was no cramp, it was something else entirely that's been bothering him and he can't help wondering what could have sent him into this funk. Is it that, after all that adventure in the town where they were celebrating Frontier Days, there's been an inevitable letdown? Or does this feeling have anything to do with Roy's leaving? He was a nice guy but you could hardly say he and Ziggy were best friends. Whatever, this bus ride, which has seemed full of adventure up until now, seems suddenly stale, dry and endless, like the landscape around him; and once more he's struck by the way time changes shape so quickly: it seems ages ago that he and Roy were walking through the cowboy-filled streets on the way to freeing Lennie from the hoosegow.

Of course, something dramatic like that can't be happening all the time, can it? But he remembers the feel of the heat on his skin, the buzz of the crowd, the smell of cotton candy and sawdust, the sense that something was about to happen. Moved by the memory, he suddenly wishes he could tell Maggie the story. He knows she'd get a kick out of it. What's she doing now, he wonders—reading one of those romance novels—and what's the weather like back in Detroit? Gray, probably, maybe drizzling, but she'd be in the kitchen where it's warm and cozy. Out here in Okie country, he feels a strong need to connect with the place he's left behind, if only to reassure himself that he still belongs there, that he'll be welcomed back when he returns.

Wouldn't it be a surprise to Maggie if he called her? The agreement was that he wasn't going to get in touch with her until he was out in California but, given everything that's already happened on this trip, he's going to be late getting there, which means that he's dealing with a special situation. It would be a good idea to give her an update on what's happened so far, wouldn't it? And calling her would go a long way toward getting him out of the dumps.

By the time they reach the next rest stop, he's decided that's just what he's going to do. His fist full of change, he closes the folding door of the outdoor phone booth attached to a diner, and in the stale air he listens to the musical sounds of the dropped quarters. An invisible insect buzzes somewhere near him as his eyes run across the initials and phone numbers a dozen previous occupants have scribbled and scratched onto all available spaces in the booth. There's even a number for "Trish W." on the ceiling. Ziggy's trying to figure out how the writer managed to keep the numbers aligned so neatly at that height as he listens to the phone ringing in Detroit. As the ringing continues, he wonders: Maggie couldn't be out, could she? Is she visiting one of the kids? Is something wrong? The uncertainty stirs an obscure agitation. It could be anger, it could be fear—whatever it is, it increases until, just as he's about to decide that he's picked the wrong time to call, he hears her answer at last.

"Maggie?" His relieved greeting comes out like a vaguely accusatory shout as he leans over the receiver, a man trying to light a cigarette in a windstorm with a single match.

"I was in the basement putting things in the dryer," she explains, sounding a little out of breath. Disappointingly, the voice that comes to Ziggy over the phone is tinny and distant, the voice of a stranger, and this puts him off for a moment. "Is something wrong?" that voice asks.

"No," he says abruptly. "There's nothing wrong." For some reason her question has irritated him.

"Where are you?" she asks after a moment.

This isn't starting out the way he'd wanted it to. "I'm somewhere on the border between Oklahoma and Texas," he says. When he pulls back momentarily, the phone, tethered to its coiled metal cord, resists. That bugs him but he sighs, trying to calm himself. What is it he wants to tell her? Certainly this geographical information can't mean much to her. What difference does it make to Maggie where on the map he might be? "I'll tell you one thing," he says. "I've come a long way."

"I'll bet," she says. All at once she sounds more like the Maggie he knows. "How is the trip going so far?" she asks.

He laughs to himself, pleased that he's no longer talking to a stranger. "You wouldn't believe half the stuff that's happened," he says. "We're running late. We've had weather problems and . . ." His voice trails off.

"By the way, what time is it there?" she asks. He tells her. "Hmm," she says, "think of that," and he realizes with a pang that Maggie's never been outside the eastern time zone.

He looks at his watch, the second hand making its relentless, jerking way around the circle. "Maggie," he suddenly blurts out, trying to convey to her what he's seeing around him, "from where I'm standing I'm looking at an empty highway. I mean, there are no cars, no trucks, nothing. I can hear a train somewhere, though, pretty far away. It's really dusty and sandy here, very dry, and the wind keeps making little tornados. And there are hardly any trees. What I'm looking at, I could believe nobody lived around here, or maybe nobody but the Indians. There's a couple of them in this diner but they sure don't look like the Indians in movies. There are lots of cowboy hats too, and boots, but you wouldn't mistake anyone there for John Wayne. At the gas station next door there's a pit with a bunch of live rattlesnakes. They're all packed together and they're hardly moving but they're real rattlesnakes. Boy, do they stink." He can't think of any more to say.

"That sounds pretty interesting," Maggie says. Which is generous of her, he thinks.

"Yeah," he answers with a feeling of futility, "it is. Real interesting."

"Well, I'm glad you called," she says a minute later. "I'm glad you're safe and having a good trip."

"Take care of yourself," he says, then adds, "I know you will."

Though he's warmed by the momentary contact with Maggie, the deflation sets in almost at once. Why did he spend his time giving her a report of what things looked like from the phone booth? Why would she care who's in the diner and what could possibly interest her about a bunch of half-dead rattlesnakes in front of a beat-up gas station on the Oklahoma-Texas border? He should have told her about the storms and floods they passed through, the bus's breakdown, Frontier Days and what happened to Lennie, and the bank embezzler who was traveling with them. Why didn't he tell her about some of the people he's met along the way? He left everything important out and just gave her a description of some Godforsaken stretch of highway. And he didn't even bother to ask her about how things were going back home. How dumb can you get?

Ziggy steps into the harsh, dry heat and shuffles his way back into the diner, a bad taste in his mouth from that unsatisfactory phone call. He'd really wanted to talk to Maggie and it had been great, actually, even for a couple of minutes, hearing her voice; but still, what he'd told her could have given her no idea of what he wanted to say about this trip. He looks around the diner, where he glimpses Sharlene, by herself in a booth, which is unusual. Remembering Roy's injunction to look after her, he starts walking in her direction.

When she sees him, she gives him a wave of her hand. "Hi, come on and join me."

He takes the seat opposite her and sinks back against the warm plastic, taking in the bright, shiny spaces around him. As he'd said to Maggie, there are a couple of fat Indians here and a quartet of old white guys wearing cowboy hats. Well, he hadn't been lying about that, anyway. A steel guitar twangs from the jukebox.

"What's the matter?" Sharlene drawls. "You look kind of down."

Ziggy pulls himself straight and flashes a quick smile. "Nothing," he fires back. "A little tired, maybe." He gives her a wink.

She shakes a finger at him. "You're a man of mystery, for sure." Then she returns to the Moon Pie she's eating with obvious delight. She's a little heavy, as Roy said, but she's pretty and there's something about her: she's almost always smiling, as if she knows there's a pleasant surprise waiting for her just around the corner. Just now she chews on her Moon Pie and nods to Ziggy as if to say, OK, I'll pretend to believe your story if that's what you want. Her blue eyes go big as she takes another bite and when Ziggy realizes he's watching her slowly lick a piece of marshmallow off her lip, he feels the need to turn away, toward the stretch of highway outside their window that seems to run through the middle of a whole lot of nothing.

"I just love these little critters," Sharlene says, wiping away some crumbs of chocolate, her big silver earrings catching the light as she leans back. "I don't know if I could ever get tired of traveling like this." She flashes him a smile. "I mean, this is just like one big vacation, isn't it? Like being on one of those cruise ships."

Ziggy laughs. "I'd hardly call it that."

She cocks her head. "Aww," she says, "all you have to do is use a little imagination."

"I don't know," he says. "Maybe I'm just not the cruise ship type." He's still thinking about how he messed up that call to Maggie.

"You've got to admit," she says, "all this stuff we're seeing is interesting." She looks out the window. "Those rocks and things."

The truth is, all he can see out there is emptiness. To be polite, though, he says, "I guess. Where you from originally?" he asks, not sure whether she's already told him.

"I was born in Florida," she says, "but we left there when I was only three. My mom moved around quite a bit, so I guess I got used to that long ago."

"Didn't you say you're going to California to see your mother?" he asks.

She makes a face. "Me and my mom don't really get along so great." She sticks out her lower lip. "I'm not looking forward to it especially." She falls silent for a few seconds, then, suddenly looking directly into his eyes, she says with great seriousness, "I bet you have cancer."

Ziggy's thunderstruck, his heart is racing as he looks into the wide blue eyes of this young woman in a denim shirt embroidered with roses. He feels terror and rage at the same time. What does she know and why is she smiling like that?

"Am I right?" she teases. Ziggy's mouth moves but no words come out. "You see," she says, "you seem to me like somebody who doesn't really want to be on this trip, somebody who'd rather be at home. Cancers, or Moon-children as some people like to call them nowadays, they're like the crab, everywhere they go, they travel with their shells."

At last he's figured out that she's talking about astrology! He must have misheard her. Jesus!

"Now, me," she goes on, "I'm a Sagittarius—that's the archer. That's a fiery sign. Females born under Sagittarius have strong personalities and we love our freedom, we're always ready to explore and have new adventures."

Ziggy laughs, a grateful survivor. "Well," he admits, "you guessed right about me. But it sounds like the archer got all the good qualities."

"Oh, no," she says. "All the signs of the zodiac are important. Cancer men, for instance, you guys can be moody and changeable, but you'll do anything to protect your home." She gives him a big smile. "Women find that a pretty sexy combination."

I'm not so sure I did such a great job of protecting my home, he thinks, remembering those dismal days when he let what was left of the numbers slide. "You can really tell what sign a person was born under?" he asks.

She shakes her head. "Not always, of course. But if you study this stuff, you eventually get pretty good at it. See that cute cowboy that just came in a couple of minutes ago? The one with the sideburns? I've been watching him and if I had to guess I'd say he's a Gemini like my old boyfriend Ricky back in Carolina." She shakes her head and looks down at her turquoise bracelet. "Now, there was a guy, split right down the middle. He could be the smoothest talker you'd ever run into, and the thing is, he could convince himself of things he didn't really believe. I could see right away that Ricky was fooling himself, he said he wanted us to live together, he was going to get a job." Her eyes go distant. "His daddy had run out on the family," she goes on, "and he wanted to show he could be a responsible guy. Shoot, I could tell from the beginning he was a wild boy, that was what I loved about him. But every now and then he'd have to start talking in this deep grown-up voice about responsibilities, and the two of us played house for a while. I'll admit it was fun in a way for a time. But then I could see Ricky was starting to feel hemmed in. He couldn't talk to me about it, he thought, so he got out of the situation the only way he knew how. He got drunk and went to a bar and misbehaved very openly with somebody he shouldn't have, and we had one heck of a fight and that was enough for him, he could leave me and all that stuff I'd got tangled up with in his mind." She's quiet for a while. "In a way it was a relief when it was over," she says, "but now and then I miss him." She shakes her head and smiles. "Mm, that little man was something in the bedroom."

Ziggy looks away, flustered and amused at the same time. He imagines talking to Maggie about this back on Dubois Street, a cup of coffee in his hand, and it makes him feel better. Believe me, he'd tell her, I wasn't prying or anything. She'd just tell that kind of stuff to anyone who'd listen.

Sharlene wets her finger with her tongue and reaches down to the table for a tiny crumb of Moon Pie, which she deftly inserts into her mouth. Still savoring this last remnant of the sweet cake, she says, "I don't miss him that much, though, no sir. Old Ricky, he's history."

If Oklahoma was desolate, Texas is even more so to Ziggy. Flat stretches of bare, baking wasteland pass by the window, too hot for living creatures, and it seems as if, even on the bus, the energy has been sucked out of the passengers, including

Lennie, who's fallen into one of his rare silences. As for Ziggy, he can't help going back to that time in the diner when he thought Sharlene told him he had cancer. The terror he'd felt at the moment was natural enough: Eddie Figlak went that way, after all, and so did Steve Koss, who was younger than either Ziggy or Eddie. What was more surprising was his instinctive sense that she was right, that she'd glimpsed something dire in him. Hadn't she guessed his astrological sign? That was weird enough in itself.

Somewhere near Amarillo, the bus driver makes an announcement. "I'd like you to keep your eyes open for something that's coming up on the left side of the road in a mile or two. I won't tell you what it is but I promise, you'll find it interesting. I'm told that some people around here even call it one of the Seven Wonders of Potter County."

"What do you suppose it can be?" Lennie asks, suddenly roused. "The world's biggest Stetson hat?"

Ziggy leans toward the window, trying to get the first view of the promised sight. "We're getting warmer now," the driver says. At last Ziggy glimpses something, a dark, slant shape coming out of the earth. There are more, it's immediately clear, and his first thought is that somebody in Texas has put up something that looks like a cross between Stonehenge and the Leaning Tower of Pisa. But these aren't stones, he soon realizes, it's a line of cars stuck at an angle into the earth—Cadillacs, actually. The driver slows as the bus passes this apparition of about a dozen shiny Cadillacs planted nose-down, tailfins high, into the Texas earth. "Kind of shows that all the kooks aren't in California," the driver comments before resuming his normal speed.

"Hey, crazy," Lennie exclaims, craning his neck to get a last look. "I love it. That's a pretty powerful statement, isn't it? Sort of like Ozymandias, isn't it? The tailfins of a vanished empire."

Ziggy nods though he doesn't know what Lennie's talking about. In his present state of mind there's nothing about that clutch of buried Cadillacs that brings him any cheer. Whatever sour mood has overtaken him recently, he hasn't been able to shake it off. But then, Cancers are moody, didn't Sharlene say that? There are no more half-buried cars in the landscape he sees out his window; it's just an unrelenting stretch of dry, dusty emptiness—even here on the bus, he can feel it in his throat. Why did he ever choose to leave the old neighborhood that, downtrodden as it might be, was at least still a place where people lived, went shopping for kielbasa or out for a drink, listened to a ball game? It wasn't barren like this place he's come to.

Ziggy hasn't been to church much lately except for an occasional Christmas or Easter mass, but just now he can't help remembering the problems the old monsignor had just after the war with a priest from Poland who shook up the parishioners at St. Connie's with his Polish sermons in which he seemed to confuse Detroit with the old country; so that his listeners couldn't tell whether he was referring to Warsaw or the streets outside the church when he warned of fire falling from the sky, and miles and miles of emptiness and ruins where once-grand buildings had stood before God's punishment fell upon the city. Monsignor Baran, who'd listened to complaints from frightened parishioners, handled the situation with his usual aplomb and had the priest quietly transferred to the Polish seminary at Orchard Lake; but Ziggy wouldn't be surprised if some of the people who'd heard those sermons remembered them years later when the bad times came down on Detroit, causing large tracts of the city to fall into vacancy and disrepair, as if the prairie was bent on reclaiming the place for itself.

"Those Cadillacs were something," Lennie says, smiling to himself. "I guess Texas is about the last place I'd expect to see something like that, though." He shakes his head. "Well, live and learn, I guess."

For Ziggy, though, those Caddies are long gone. Out here he feels that he's in danger of being swallowed up by the landscape that's no longer just flat. There are strange shapes on the horizon, the land is twisted into eerie formations that look as if they'd originally been intended to be something other than just rocks. This is stranger than the empty prairies of Texas. You can tell from the look of things that it's even dryer out there, and the plants are what you'd expect to find in the desert. The soil itself has changed color, as though they've wandered on to another planet. I'd hate to be lost out here, he thinks, imagining the baking heat, the dry earth scorching to the touch. What the nuns were talking about, maybe, hell without flames.

"We're stopping." It's Lennie, who gives him a gentle nudge.

Blurrily, Ziggy orients himself, recognizing that he must have drifted off to sleep. "Where are we?" he asks, still trying to shake off the sense that he's just come from someplace else.

"God's country," Lennie says. "Tucumcari, New Mexico. It's our dinner stop."

There's the usual bustle among the passengers at the prospect of a bit of relief from the cramped quarters of the bus. "Look at that," Sharlene says excitedly. "They've got pool tables." She makes sure to bring the case with her pool stick when she leaves the bus.

"Tucumcari, New Mexico," Lennie reads the name aloud. "Can you believe that name? They might as well have called this town Timbuktu."

The place they've stopped at isn't much to brag about, a low mustard-yellow stucco building housing a diner and bar, the sign outside spelling POOL in red neon. Inside, a couple of ceiling fans turn halfheartedly above a counter and a scattering of tables. A low archway leads to the bar next door, a window-less room where a couple of pool tables are visible. In the dim lighting in the bar section Ziggy can make out a crudely done mural on the far wall, undoubtedly the work of a local artist: a desert landscape of red rock with giant cacti in the foreground, an iguana looking on as a lone Mexican in a serape and sombrero rides by on a burro. The other end of the mural depicts an outsized rattlesnake coiled on a rock, ready to strike, and an eagle silhouetted against a dark blue sky.

Sure enough, once she's got a look, Sharlene heads straight for the pool tables. She extracts her pool cue from its case, screws together the two sections and begins knocking balls around with what seems—even from the table where Ziggy and Lennie are sitting—to be a lot of skill and confidence. As he munches his taco, though, Ziggy's aware of the half dozen or so men at the bar watching her. Off by himself near the end of the bar is a short cowboy with a thin mustache who seems to be deliberately ignoring the newcomer. After a minute or so, he ambles to the jukebox, where he takes a long time making his selection. When he does at last he smiles to himself as if he's accomplished something pretty special. From the looks of Sharlene, she approves of his choice, nodding her head to the music. When she catches the cowboy's eye, he winks at her and she nods back. "Desperado," the singer wails, and Sharlene seems to be humming the song to herself as she resumes her feats with the pool stick. Other men from the bar shout encouragement to her, but the little cowboy just smiles quietly to himself. Clearly, Sharlene is responding, laughing at something one of the onlookers has said, once even taking a bow after a shot. In the dim light the whole scene seems to be taking place under water.

"Something's going on over there," Lennie says. He takes off his glasses momentarily and runs a hand through his hair. He needs a shave and now, with his glasses off, he looks older, like the man he'll be in twenty years.

Ziggy nods. "I think you're right."

Lennie puts his glasses back on. "Good thing Roy isn't still with us."

"Yeah." Ziggy takes a sip of his beer. "Looks like Sharlene's found someone she likes." I'm tired, he thinks, I'm too old for all this stuff.

In a few minutes the cowboy and Sharlene are playing a game of pool together, and there's a lot of spirited byplay between them, all of which is accompanied by comments from the men at the bar. Apparently the cowboy has invested a number of quarters on the same song, since "Desperado" is playing again and now the cowboy is crooning along in a hammy way. Sharlene gives every sign of being appreciative.

"Poor Roy," Lennie says. "He'd have a hard time letting go."

By now, Ziggy thinks, Roy must have seen his son. One way or another, he'll have found out whether his trip was worth it. "I don't think old Roy is thinking about Sharlene just now," he says. Meanwhile, the cowboy has persuaded Sharlene to lay down her stick and the two of them dance together while the men at the bar applaud.

"Is it just me," Lennie says, "or does that guy remind you of Wayne?"

Ziggy nods. It's Sharlene who's doing the choosing this time, he can see, and even a whole box of Snickers bars wouldn't be of much avail now.

When dinner is finished, Ziggy and Lennie step outside into the dry heat of the New Mexico evening. Lennie pops a stick of gum into his mouth and sings, "I left my heart in Tucumcari." "You know," he goes on, "this trip is starting to get to me, I guess, because I have to admit I miss Amelie Lathrop. Think of all the information I could have gotten about the graves of our presidents that I'm going to have to learn by myself."

The bus is due to leave in a few minutes and some of the passengers have re-boarded already, but Sharlene isn't anywhere to be seen. Finally, just as the last of the passengers are returning, she trots back to the bus and says something to the driver, then climbs aboard. Moments later, she's standing beside the bus with her luggage. Recognizing what's happening, Ziggy approaches her.

"I decided I'm going to stay here a while," she says. "It feels good to play a little pool again." The cowboy, who's never been introduced, has apparently decided to stay indoors and wait for her.

Ziggy looks out over the desert landscape, where a round white moon is pasted in the sky over the darkening hills that form a wall on the horizon. He knows he has no chance of changing her mind: she'll do what she wants to do. Still, he feels protective. He's just going to have to believe she can take care of herself. "What can I say?" he tells her. "Have your adventure, Sagittarius. Don't forget, though, to find your way to California."

She gives him a quick peck on the cheek. "I guess California's still going to be there for a while. And who knows? We might be destined to meet again. So long for now, Moonchild." Then she grabs his wrist, pulls him toward her and whispers, "I don't know what it is that's taking someone like you so far from home, but I hope you find what you're looking for."

The gloomy silence on the bus after the departure of Sharlene is broken by Lennie, who asks, "Ziggy, I never asked you: why are you going to California? Visiting relatives?"

The bus is plunging down an incline into a valley, though valleys usually have rivers, and the closest they've come lately to anything that might be called a river has been when the highway has occasionally crossed a wide shallow, river-shaped gouge in the earth that somebody on the bus called a dry wash. He certainly was right about the dry part. "It's complicated," Ziggy says. "Sometimes I'm not so sure why I'm going there at all."

"Well," Lennie says, "you've been very patient listening to my stories. Try me. I actually like complicated."

At first Ziggy isn't so sure he wants to be talking about this to somebody he's only known for a couple of days. It's pretty personal stuff, after all. Then too, he knows that if he tries to put his feelings into words he's going to have to be able to make his motives clear to himself, which might not be all that easy. But Lennie's a decent guy, after all.

"OK," he says, "I used to be in the numbers business back in Detroit. This was a while back." He pauses. "I wasn't the top guy in our organization but I was pretty high up."

Lennie cocks his head, as if he's trying to get a good look at Ziggy for the first time. "Wow," he says. "you mean like in 'The Godfather'?"

Ziggy shakes his head. "No, no, there were no guns, no rough stuff. Sure, it was illegal, but it was just a bunch of Polacks playing numbers. Polacks running it, Polacks playing." He adds quickly. "Actually, there was a fair amount of change involved. I'm talking about the war years, when Detroit was a three-shift town and everybody had money but there wasn't much to spend it on, and then after the war, times were flush." After a moment, he adds, "I did pretty well for myself, pretty damn well."

Lennie nods appreciatively and Ziggy's quiet for a while, basking in the memory of those times. Yeah, as unreal as it might seem out here in the middle of nowhere, all of it actually happened. But he's supposed to be telling Lennie about why he's going to California. "OK," he says, "to make a long story short, our numbers house got busted in the fifties and some of my friends went to prison. I was lucky. But . . ." He shakes his head, recognizing that there's no way he can explain what followed. "Nothing was the same after that. My life got scrambled, the numbers went all to hell and I pretty much lost everything." He lights up a cigarette and inhales deeply. "Well, no crying over spilt milk. Those days were over long ago."

It's a couple of seconds before Lennie says anything. "But . . ." he suggests. "I see a 'but' coming."

Ziggy nods, looking into the cloud of smoke he's expelled. "Yeah." He wants to put this as clearly as possible. "What happened after that raid, I take the blame for myself. I just kind of lost control of things, I started drinking, I let things slide." Well, he thinks, it isn't pretty but it's true. "OK," he says, "I know I'm never going to get any of that back." That's true too, and he accepts it, had to accept it quite a while ago. "That was a big change," he says, "and, believe me, it wasn't easy making the adjustment." He thinks about that for a moment. "In the old days," he goes on, "I was the guy in the neighborhood you went to if you wanted something fixed. The pastor would call me first if he wanted to put on a shindig and needed support or if the high school football team needed uniforms." The monsignor was even hot for me to be head of the East Side Homeowners' Association, he could tell Lennie, but the good father sure pulled back in a hurry after the raid.

He's started to drift, though, and he pulls himself back. "There was this other guy," he says, "an undertaker named Przybylski. He had the bucks too and he used to love it when the monsignor came to him buttering him up before hitting him for a contribution. But Przybylski never liked the numbers. Even though everyone in the parish played—even some of the priests—this undertaker always acted as if he thought he was above that kind of thing." Ziggy wrinkles his nose, remembering. "He had a big smooth face with a tiny mouth and he was the kind of guy, you could believe, who went to bed every night in freshly ironed pajamas. As far as anyone knew, he didn't drink. I never liked the way he used to sit there at the bar with his glass of Vernors ginger ale and kind of smile to himself."

"I can see how someone like that could get under your skin," Lennie offers.

"You said it," Ziggy says. "There was this other thing: Przybylski inherited his funeral home from his father. He never really had to work for anything like the rest of us. He'd just sit there quietly, watching and waiting. He knew that sooner or later we'd wind up with him."

"And how is this guy connected to this trip?" Lennie asks after a while.

Ziggy takes a brief drag on his cigarette. For a moment he's back in Detroit on the night of Eddie Figlak's wake, his old friend's corpse suddenly popping up in the casket, the place going crazy with people stampeding to get away from what they didn't want to believe they were seeing; then there was all the stuff that happened later at Connie's. He exhales the smoke. "I found out recently," he says, "that Przybylski might have had a hand in tipping off the cops who made the raid that finished the numbers."

"Yeah?" Lennie nods expectantly.

"Przybylski left Detroit a while ago for California." He thinks a moment about what he's going to say. "I'm going out there so I can find out from him if that's true or not."

"Wow," Lennie says again. "What are you going to do to him?"

Ziggy shakes his head. "I just want to hear from his own lips what happened. That'll be enough for me. Then I'm going back."

Lennie's silent for a while. Then he says, "That's impressive. You're on a real quest."

Ziggy laughs. "If you say so."

After a moment, Lennie asks, "What do you think he's going to say, after all these years?"

Ziggy shakes his head. "I don't really know."

"You must have imagined it, though. Right?"

"Yeah," he nods. "I have. But lately, I don't know, the whole thing seems kind of unreal."

Lennie nods, keeping his thoughts to himself. Then he asks, "You're sure he's still alive?"

Ziggy snorts. "He'd better be, or else I'm wasting a lot of time."

Lennie shakes his head. "That's some story," he says. "I wish I could be there to see that confrontation."

"You might be disappointed. This isn't a movie."

Their driver for the last leg of the trip is an unsmiling stubby crew-cut guy who has little taste for informing his passengers about the sights they're seeing. He barrels down the scorching highways as if he's being chased by the police, and the way he's moving, they wouldn't be likely to catch him. And still, after climbing one hill and dropping down another, Ziggy could convince himself they're exactly where they were an hour ago.

As the bus continues its westward movement he runs his finger across the worn timetable: Albuquerque and Gallup in New Mexico; Holbrook, Winslow, Flagstaff, Glendale and Phoenix in Arizona; Blythe, Indio and San Bernadino in California, all stand between him and LA, almost another full day to go. It's hard to believe that even though he's already traveled across the whole breadth of Michigan, down through the storm-battered Illinois prairie and the green Ozarks of Missouri, all the way into hot, dusty Oklahoma and Texas with its cowboy hats and buried Cadillacs, and been in the sand-colored state of New Mexico for a while now, he still has almost a thousand miles ahead of him. It makes him wonder if he's actually going to get to California. Years have passed, for sure, since he last walked on Dubois Street.

For his part, Lennie's gone quiet once again, curled over in his seat like a man studying a prayer book. Occasionally he makes a comment on the scenery. "Look at that," he says at one point, "that's got to be actual tumbleweed, just like in the movies. Did you ever see *Them*? It's a great sci-fi flick about giant ants in the desert, and there's a scene in a sandstorm near the beginning where the wind is howling and dark patches of tumbleweed are being blown through the swirling dust. It's all so creepy and ominous—you just know something horrible has happened out there."

Ziggy hasn't seen the movie but he watches the wind-driven tumbleweed plants bouncing seemingly weightless across the desert floor. How far, he wonders, will one of them go before it stops? This is a strange country indeed.

"We could be on the dark side of the moon," Lennie says later. "Think of how hard it has to be for any creature to survive in that kind of unforgiving environment." He looks toward the distant horizon. "What's amazing," he says, "is that, even though it's so dry out there, we're actually traveling across the bottom of what used to be an ocean. Imagine: scientists who search through these rocks are likely to find not just fossils of dinosaurs but traces of giant clams and icthyosaurs as well as whales, and my personal favorite from childhood, the megalodon or giant shark."

So that's where we are, Ziggy thinks, traveling along the bottom of a dusty sea on the dark side of the moon. He can believe it. Gigantic whales and dinosaurs once lived here, leaving their outsized skeletons in the layers of sediment that make up these huge, twisted and silent rock shapes. Possibly the giant shark prowled this very highway: the tiny creatures aboard this bus would just be appetizers. When Ziggy'd paid for his ticket in Detroit he never imagined he'd be traveling through any place like this, where in the blowing sand an isolated cactus could be an ancient Indian spirit intently watching the passing bus from the depths of the desert. The image chills him. He realizes that an old depression has found him out again and he feels lost among these alien shapes and eerie vistas. He may have told Lennie that he's going to California in order to ask Przybylski a question, but out here in these vast desert expanses it sure doesn't feel like he's the one who's making choices; he could easily believe he's being pulled westward by some unseen force. What that force could be isn't something he wants to think about.

"We're going to be very close to Death Valley pretty soon," Lennie says. "Some of the hottest, driest and lowest spots on the planet are there."

Ziggy nods. Death Valley. Sounds about right for the way he feels just now.

Chapter Six

Joshua trees, that's what Lennie said they were, those weird shapes out in the desert trailing long black shadows in the morning light. With their branches raised toward the sky they look like damned souls in Hell begging God for water. Ghost trees, they should call them. They certainly aren't anything like the elms of Ziggy's childhood or the big chestnuts that line Dubois Street, comfortable city trees that provide welcome shade in the summer and rustle excitingly just before a storm. God, he's come a long way from home. This is the last leg of his trip and as far as he's concerned, it can't be over too soon.

Lennie's quiet too—is he remembering Brooklyn? The bus is fairly empty for this final stage of the ride. As far as Ziggy knows, he and Lennie are the only two passengers who've been aboard since Chicago. Though others have joined the company along the way, there doesn't seem to be the old camaraderie among the remaining travelers. Maybe it's the place they're passing through, but just now the others onboard seem to be locked into themselves, like a busload of fugitives intent on staying unrecognized. Or maybe they're all thanking their lucky stars they're inside this bus, where the air-conditioning is at least pumping away at half-speed, and not out there in the desert, where before the day is over the temperature will reach well over a hundred degrees. Even the driver, the same no-nonsense guy who took the wheel a couple of states back, seems to be in a desperate hurry to get out of here, and the bleak landscape flies by in a blur, making it seem all the more unreal.

Still, Ziggy reminds himself, it's really happening, I'm already in California, though the desert towns he's glimpsed through the window are hardly what people think about when they hear that word. These desolate settlements look like the places where the pioneers gave up hope and just stopped— little more than speed bumps consisting of a shabby gas station that doubles as a general store set among a handful of other low flat buildings on grassless plots, a couple of trailers, maybe a dog lying under a pickup truck, and nothing but desert as far as the eye can see. No wonder they're always reporting UFO sightings from places like this. What was that movie Lennie mentioned that had a dust storm in the desert? He can imagine something like that here.

At least the towns provide some contrast. Once they're beyond the settlements, the same bleak landscape continues to roll by his window hypnotically until he drops into a half-sleep, only realizing he's drifted off when he comes suddenly awake. Because of the unchanging scenery it's impossible to tell how long he'd left consciousness behind, but enough of its traces linger to identify where he'd gone to: he was back in Detroit on V-J Day, when the war ended.

It's no surprise his memory carried him back to that particular day, which was one of the memorable moments in the city's history. He'd been downtown with the crowds who pushed through Campus Martius in front of City Hall as capless soldiers and sailors climbed atop streetcars that were no longer moving, stopped by the throngs that had poured into the center of the city, driven there by the pent-up need to celebrate. Old men waved bottles of beer, teenagers were shouting, everybody was happy. Drunks got warm greetings from people who were sober, thousands were screaming, singing and dancing while sirens and whistles blew, even a trumpet and a sax joining in. Kids shinned up lampposts and total strangers kissed each other—Ziggy saw a nun hugged by a trio of soldiers. Flags were waving everywhere, black people shook hands with whites in the same place where two years earlier they'd chased each other with baseball bats. Arms were moving like trees in a storm, they rose and fell in swimming motions. Horns blew, horns were stuck, all the prewar Fords and Chevys were stopped in their tracks, unable to move, but the drivers were smiling. Here and there someone was openly crying with joy.

That was a great time for the city, all right, but as he re-experienced it moments ago, he doesn't remember feeling all that happy, he'd been watching apart from it all. Yes, there was something holding him back, wasn't there? It doesn't take him long to grasp the underside of that memory: of course, the war ended only a few days after he'd broken off his affair with Helen Nadolnik, and as those celebrating crowds pushed against him he was still caught up in a tangle of feelings about her. Jesus, Helen!

Even now it's hard to believe he did some of the things he did back then, but he'd been a desperate man. Vince's death tore a huge hole in the neat map he'd constructed in his head, and only Helen seemed to realize how much his friend's abrupt removal from the world had shaken him, the sudden questions it raised about life and what we were all doing here. Hadn't he seen the mark on her hand where she told him she'd put the burning cigarette just to prove to herself she was actually alive, hadn't he touched it, kissed it?

And yet in the end none of those questions got answered in their secret meetings, though in the fierce combat of sex it often seemed as if the answers were almost within reach. When Ziggy could no longer deny that, for all the passion and excitement, the two of them were no closer to solving the mysteries opened up by Vince's death, he realized what he was risking in this pursuit of unanswerable questions; and there came a day during the week the war ended when he was in Helen's apartment above Mrs. Kubek's, listening to the ticking of the brass clock on the wall, looking down at the familiar brown rug as if he'd lost something there, and he was saying, "It has to stop. It can't go on."

Helen drew on her cigarette and exhaled. "I always knew it was going to end this way, Ziggy" she said. She'd got up and he stood too, both of them on that small rug like castaways on a desert island.

"But it's not ending," he said. "We're still going to be friends." It sounded hollow, even to him.

"How can you say that, Ziggy, after what we had?" He'd never seen her look so angry.

He stood there, a few feet away from her, in his tan summer suit, a straw hat moving slowly in his hands like the steering wheel of a car being put through the most careful of turns. He'd prepared himself for how tough this was going to be, but he hadn't been prepared for the way time seemed to have stopped: they stood there for eternities saying nothing more, the clock ticking, the war on its way to ending, she in her pink flower print dress with the big shoulders, her hands clasped before her so that the knuckles were sharp and pointed, the thin white curtains behind her scarcely moving in the summer breeze, the strains of "Sentimental Journey" coming softly from the large brown console radio.

Then Helen's nostrils flared as if she'd smelled ammonia. "All right," she said. Nothing was moving. How white her face was, he was thinking. She stood there in her pink dress, still as a corpse, saxophones crooned, the curtains hung like smoke. He had a sudden thought of Niagara Falls, tons of white water falling with the force of stone, the shuddering roar, the mist. One afternoon in a bed in the Jewish hotel in Mt. Clemens he'd actually promised to take her there. "You won't believe it," he said, remembering how he'd felt the first time he'd seen them. Now, standing on the brown carpet, he was thinking, Jesus Christ, what am I doing? And at the same time, Hold on, in five minutes it will be over, you'll be walking down the steps, this thing you thought you could never do will be over.

And it was. Though a couple of days later, among the crowds celebrating the end of the war, he found himself thinking that if he and Helen were there, they could kiss openly and everyone around would smile at them. It took a while for it to be over, really. In the end he knew it was the right thing to break it off with her, but his mother would have said that God never forgets. She'd also say that though he'd survived that business, Ziggy still has a lot to answer for.

He's still caught up in this reverie when it occurs to him that there's been some subtle change in the sounds around him and he realizes that the bus is in the midst of a long climb, its gears whining with the effort of the ascent. The land keeps rising continually until it seems as if they're pulling themselves upward out of a bottomless hole, and Ziggy's just about accepted that they'll keep climbing forever, when suddenly the sound changes again and he knows they've reached the top of something. In a moment he feels a weight lifting as the bus begins its downward plunge: the desert is behind them at last, he realizes, they're on their way to the coast, and he feels a sudden irrational joy, as if he's just found twenty dollars in his pocket. When they come to a settlement now the houses are more thickly clustered and there are all sorts of plants growing around them, a whole different set of colors: brilliant reds, fiery yellows, rich greens and purples. What's more, there even seems to be a bit of a mist in the air. Can there really be humidity on this side of the mountains?

Lennie is at his side now, leaning toward the window. "Hey, we made it, pardner," he says, caught up in the excitement of the change. "Think of those pioneers plodding along with their covered wagons through hundreds of miles of prairies, hoping the cloud of dust on the horizon means buffalos and not Indians. Then they have to navigate that long stretch of desert we were in where the only road sign they'd see would be a bleached skull along the side of the trail. And after surviving all that, what do they get for their troubles? Another long slope to climb. Hell, at that point a lot of them must have been ready to just give up; but then, coming down the last mountain like this, they must have thought they'd suddenly landed in Hawaii. You almost expect grass skirts and hula dancers. Look at all the colors, all the stuff growing. It's enough to get a dead man's pulse racing."

Ziggy doesn't say anything. If he were to try to describe what he's feeling now he'd have to start by saying he's just been stabbed by a surprising jolt of fear. But what is there to be afraid of? This place is a hell of a lot more attractive than what they've left behind, isn't it? With each mile there's more evidence that they're entering a more populated area. Ziggy pays silent attention to the successive towns with their stucco houses and tile roofs, and before long the driver is announcing the last stop on their journey.

In downtown LA, Ziggy and Lennie, their bags in their hands, stand in the terminal among the dispersing passengers. "Are you sure there aren't any more stops?" Lennie says. "I expect to hear some announcement that I have five more minutes to board the bus."

Ziggy nods, looking warily at this alien place to which he's come. "Hey," he suggests, "how about a cup of coffee before . . . ?"

"Sure," Lennie says, apparently no more eager than Ziggy to move to the next step. It's early afternoon and the city buzzes noisily outside the coffee shop. For all the distance Ziggy's covered, the bus trip seems like a period out of time. Now that the traveling is over, things seem to have speeded up alarmingly and he wants to slow them down.

In the coffee shop, though, neither man has much to say. "Well," Lennie declares abstractly, "here we are in LA after all, aren't we?"

"It sure isn't very glamorous around here," Ziggy observes, depressed by the shabby surroundings.

Lennie nods. "I've got to get up to West Hollywood, to a place called the Tropicana Motel. I sure hope it's better than this." At the moment, Lennie doesn't look very confident about his future as a stand-up comic.

They fall into a silence and Ziggy has to fish for some way to keep the conversation going. "So how are you going to be practicing your comedy while you're doing other jobs?" he asks.

"It takes a lot of work to build up a twelve-minute sketch," Lennie says. "There's a lot of trial and error. That's where the comedy clubs come in. I can try things out there."

"Tell me one of your jokes," Ziggy says.

Lennie looks around suspiciously. "What do you mean?"

"I'd just like to hear one," Ziggy says.

Lennie glances around once more, then leans toward Ziggy and whispers, "The place I used to live in was so crummy, even the cockroaches were wearing flea collars."

Ziggy laughs softly. "That's pretty good," he says. "Thanks."

The two of them drink their coffee in silence after that, taking in the scene around them: a couple of tough-looking women carry their coffee to a table, their jeans stuffed into their boots so that they look like aviators from the First World War. A scowling black man with a salt-and-pepper beard and a shaved head is reading a book in the corner. On the other side of the room, a furtive Hispanic man and woman are bent toward each other whispering, as if in prayer; and a preening young white guy in jeans whose tee-shirt sleeves are rolled up to call attention to his muscles, looks at the women and nods in response to something nobody's said to him.

"It's hard to believe that trip's really over," Lennie says spiritlessly.

Ziggy smiles. "Amen."

"All of a sudden I feel as if I've walked all the way from New York," Lennie says, and Ziggy waits for more, but he finishes his coffee in silence.

"Well," Ziggy says after a while. "I guess here's where we say adios."

"You've got that number I gave you?" Lennie asks. "Just in case you have any news about that undertaker of yours."

"Yeah," Ziggy says. "Right."

Seconds later they shake hands and part company, possibly forever. Ziggy is alone in Los Angeles, and it occurs to him that now he has no one with whom he can talk about the trip he's just taken who'd understand him. Is it just going to fade away then?

He knows he has things to do and he ought to be doing them, but he isn't ready yet for any purposeful action. Just now nobody in the world knows where he is, he's completely out of touch, and it gives him an eerie feeling somewhere between giddiness and terror. Without any real sense of destination, he takes a walk around the area. Jesus, this is a seedy neighborhood, he thinks, but isn't that where they always put the bus station? Still, it's a different kind of seediness from what he knows in Detroit, though he can't put his finger on that difference. As he makes his way down the street, he has the sense that there's something off about this scene, and it isn't just that there are palm trees out here. No, it's more than that. It seems somehow too bright—he feels exposed on the wide, sunny streets—he keeps looking for shade, like an escaped convict fleeing the searchlight. No wonder they wear sunglasses all the time here.

It's only after a couple of seconds that he realizes he's seen something out of the corner of his eye that makes him wish he'd been paying more attention: a guy who just turned the corner looked familiar for some reason. Then it strikes him: the Indian who harassed him in Chicago. Could it be? The thought pulls him up short. No, he decides, it was just someone of about the same general build, dressed like the Indian. A bum's a bum, after all, and there are plenty of them all over.

Still, maybe that Chicago Indian was right in his prophecy. It's not that the trip turned out to be a disaster or anything like that. But Ziggy's certainly feeling a letdown now that he's here.

There's not much inducement for him to stay where he is, and he has to get some things settled soon, doesn't he? All along he's had the idea of crashing with Father Teddy as a way of at least postponing the time when he'll have to stay with Charlie and Gloria, and he'd assumed it would be a done deal. Now, here in the dingy neighborhood surrounding the bus station, he realizes how cockeyed that idea might turn out to be. There are a thousand reasons why he might not be able to pull it off, beginning with the possibility that Teddy no longer lives at that address. Then what?

Recognizing that if he's going to find out, it's better to do so sooner rather than later, he goes to a phone booth whose graffiti informs him that "Janna Sucks," as well as listing a number "gerinteed" to provide a good time amid a clutch of names, some of them accompanied by crude drawings of animals and an occasional bit of Spanish. He pulls out of his wallet the piece of paper on which Father Bruno had written the address: "Teddy K., 605 Oceanside Lane, Venice CA 90291." Luckily, a search through the phone book comes up with a number. A good sign! Then he steels himself to his next task and looks through the P's for Przybylski. Nothing. He looks again, checking his spelling, and gets the same result. For an instant the bottom drops out of everything. If there's no Przybylski in Los Angeles, what's the point of his coming all the way out here? Of course, he might live in one of the suburbs. But why didn't he try to find out this information when he was back in Detroit? Is it because that might have discouraged him from taking the trip when he really wanted to?

All at once it's very important that he get in touch with Father Teddy, who's at least one connection to Detroit, one possible justification for this long trek of his. He lights up and dials, his hands shaking.

The phone only rings once before it's answered enthusiastically. "Yes, yes?" the man on the other end of the line practically croons, as if he's been waiting all day to be informed that he's just won the lottery. Ziggy hopes he isn't going to disappoint him too much. "Teddy?" he says. "Father Teddy Krawek?"

The voice he hears is suddenly filled with suspicion. "Who is this? What do you want?"

Ziggy waits before going on. "It's Ziggy Czarnecki from Detroit," he says, trying to sound cordial. "St. Connie's. I'm sure you must remember me."

It takes the other man several seconds to process the information, during which time Ziggy pulls down a long drag on his cigarette. "Yeah," the voice responds at last, sounding a little relieved. "Sorry if I seemed suspicious. It's just that it's been a long time since anybody addressed me as a priest." Then he adds, "Or called me Teddy."

"Sure, sure," Ziggy says. "What do you call yourself now?"

"Ted," the man says. There are vague traces of the voice Ziggy remembers from Detroit, but even after only a few sentences he has the sense that some change has taken place: he doesn't sound like a priest anymore.

"Oh, OK," Ziggy says. "It sounded as if you were expecting someone else when I called," he offers tentatively.

The ex-priest hesitates a moment before responding. "Yeah," he admits. "I was hoping it was a woman."

A woman? This is a complication Ziggy hadn't expected. "Ah," he nods. "Your . . ." His voice trails off.

"Yeah," Ted answers. "We've been having our differences and I kind of hoped she was over it." Ziggy watches the cars in the street. "By the way," Ted says, "where are you?"

"I'm here in Los Angeles, near the Greyhound station," Ziggy answers, recognizing that they've come to a critical point. "I came on the bus. In fact," he says, "that's why I was calling you. I talked to Father Bruno not long ago and he mentioned you."

"Oh, how is old Bruno?" Ted asks.

"He's doing fine," Ziggy says, though that wasn't really the impression he'd got when he saw the priest. Ted says nothing more and Ziggy realizes he's got to get to the point. "I was . . ." he starts, "I was hoping I might be able to stay with you a couple of days. You see, I have kind of a project I have to get finished here." Having said it, he realizes how stupid it all sounds. Why couldn't he have tried to settle some of these things in advance? He barely knows the ex-priest and he's hitting him with quite a request out of the blue.

It's obvious Ted is thinking the same thing. For a long time he doesn't say anything. At last he speaks. "This is kind of an awkward time, but . . . I mean, my situation right now is kind of in flux . . ."

The woman, of course. "I should have given you a little more warning," Ziggy offers.

Ted, though, doesn't appear to be listening. "Well, yeah," he says, as if to himself, "on the other hand, this might be just what the doctor ordered." He considers this for a moment. "You see," he goes on, "Linda moved out last week so I've got the room, at least for now." Once more he's silent. "And anything would be better than living alone again," he says after a while. Uh-oh, Ziggy thinks, am I going to have to hold hands with him to get him through his loneliness? But at least it sounds promising. "And, who knows," the other man's voice suddenly lifts, "maybe if I've got someone staying with me, she'll decide to come back. Hah, that's the kind of problem I wouldn't mind having. Yeah," he says with more conviction, "sure. Where are you? Oh, yeah, you said: near the bus station. The one downtown?"

When Ziggy explains his situation, Ted tells him he'll be there in a half hour. "I'll be driving a green Valiant," he says.

He's as good as his word, though he'd have been more accurate if he'd described his car as a beat-up green Valiant.

There are a few dents on the driver's side of the car, which may be ten years old and probably hasn't been washed since it was bought. But then, Ziggy thinks, I wasn't really expecting a shiny new Cadillac.

Ted bounds out of the car. He's wearing chinos and a faded blue tee shirt. "Ziggy, it's good to see you," he says with some of the old priestly affability, though it's in fact an awkward moment, the two of them not really having been friends in the old days, and they shake hands formally. Looking at the man with the short gray beard, you'd never guess his former profession. In his fifties now, he's become pudgier with the years, softer, with pouches under his eyes; his sideburns are low and his thin sandy hair has been allowed to grow long. Father Teddy, a hippie? Still, once his greeting is over, something flickers in his gray eyes that reminds Ziggy of the boyish priest of decades ago, the look of someone who's lost something and isn't sure whether he wants to find it.

Ziggy, who should have guessed it from the phone call, finds out right away that Ted isn't shy about talking about his life. On the way to his place he manages to cover a lot of ground, detailing his various travels and jobs since he left the priesthood. He's been a janitor, he tells Ziggy proudly, a coffee roaster and a telemarketer. Currently he's working part-time at a used bookstore in Santa Monica called Old Words.

"You probably want to know why I'm not a priest anymore," he suggests.

In truth, Ziggy could live without that particular piece of information, but he can see that Ted wants to be asked. "Sure," he says.

"Ah," Ted's voice goes a little dreamy, "that's a kind of mystery, isn't it?" He's silent for a time, and Ziggy can imagine he's remembering those days. "There are times when I wake up," he goes on, "and it's as if a breeze comes from a certain direction bringing some kind of smell—maybe incense," he laughs to himself, "and I find myself missing all that majesty, the . . . the bigness of life, the drama of salvation." He shakes his head. "Why did I leave it? I guess in the end I lost the talent for it." He's quiet for a moment. "It was like playing an instrument. I used to be able to play it beautifully, I could play it naturally, and then all at once I lost the gift. So I had to say goodbye to the majesty, but what I've found is fine, it's not negligible, is it, life?"

Ziggy can only shake his head. Staying with this guy may be harder than he thought.

"It's actually a dream I've had," Ted goes on. "I'm on stage and sometimes I'm holding a horn, sometimes it's a violin, and the audience is waiting for me to play but the instrument is totally alien to me—I literally don't know which end is up." He sighs. "Linda says it's important to work these issues out in dreams. Sorry," he says at last, "I guess your being here just brings up all those old memories."

Ziggy's been paying attention to the exit signs on the freeway and notes that they're getting off in Santa Monica, where Ted said he works. They move along a wide bright roadway until at last they come to the ocean, and Ted turns left onto a street that's separated from the Pacific by a park with vivid green grass and tall palms whose trunks are covered with a rough bark as they climb toward feather-duster tops far above. But Ziggy's eyes are carried beyond the palms to the Pacific itself, a vast sheet of blue spread out below them, sunlight and ocean as far as the eye can see. He's seen plenty of pictures, of course, he's seen it in the movies, but the reality takes his breath away.

"I thought we'd come this way," Ted says. "It's nicer."

Ziggy's barely listening, caught up in the sense that he's looking at the western ocean for the first time. Can it really be true that the first bit of land you'd bump into out there would be Hawaii? And if you kept on going you'd wind up in Asia. Whatever he'd come to California looking for, at least he's got this.

Soon they're in Venice, which is considerably less tidy than Santa Monica. There are many canals, though, which vaguely remind Ziggy of his long-lost place on Harsens Island. Ted turns away from the canals and pulls up in front of a tiny bungalow, like something out of a children's story, with not only a scruffy palm tree that's dropped some of its dead fronds onto the lawn, but also, among the fronds, an old brown sofa, which is pretty much in keeping with the décor of other places Ziggy's seen in this neighborhood—where furniture and sculpture abound on people's lawns.

"Be it ever so humble," Ted says, ushering him in. The place is even smaller once Ziggy's inside, a fact that's exaggerated by the abundance of plants that crowd the room. In pots on the floor, on windowsills, hanging by cloth holders from the ceiling, they turn the room into a jungle. Ziggy's never seen so many plants outside of a greenhouse and Ted quickly explains that this is Linda's influence. "She's got a passion for living things," he says, "a real gift." Then he adds, "Linda saved my life." Ziggy nods, still marveling at the idea of the former priest caught up in romantic tangles like everyone else.

It's clear Ted wants to talk about this Linda, and Ziggy asks, "Linda's the woman you're having a fight with?"

Ted runs his hand through his hair. "Oh, not so much a fight as . . . I guess, we're temporarily out of alignment." He smiles. "Linda's a very passionate person and she can be pretty volatile." He seems to want to say more but suddenly breaks off. "Look, you don't mind sleeping on the sofa, do you?" he says, and Ziggy's first thought is that he means the one on the lawn; but he sees another, just as beat-up, in the room. The rest of the furniture is a mismatched jumble of styles that might have been picked up at yard sales. Bright strips of red and yellow cloth with bold designs hang on opposite walls.

"Sure," Ziggy nods.

"I thought maybe we'd go for a little walk along the beach," Ted says once Ziggy's settled. "It'll help you get oriented to the neighborhood."

As they walk along the paved strip in the sand, accompanied by other pedestrians as well as bicyclists, roller-skaters and skateboarders, Ziggy listens and takes in his surroundings. In the dazzling light, his eyes keep being pulled out over the large stretch of sand to the ocean, but his gaze constantly returns to something closer at hand. Women in the scantiest of bikinis are stretched out on blankets, their dark skin glistening; a couple of blond young guys in baggy shorts carry surfboards like African tribesmen advancing behind their shields, while in an enclosed area a clutch of shirtless muscle-bound men, oblivious to everything that's going on around them, pump iron, their animal grunts accompanying the clang of metal. A pair of young guys with shaved heads and dressed like Asian monks are chanting something in a language that isn't English. Kites of all shapes soar in the blue sky high above, their colorful tails fluttering behind them. Ziggy's suddenly assaulted by the smell of sun tan lotion and Mexican food, mixing with the briny tang of the ocean. A warm breeze strokes his bare arms, occasionally carrying bits of sand. Who'd have believed Ziggy if he'd have told them he'd be walking along a beach in California with Father Teddy Krawek, once a sanctimonious asshole and now an aging hippie who can't stop talking about his girlfriend?

Ted has been explaining his situation to Ziggy: he and Linda have been living together for about a year. "We've had these conflicts before," he says. "Basically, she needs her space and I respect that in her."

"What are you two fighting about?" Ziggy asks, thinking that these things seem to be a lot more complicated these days.

Ted shakes his head. "It's stupid, really. She wanted us to go on this weekend retreat run by this guru who calls himself Dev Shakramuti. I told her I thought the guy was a phony and she actually agreed, but by that time the whole conflict wasn't even about that anymore. She accused me of throwing my weight around—me, can you believe it?" He sighs and Ziggy watches a plane climb over the Pacific. "Well, I've known Linda long enough to understand that once one of these dramas gets started, it has to play out to the end." He smiles. "I didn't always know that. You know, I was pretty close to despair when I met her." He's silent a while, working something through in his head. "Well," he says at last, "I guess I have to play the bad guy in this story. It isn't fair, but it's going to be OK." He looks at Ziggy. "Boy, have I learned a lot about human relations from Linda. I'd have been a better priest if I knew then what I know now."

They walk on in silence until Ziggy says, "You still miss those days, you said?"

Ted shrugs. "I can't go back. I know that. I miss the certainty sometimes, I guess." He shakes his head. "But, no, I couldn't go back there now."

Clearly, what he can go back to with enthusiasm is talking about Linda. She grew up in a middle-sized city in Ohio, he tells Ziggy. "She was young and starry-eyed like a lot of us, she married too early and walked right into a disaster. Fred, her husband, was someone who was vain and insecure, and because he was so scared he wouldn't measure up, he had to be in charge, he was a know-it-all. Of course, given the way she was raised, Linda felt it was her job to support him by agreeing with him even when she knew he was full of it. Apparently he went from job to job, mostly in sales of some kind, and he had to get himself pumped up, usually at her expense. In the end, for all the support Linda gave him, he accused her of undercutting his confidence. The creep had the gall to use that as an excuse to justify his affair with one of his prospective clients.

"That was the last straw for Linda," he says. "Ohio had become just a place filled with relatives and gray skies, Ohio was history, and she headed for California, where she decided she was going to reinvent herself."

A very tall woman in a bikini and red baseball cap speeds past them on a skateboard and Ziggy wonders, is she someone from Ohio who's reinventing herself? It's doubtful that Ted sees the woman, though, he's so caught up in Linda's story.

"Unfortunately," he goes on, "in her first year she almost managed to kill herself with drugs and booze. She tried everything sexually—threesomes, lesbianism—but in the end she decided that it wasn't who she was. Finally she found her own path and she's at peace with herself. It's not perfect, of course, but, she's making her own decisions, she's leading the life she wants to lead. You know, I couldn't tell you how many jobs she's had, and some of them were pretty strange. But she's at a nursery now, working with plants, and she says it's what she was born to do. I believe her."

Ziggy certainly hadn't expected to learn this much about Ted's girlfriend's private life. In fact, there are certain things he'd just as soon not know. But Ted goes on talking about her. "She came into the bookstore one day looking for something on plants. She and I clicked from the beginning, I asked her out for coffee that same afternoon. That's when she told me I had the soul of a poet. Boy, I needed someone exactly like her at exactly that time. You wouldn't believe how low I was. Linda saw it right away. 'Even when you make jokes, your eyes are so sad,' she told me. "She saw right into me, Ziggy, she really did."

Ziggy nods obligingly. This guy could talk your ears off, though. But then, he used to be a priest, didn't he? They're trained to do that. By now the two of them have apparently come to the end of their walk and have turned homeward. Ted laughs, as if he's suddenly come out of a spell. "Hey," he says, "here I've been talking about myself all the time and I haven't let you get a word in. I don't even know why you're here in California."

"Well, it's private business," Ziggy says. "But the kind of business where you might be able to help me."

Ted looks at him expectantly.

"Remember Przybylski the undertaker?"

Ted nods. "Sure."

"You know he left Detroit in the sixties and came out here."

"Yeah, I heard that."

"I was hoping to find him. I wanted to ask him something. You wouldn't know where he is, would you?"

He shakes his head.

"I was figuring he wouldn't be too hard to track down, being an undertaker and all."

"No," Ted says, "I don't know anything about him being out here. But LA's a big place. We can look him up in the phone book."

"I already tried," Ziggy says, and his heart sinks at the memory of his earlier failure.

"Did you try the Yellow Pages?"

"No—no, I didn't." Ziggy's suddenly filled with hope. "I didn't have the Yellow Pages where I was."

"Well, we can do that back home."

That puts a spring into Ziggy's step on the return trip. Unfortunately, back at Ted's place, the Yellow Pages yield no listing for Przybylski's funeral home, which baffles Ziggy. It's hardly likely Przybylski would have shifted to selling cars, is it? Or did he fail in LA and move on to someplace else? There's something here I'm not getting, Ziggy thinks. Trying to keep back the sense of failure and futility, he takes a deep breath. Well, it's time to give Przybylski a rest for a moment and take care of other essential business. "Can I use your phone to make a collect call home?" he asks, and Ted tells him to go ahead. "I have to water these plants anyway," he says.

As Ziggy makes the call he's aware of the sound of water being poured on the plants, and the room is soon filled with the rich smell of wet earth. "Maggie," he says when he hears his wife's voice, as before momentarily unfamiliar. "I'm out here in California, in LA."

"Are you with Charlie and Gloria?"

"No," he says, getting used to her voice all over again, "that's what I wanted to tell you. I'm going to be staying for a couple of days with Ted Krawek. You remember Father Teddy?"

Maggie is silent for a few seconds. "What . . . ?" she begins, but stops there.

"It's a long story. He's not a priest anymore," he lowers his voice. "He's got a girlfriend. I'll tell you about it later." The thought of all the adventures he'll be able to tell her about at the kitchen table warms him; it almost makes up for his striking out on the Przybylski business.

"I'm sure you have your reasons," Maggie says, unconvinced. "Are you going to tell Charlie about this?"

"Oh, yeah," Ziggy says. "I'm just going to be here a couple of days. I'll get to Charlie's eventually."

Maggie sighs. "He and Gloria are going to be upset that you're not coming there right away."

He laughs. "Hey, Maggie, not that upset."

After a while she asks, "What's it like out there?"

He sighs, trying to summon up his first response to the Pacific. "I wish I could tell you. It's different, though, that's for sure."

She waits a few seconds in case he has more to say. Then she asks, "Have you found out anything about Przybylski?"

"No," he confesses, "no, I haven't. Not yet." Blessedly, Maggie doesn't press him on this, doesn't ask him whether this means his trip has been a total waste of time. In the silence Ziggy hears the water that's moved down through the soil of the hanging plants splashing softly against the trays beneath the pots.

"When are you planning to come back?" Maggie asks.

"As soon as I can wrap this up, Maggie," he says. Whatever that might mean. "As soon as I can. Oh, have I got a lot to tell you," he adds, practically in a whisper. "Any news from around the neighborhood?" he asks.

"No, nothing here. But remember Father Bruno, who used to be at St. Connie's? He died of a heart attack yesterday."

The blow is sudden and surprising. Even when he was in the parish, he wasn't one of the priests Ziggy had that much to do with. But now he's gone, like that. Another one. And Ziggy sensed it too, the last time he was with the priest, didn't he? He doesn't press Maggie for details. Moreover, he decides on the spot he isn't going to tell Ted, at least not right away.

All at once the image of Father Bruno gives way to something else, the memory he had on the bus of his affair with Helen Nadolnik thirty years ago. Ziggy knows himself, he certainly knows that his younger self, caught up in all the confusion of that time, wasn't likely to turn away from Helen—if it were to happen all over again that younger Ziggy would do the same thing. Still, his successor has some sense of the hurt those actions caused his wife.

"Maggie," he says quietly.

"Yes?" she asks.

He hears water dripping from Ted's plants. "Thanks," he says.

"For what?"

"Everything," he says.

"Are you OK?" she asks.

"Yeah," he answers. "Don't worry. I'm OK."

Once the call is over, he forces himself to call Charlie right away and, to his relief, he gets the answering machine. He briefly gives his information, conveniently neglecting to include Ted's phone number, and is relieved to have got that job done.

After the call Ziggy goes outside and has a smoke on the sofa, having already been told that Linda doesn't allow smoking in the house. He exhales into the mild afternoon air, and watches the spokes of a bicycle wheel glinting in the sun as the bike slowly crosses an arching bridge over one of the canals. Jesus, Bruno's dead and I'm here in California sitting on a sofa on an ex-priest's lawn. A powerful emotion grips him, though he couldn't say whether it's a pleasurable

135

or painful feeling. Well, he tells himself, I'm here, I've come all the way across the country. That's something, isn't it? He doesn't want to let himself think what follows naturally from that, that it's something, whether or not he tracks down Przybylski. It's true, though, isn't it? He wouldn't want to give up this trip. He couldn't have invented what he's seen so far. Like Ted, the former Father Teddy.

"Do you know much about plants?" he asked Ziggy, and when Ziggy shook his head, he started talking about a kind of plant called a bromeliad, that didn't have to have its roots in the ground. "They call them air plants," he said. Ziggy was still wondering why he was getting this lecture on plants when Ted got to the punch line. "Linda thinks I'm too much of a bromeliad."

Of course, Linda. "And she isn't, you're saying, she isn't one of . . . those?"

He smiled then. "No, Linda's very earthy." Ziggy was grateful he didn't follow up on that with a review of her sexual history.

Ziggy's had his glory days all right, and he's had his days in the toilet. After he lost the numbers he could have cracked up the way so many people in the movies and TV do, buckling under the stress. And he almost did, by God, almost managed to bury himself with the booze, crying over spilt milk. How he managed he has no idea. Maggie certainly had a lot to do with it, though sometimes he's had the uncomfortable thought he was only able to get through it all because he inherited something of his old man's stubbornness. Whatever the reason, he didn't crack up. The problem is, you pay a price, don't you? He's had to behave all these years, punch his clock, eat his lunch, take his lumps. There's none of the old wildness and adventure that used to make his blood sing. One of the worst things about getting old, he thinks, is that things get boring. But here he is, isn't he, in California, rooming with an ex-priest who waters his girlfriend's plants with as much devotion as he might have given to saying the mass. Is Ziggy ever going to see this woman? Who says life can't still be interesting? The taste of tobacco on his tongue carries the sharp tang of mystery.

The next morning Ziggy's alone in the tiny plant-filled house trying to catch hold of a dream that remains just out of his grasp. All he knows is that Father Bruno was in it: he was drinking ginger ale, he was laughing, then he was crying. Ziggy can't remember any other details about the dream. His back is aching from the night's furtive sleep on Ted's lumpy sofa, and after a cup of warmed-over coffee he's decided to go outside for a smoke. Just now things are peaceful and pleasant in front of the ex-priest's house. Ziggy has no inclination to go to Charlie and Gloria's, and if there were any way to skip that visit entirely and just return to Detroit, he'd do it. There's no real way he can pull it off, though, now that he's out here. He'll have to spend at least a couple of days there. The problem is, when he'd accepted that possibility back in Detroit he still thought his main business out here was going to be with Przybylski, so it had been easy enough to imagine his stay in Burbank would be bearable—Charlie's would just be a base of operations. But now it's likely he'll have nothing to distract him there and the prospect of long, boring days weighs on him, even though he's sure Charlie has better sleeping accommodations than what he'd had last night. Everything's been made worse by his failure to find Przybylski.

Well, there's nothing he can do about Przybylski just now, is there? For the moment he's going to be content to sit here on the sofa and watch the southern California world go by. He knows from what Ted told him that the fiery red plant is a bottlebrush, the one that looks like a bird is naturally called bird of paradise. The purple stuff on the roof across the street is something he's already forgotten. On their walk yesterday, Ted pointed out lemon and pepper trees as well as mock orange. "It's got the greatest smell," he said. It's certainly true that the colorful vegetation that surrounds these little houses of Venice gives them a bit more glamour. Ziggy closes his eyes to take in the smells around him and in the distance he hears a sound. Is it a roller-skater? Is it a skateboarder ? The inside of a seashell? It's so faint you can hardly hear it.

He's lying on a sofa somewhere, but outside, on a stranger's lawn in a place he's never seen before, looking at strange plants. No, it's Ted's, Father Teddy's, in California. But how does he know this? His heart pounds with terror. On the thin grass at his feet is his cigarette, still burning. So he can't have been out that long—what, a couple of seconds? That makes him feel better, but he still can't understand what just happened to him. It's like that time in the john in Oklahoma. He remembers how that scared him. Now he has to force himself to breathe slowly to stem the rushing panic. Jesus, not out here, please. After a second he reaches down and picks up his cigarette. Even though he can taste the grass as he takes a puff, it calms him. He decided after that first episode that it might be dehydration. That could be the explanation of what just happened to him now as well. He's certainly been on an irregular schedule, anything could have caused a brief—what? He didn't faint, after all, just blacked out for a second or two, though even that way of putting it is too strong. He takes another puff on the cigarette. Then he realizes that Ted's phone is ringing.

When he picks up the receiver at last, he hears the enthusiasm in the ex-priest's voice once more. "I've got the greatest news," he announces. "Linda showed up this morning at the store and we resolved all our differences."

"Great," Ziggy says, catching his breath, anything but happy about this news. This Linda, whom he's never seen, this woman who's forbidden smoking in Ted's place, this person who saved Ted's life and then compared him to a plant—Ziggy can only see her as an intruder who's going to put him out on the street, or at Charlie's, which would be just as bad.

"You sound out of breath," Ted says.

"I was outside when the phone rang. I had to hustle in."

"Oh, sorry," the other man says, like someone who has an excess of generous feelings to distribute. "By the way," he adds, "don't worry. Linda says it's OK for you to crash at my place for another day or so. She's staying with a friend who really needs her help and she may have to stay there a while longer."

Ziggy's relieved and for a few seconds he just stands there holding the phone, assimilating this new information, his breath steadying. "I'm glad you two got over your problems," he says. Actually, he welcomes the distraction from his own concern about what just happened to him.

"Oh, Linda's a fire sign and needs her space, that's all," Ted informs him. "The thing is, she really wants to meet you so I asked her to come to dinner tonight. You're going to love her, I guarantee."

So he's going to have a chance to see this wonder woman with his own eyes. Not that he'd have any say in the matter. "I'm looking forward to meeting her," he says, at least half-meaning it. His spirits have actually lifted in the last minute or so. He just nodded off there on the lawn, something that could have happened to anyone. After all, how much sleep did he manage to get last night on that beat-up old sofa?

When Ted shows up in a couple of hours he's carrying a couple of shopping bags. "What did you do all day?" he asks.

"I went back to the beach," Ziggy tells him. This time he found he was a little more used to all the space and sunlight, the bright colors. The cheap sunglasses he bought helped. "Mostly, though," he says, "I just took it easy and rested around the house. It sure beats sitting on a bus."

"I should have let you drive me to work so you could have used the car and had a look around," Ted says. "I'll have to do that tomorrow." He's busily unpacking the bags as he talks. "I'm going to fix some of my killer lasagna," he announces, and begins to bustle about the kitchen readying the place for Linda's arrival, boiling water and shredding cheese, chopping vegetables and opening cans of tomato sauce. A priest who does his own cooking, Ziggy thinks. He's going to have to tell that to Maggie. He wonders if Ted misses old Mrs. Rowinska, who did all the cooking for the priests at St. Conrad's.

"Need any help?" Ziggy offers, not really having much to offer.

"Only moral support," Ted says. Before long the tiny house is filled with the smell of food.

"You sure it's OK if I stay here?" Ziggy asks after a while.

Ted looks up from chopping onions, his eyes glistening. "Like I said, Linda's really eager to meet you. I told her about your problems with Przybylski and she said she wants to help."

That gets Ziggy's attention. "How can she help?" he asks.

"Oh, she's quite a woman," Ted says. "I told you she worked at a lot of different jobs. One of them was with a private detective. She knows a thing or two about finding people."

"Nice," Ziggy says, more impressed by Ted's ardor than his girlfriend's resume. He is getting more interested in meeting this woman, though. All at once he remembers Father Bruno. He really ought to tell Ted about that, but this is hardly the moment. He's not going to be the one who puts the damper on the ex-priest's big night.

Soon enough there's a knock, and a blonde in a short skirt and orange tights walks through the door. Ted darts across the room like a torpedo and, after a protracted clinch, he releases her and leads her toward Ziggy. "Linda, this is Ziggy Czarnecki," he says. "Ziggy, Linda Laing."

Ziggy nods but before he can finish saying that he's pleased to meet her, Linda is hugging him amid a jangle of silver jewelry and the smell of some sweet, dry, earthy scent. "I've heard so much about you," she gushes. "It's so good for Ted to have someone from his old life visit him."

We weren't exactly friends, Ziggy wants to tell her, but he gets the impression that small details like that aren't so important to this short, solidly built woman with a wide pleasant face and shoulder-length blonde hair. When she smiles at him there's an ironic twinkle, as if she and Ziggy are sharing some joke. When her smile stops she looks wary, even a little tough, but the smile returns easily, accompanied by a tilt of the head that reminds Ziggy of some forest animal he can't quite place. He guesses she's in her forties, but she moves with the quick grace of someone younger. This is the woman who saved Ted's life, he reminds himself, Linda the Lifesaver.

By now she's moving around the room examining the plants. "I see Ted's been taking good care of you," she whispers to one of them. "That's right," she says, stroking another one. "Look at the sheen on those leaves."

Ted hands her a glass of red wine and gives Ziggy the beer he asked for, and the three of them sit down around the Salvation Army coffee table, though Ted springs up every now and then to look after his meal. There's music playing dimly in the background, drums and bells and some kind of stringed instrument, but it's barely audible. Ziggy, who's only had a couple swallows of beer so far, is in a surprisingly mellow mood. Linda the intruder has quickly become Linda the pal. She's a little flakey, maybe, talking to plants, and her outfit—a colorful peasant blouse, denim miniskirt over those tights, along with the jingling silver bracelets and the hoop earrings—may be a little loud, but she seems perfectly comfortable in it. She reminds Ziggy of Sharlene and, given their ages, she could be the traveling pool-shooter's mother. She's actually pretty attractive, and likeable too. He's happy for Ted.

His host, for his part, is beside himself with unconcealed joy, practically dancing from the kitchen to the main room to refill drinks and then back to check on his lasagna, whose aromas are coming through more and more strongly.

"Ted says you come from Ohio," Ziggy ventures, hoping Linda won't be upset that he knows something about her past. But then, she and Ted don't seem to be very secretive types.

She squints over her wineglass as though trying to see all the way to the place where she grew up. "I've made my peace with Ohio," she says quietly. "Ohio's fine for a lot of people. Not for me, though." She smiles. "I guess I need to roam."

Ziggy remembers something the ex-priest told him about Linda. "Ted said you were a fire sign," he says and she nods, leaning in his direction to hear more. "You wouldn't be a Sagittarius, would you?" he ventures.

"Wow!" she exclaims, turning suddenly toward Ted. "This guy's good. And you?" she asks Ziggy. "What's your sign?"

He finds that he's hesitant to say the word "cancer" aloud. "I'm a Moonchild."

She nods and gives him a naughty smile. "That figures."

Ziggy takes a swig of his beer. He's having a good time, no doubt about that. For a moment he thinks it's almost like being on the bus again, encountering something new along the way. Many a person his age wouldn't have been able to manage that trip, he reminds himself, and it makes him feel younger.

As though she's guessed what he's thinking, Linda says, "Ted tells me you came all the way from Detroit on the bus. That must have been something."

He nods.

"I've always wanted to do that," she says. "It would be great to go all across the country that way, with a backpack, maybe a tent. You could stop where you wanted and camp out, catch the next bus whenever the spirit moved you." She calls to Ted in the kitchen. "What do you say, sweetie?"

"Sure thing," he says, though Ziggy doesn't have such an idyllic view of what that trip would be like, even for a younger

guy like Ted. But at this point, he knows, Ted would enthusiastically agree to a swim in shark-infested waters, as long as
Linda suggested it. On the other hand, Ziggy doesn't mind at
all being seen as a bold adventurer, and with Linda's encouragement, he tells the two of them about the Midwestern
storms, Lennie's brief imprisonment and the arrest of the
woman who said she was visiting the graves of presidents.

"Hmm," Linda frowns after he's told the last story. "Who
knows the real reason those cops took her off the bus. After
all, there are a lot of strange things going on in our country
these days. Maybe that woman was in one protest too many.
You never know."

Ziggy nods amiably. If that's the story she wants to believe,
it's no skin off his back.

"But you stood up to the cops when you got that poor
Lennie guy out of the hoosegow," she says. "Good for you."

"He wasn't a real deputy," Ziggy says.

Linda shakes her head. "Sometimes the ones who want
to be cops are worse than the real ones. Give yourself more
credit." She lifts her glass. "To Ziggy, champion of freedom."

As the beer and wine keep flowing, Ziggy feels perfectly
at home here in California.

Later, at the table, Linda turns to him and says, "Ted told
me about your problems looking for that undertaker. Why are
you looking for him, if I might ask?"

For a moment Ziggy isn't sure how he wants to answer
that question. After all, he hasn't even told Ted this part of
the story. And does he even know himself at this point why
he wants to see Przybylski? Around him many candles are
burning, some on candlesticks and some in little colored jars
like the votive lights in church. OK, he thinks, if I can't make
this sound like a halfway sane project, maybe it means I'm
crazy. But he finds that he wants to tell this woman he's just
met, he wants somebody else to know how he feels.

"I don't know if Ted told you," he begins, "but back in
the old days I was pretty big in the numbers." He's happy

to be able to present himself as a person of consequence, if only in the past, though he doesn't want it to sound like he's bragging. "OK," he says, "it was just some Polacks in Detroit, but we had a very nice thing going in the neighborhood and, really, all over the east side of the city. We didn't hurt anyone and we made a lot of people happy." He interrupts himself. "I know I might be making it sound like a social service agency. Some of us made a lot of money doing it, but if you took a vote in the parish, I'd say the numbers would have got an overwhelming approval." He points toward Ted. "Even from the priests."

Ted raises his hand. "I confess. I would have voted against it. But I was younger, dumber, there was a lot I didn't know."

Linda leans toward him and kisses him. "But you were always sweet. I know that."

"So there came a time," Ziggy goes on, "when the cops raided the numbers and came to my house; they kept my wife and kids in one room while they searched the place . . ." He breaks off. "This is too long and too complicated a story," he says. "The fact is, after that, everything was different: some of my best friends went to jail, I went into a tailspin, the numbers went to hell." He sighs. "Well, what I'm trying to say is that everything changed." Saying that aloud here in faraway California isn't easy. He takes another sip of beer and the other two wait for him to resume. "Maybe everything comes to an end eventually," he says with a shrug, "maybe it happens no matter who does what, but not long ago somebody told me that this undertaker Przybylski might have helped the cops, he might have given them some information." Linda nods encouragingly, sending her earrings into motion. "Now here was a guy," Ziggy says, "who never liked the numbers, he kind of stood aside from everyone, he just buried them, and that bugged me big-time. When I heard he might have fingered me, I decided I wanted to come out here and ask him to his face if he really did that."

"You came all the way out here to ask a question?" Linda says.

He nods.

Linda's bracelets glisten in the dancing light. "Wow!" she says, turning toward Ted. "I knew I liked this guy. Now I know why. You're one of the seekers, Ziggy. You didn't come out here just to see the sights, go to Disneyland, get some sun." She leans toward him, fixing him with her blue-eyed gaze. "For me," she says, "there are only two kinds of people, those who are seekers and those who aren't. You, me, Ted, we're seekers."

Ziggy has certainly never thought about it that way but if she's including him in some special group, he's not going to complain tonight. He wants to be honest, though, he wants to make himself clear about the way his feelings toward this mission of his have been changing. "The truth is," he says, "I don't even think what he did or didn't do bugs me the way it did when I first heard about it. I mean I'm not trying to find justice or anything like that. Still, I damned well want to find out what happened, if you know what I mean. I'm not going to punch him out or anything, I just want to find out what happened."

"In other words," Linda says, "you aren't willing to let sleeping dogs lie."

Ziggy shrugs. "I guess."

She smiles encouragingly. "And that's why you came all the way out here?"

"And by bus, let's remember," Ted adds, "Which is pretty heroic in my book."

"Yeah," Ziggy says. It's quiet for a while. The music plays dimly, Linda's bracelets jangle as she reaches for her wine, flames are pulsing and jittering all over the room, green leaves shine in the dancing light. "The problem is," Ziggy goes on, "Przybylski seems to have disappeared from the face of the earth. I mean, there's nothing in the phone book."

She turns toward him with fire in her eyes. "LA is full of people who don't want you to know where they are," she says. "There are lots of ways to find them."

Ziggy shakes his head. "I could understand a guy who might want to run away from his creditors if he owed money," he says. "But Przybylski's business was doing fine."

Linda nods. "That is interesting," she says, "but that just makes it more of a challenge. Look, I suppose Ted already told you I used to work for a pretty damned good P.I. named Art Shamsky. And he owes me lots of favors," she says. She fixes Ziggy with her gaze. "Let me work on it," she says. "I won't let you down."

"I'd really appreciate that," Ziggy says sincerely. "The problem is, I'm only here for a few more days."

She reaches out suddenly and takes his hand in hers. "Listen, Ziggy. If this guy is in the greater Los Angeles area, I'll find him for you. I promise."

Ziggy's taken aback by her intensity. "Well," he says, "thanks."

Ted raises his glass. "Here's to finding Przybylski," he says.

"We'll solve this mystery," Linda adds. "Someone can't just disappear into thin air like that." She laughs. "Not with all those syllables."

There's a sheepish grin on Ted's face when he says, "Linda always gets her man."

"Damned straight I do," she says, putting on a southern accent. "And don't you forget it, mister." Leaning toward her, Ted seems to be panting with the desire to lay his hands on her, and from the look she's giving him, Ziggy's sure she's eager to reciprocate. All at once he feels like a fifth wheel. Maybe the two of them are already regretting letting him stay here.

Not long afterwards, Linda says, "I guess I'd better get going," and an eager Ted accompanies her to the door. "You know," he says, "I'll follow you to Sarah's place. I'd like to pick up that book you mentioned when you were at Words." He turns toward Ziggy. "Don't wait up for me," he says. "I won't disturb you when I get back." Then he adds softly, "We have a bit of catching up to do."

"Sure, sure," Ziggy says.

At the door Linda gives him another squeeze. "Remember," she whispers into his ear, "you can count on me." When she steps back, she says, "Repeat after me: 'We're going to find this guy.'"

Ziggy smiles. "We're going to find this guy," he says obligingly. He certainly wants to believe it.

Chapter Seven

≈

The next morning at breakfast, Ziggy quickly learns that Ted is as good at frying eggs as he was at making lasagna. He isn't surprised to find out that one of the ex-priest's many jobs was as a short-order cook. A man of many talents, his former parishioner has to concede.

"I sure need this coffee," Ted sighs. Though he's bleary-eyed, he looks happy, and Ziggy can only guess that he and Linda managed to get in a good deal of catching up last night. He has no idea when Ted came in, since he slept very soundly and apparently dreamlessly. At last, he feels, the kinks from the bus trip are being worked out—he feels ten years younger this morning. Still, as pleasant as things are here at the ex-priest's house, he has to fight the sense that he's just drifting. The fact is, it's become harder lately to conjure up an image of Przybylski beyond the vague memory of a thin smile and a glass of Vernors ginger ale on the bar. If the man turns out not to be in Los Angeles, what's Ziggy doing out here? But that story isn't over, he has to remind himself, it's too early to give up on finding the undertaker. Maybe he's putting too much weight on a thin thread of hope, but he might as well try to make the most of things in the meantime.

When he went out to get the paper about an hour ago, he saw that it was shaping up to be another nice day; and he experienced a rush of anticipation, since he knew he was going to have the car once Ted got dropped off at the bookstore where he works. His host has even gone to the trouble of marking up a map with the routes to some of the places of interest nearby, and Ziggy can't deny that he's looking forward to the prospect of a little drive through the streets of the city. He hasn't been behind the wheel for days now and, coming from Detroit, he may need that more than he'd realized. Then too, a little sightseeing will help him take his mind off of the Przybylski problem, not to mention the unwelcome prospect of a couple of days at Charlie's. It will at least be good to have some time to himself, to look around a bit and call his own shots. But as he drinks his coffee, he's aware that there's still a piece of unfinished business that has to get done this morning: he's got to tell Ted what he learned yesterday from Maggie about Father Bruno.

He washes down a bite of toast with his coffee before announcing, "I'm afraid I got some bad news when I phoned Detroit yesterday."

Ted looks up from his plate. "Is everything all right at home?" he asks.

"Oh, yeah," Ziggy nods. "Yeah, everything's fine. It's Father Bruno, though. Maggie said he died of a heart attack the day before yesterday. I guess I didn't want to tell you right away."

"Huh," is all Ted can say in response. The syllable escapes him as if a sudden slap in the back has expelled the sound involuntarily. The weary joy of a minute ago has gone out of his eyes and he looks momentarily confused, a man who's caught somewhere between this small plant-filled house in Venice, California and the imposing mass of St. Conrad's church back in Detroit. "Wow," he says, "that's a bolt out of the blue, isn't it?" He takes a quick swallow of his coffee.

"Were you two close?" Ziggy asks. He's completely in the dark about what a friendship between priests would be like.

Ted shakes his head slowly. "No," he says. "We were colleagues, part of the St. Connie's team, you might say, but, no, I never really did get to know him." The muscles in his face tighten and he runs his teeth over his lower lip. "Bruno had a way of keeping relationships distant," he says after a while. "At least with me, I guess. He had a kind of formal sense of humor. He'd say things like, 'How is my esteemed colleague this morning?' or 'I wonder what the reverend monsignor has up his sleeve for us his minions today.'" Ted's silent for a few moments. "I had no idea what he was like when he was by himself, what his inner life might be. He didn't open up much." Ted's laugh is curt, almost inaudible. "Of course, none of us did in those days, I suppose."

Ziggy remembers Father Bruno on Harsens Island, pulling at the stump, his face red, his tee shirt drenched with sweat. He was smiling because he knew he was eventually going to pull it free. "He used to have fun at my parties out at the island," he says. "He was strong and I guess he liked to show off his strength." The last time he saw Father Bruno, though, after Eddie Figlak's wake, there was little of that strength left. Ziggy remembers his sense of the priest settling down on the barstool like a deflating black zeppelin.

Ted's eyes narrow. "Did he . . ." He breaks off and starts again. "Do you know if he still believed?"

"Believed?" Ziggy's puzzled.

Ted's voice is hushed now, as if he's speaking in the confessional. "Did he seem to have any doubts about his faith?"

Ziggy shakes his head. "He sure never talked to me about any of that stuff." As far as he knows, Father Bruno had no more doubts about the Roman Catholic church than he had in the Oldsmobiles he regularly drove.

"Let's assume then that that wasn't a problem for him," Ted says, settling back with a sigh. "If so, he was lucky." Ziggy can see that talking about Father Bruno has opened up old questions for Ted, questions that might not be permanently settled. There's a brooding expression on his face as he moves his coffee cup idly on the table and Ziggy waits for him to go on. "Losing something like that," Ted says at last, "something that was your moral compass from the time you were a kid, that's incredibly hard, you know, and painful." He falls silent and his solemn expression is one that Ziggy hasn't seen before on the California version of the man who used to be a priest at St. Connie's. In the morning light the lines in his face pull downward, and he looks older.

"You said you . . . what, lost your talent for faith?" Ziggy ventures after a while.

The other man smiles wanly. "Yeah, that's the version I give when I want to sound flip and offhand, but the real experience was much more wrenching." He looks down at his hands. "It took a while before I could admit to myself what was happening. And when I did . . . well, I know they always say quitting drugs cold turkey is one of the most painful experiences . . ." He's silent again and Ziggy waits, knowing there's more. "I never felt so exposed, so . . . I don't want to sound melodramatic, but," he pauses, turning his cup, "for a while I even thought I was going to kill myself."

As the silence lengthens, Ziggy feels the need to speak. "Well," he says, "things worked out for you, though, right?"

Ted nods, still staring at his hands. "Yeah, they worked out. It wasn't a sure thing, though, I'll tell you that. And it's taken a lot of work. What about you," he asks, looking up, "do you believe?"

Ziggy isn't ready for that question. "Well," he stalls for time, wishing he weren't prevented from smoking at the table. Pulling out a cigarette, lighting a match, taking the first puff, all of it would consume time and that first hit of tobacco would probably clear his head. But since that's not available, he's going to have to go on unaided. "I don't know," he says. "Actually, I try not to think about it much." He could tell Ted about his mother, who saw God's hand in the most ordinary events, he could try to convey to him how hard he had to struggle against her fatalism: according to her, mere human beings—she always called them "mere" human beings—were nothing and God was everything. If you bought that, the young Ziggy felt, it robbed you of your power to achieve anything on your own. Though, come to think of it, his mother certainly did believe in the power of prayer. All that might be hard to explain to a stranger, though. He shrugs, but the man sitting across from him is looking at him seriously, waiting for more.

"I don't know," Ted says quietly, as if to himself, "it would be pretty hard to keep from thinking about it all, why we're here, what's the point."

Yeah, Ziggy wants to say, I'd like to know what the point of it all is. I do think about that, he could say truthfully. He wants to ask the other man, who after all had the benefit of training in the subject, what he really thinks happens to people when they leave you for good? Faces of the dead crowd around him: Vince Nadolnik, Eddie Figlak, Big Al and J.J., his sister Terry. They're gone, but still. God, does he wish he had a smoke.

He's got to say something, though. "Do I think there's some force out there controlling everything we do?" He laughs. "That would be a crutch, wouldn't it? All you'd have to do is sit back and wait for things to happen." He shakes his head. "The thing is, I can't say, I don't know what's out there, I sure as hell don't know what happens after we die but . . ." He's suddenly run out of things to say—as usual, he's come up against a wall. Frustrated, he looks at Ted, who's nodding helpfully, and finishes, "Well, it's not like I don't believe in anything, I'd say I believe in something, maybe not every one of the church's teachings. I guess I'd say most times I try to be a good guy and not a bad one." He hopes the last statement is true, though just now it's a lot easier to remember the times he failed to live up to that goal. Feeling the weight of that failure, he falls silent. The effort has exhausted him.

Across from him, Ted's nodding has suddenly become vehement. "Hang on to what you believe, Ziggy," he says. "Whatever foothold you have on things can slip away in an instant."

Ziggy looks at this man he's gotten to know so much better in the last couple of days than he had in the time when

Ted was a priest at St. Connie's. And still, does he know him at all?

Abruptly, Ted pulls himself erect, as if to signal he's come to the end of this particular subject. "Father Bruno was a good priest," he says, his voice suddenly crisp. "He was no saint, but he did his job, he showed up and performed his duties. I'm sure he was a help to a lot of people. *Requiestat in pace*," he mutters, making a quick sign of the cross.

"Well," he says after a while, obviously relieved to be off the topic of Father Bruno and all that the news of his death has brought with it, "we'll have to be going pretty soon. Are you ready?"

"Sure," Ziggy assures him.

Ted's focused on the present again. "OK," he says, "the routes I planned out for you should be pretty easy to follow. LA is huge: you could fit two or three Detroits into it and still have room left over. So I thought we'd just concentrate on west LA: Santa Monica, Westwood and Hollywood—there's plenty to see there. And my route keeps you off the freeways. Take the wrong exit and God knows where you'll wind up. I wouldn't try to freelance before I got a sense of how things are laid out."

Ziggy nods, acknowledging a little nervousness after hearing Ted's description. But, hell, he's been driving all his life. You don't need a college degree to do that.

"I'd suggest you come back here to Venice and start your sightseeing a little later," Ted says. "Wait till the streets clear a little."

Ziggy's looking at the map on the table. "Sounds like a good plan to me."

On the way to the bookstore Ted says, "About Przybylski. Don't give up hope. Linda's working on it."

"You really think she can find him?" Ziggy asks.

"She's a very capable woman," Ted tells him. "She's really sharp."

"Oh, I could see that," Ziggy says. But it seems to him they're going to have to be more than just smart to find Przybylski; they're going to have to get lucky too. If he's here at all, that is.

Ziggy follows Ted's suggestion and returns to the house in Venice, which enables him to get a little more familiar with the streets as well as the car before he really starts his tour. "Wait till the morning rush is over," Ted advised him. "Let the traffic settle a bit." Enough time to make another piece of toast, warm up some coffee and read the paper.

When he does venture forth he already knows that his first stop is going to be nearby Santa Monica, where he parks so that he can explore the pier he glimpsed from the car when he first came here. He steps onto the platform that carries him over the beach and lingers for a while near the amusement park, taking in the clatter of a solitary ride, the repeated pop of a gun firing at paper targets, the rote patter of a barker selling carnival games. There's not much action at this hour but the surroundings call up an enticing blend of hazy memories.

After a while, though, he sets off for his real destination, the end of the pier that juts out over the ocean. Leaning against the wooden railing, he stands there feeling the breeze on his face as he stares at the velvety blue Pacific. He closes his eyes and inhales the briny smell of the sea, the shriek of gulls and the noisy flutter of a nearby flag filling the darkness. After a few seconds, he opens his eyes to the endless rows of breakers advancing toward the shore. How far have they come to get here? When he turns back toward the land he follows the wavering line of purple hills to the town behind him, its chalk-white towers rising among the dark green tops of tall palm trees. Jesus, he thinks, Maggie should see this, I've got to take her here.

Back in the car again, he can't resist the temptation to diverge slightly from Ted's plan, and he travels north on the

Pacific Coast Highway, intending to go a few more blocks with the water on his left before turning away from the ocean. By the time he gets a chance to do so, though, he finds himself climbing a twisting road that carries him away from the built-up shoreline upward through a suddenly wild and rugged countryside—he actually sees a couple of people on horseback. The area is overgrown with trees and bushes, a mixture of greens and browns, the dense vegetation closing in on him in places, then giving way to sudden open spaces where dark twisted trees stand in the tall, waving grass, jogging his memory, even though he's never been here before. Every now and then a house is visible in the midst of this wild landscape, some of them perched drunkenly over steep ridges. How could you sleep at night when there's nothing under your floor but air? A cluster of shining glass triangles looms suddenly, like a ship riding tall waves. There's a brief glimpse of a vivid yellow wall visible among the rustling leaves, a bright blue roof juts out above the trees. Unpainted rustic dwellings are only seconds away from gleaming modern structures. Many more places are hidden away, their presence signaled by wrought-iron gates or wooden barriers. Signs at some of the entrances depict rainbows and stars and even a large eye, an arrangement of colored glass glitters in the sun. Rich hippies, Ziggy thinks. Now and then a sleek Jaguar or a dust-covered jeep is visible in the driveway. It's all very picturesque and he has to concentrate to keep his eyes on the road, and for a time he can convince himself he's never going to get back to civilization; but at last he gets to the top of whatever road he's been climbing. There, after a sudden, sweeping view of the city, he's traveling downhill again, the road corkscrewing past entrances that lead to more unseen dwellings.

When he's out of the wilds at last, on actual city streets, he has no idea where he is, so he pulls over to a curb. After a lengthy study of his map, he finds that, though he apparently wandered into a canyon, he's wound up not far off the route

Ted outlined for him. He plots his way back, careful to avoid the freeways, and, much to his relief, in a few minutes he's managed to make his way to Hollywood. The detour into the canyon has been enough adventure for the day. It's almost time for lunch and he's close to the Farmer's Market, which Ted identified as one of the places he ought to see. It couldn't have worked out better if Ziggy had planned it.

The farmer's market in the neighborhood back in Detroit is a dark, damp unheated building that looks like an old airplane hangar; and in the cooler weather the sellers who've come in from the farms crowd around fires in trash cans to keep warm. The customers who wander the concrete aisles are just people from the neighborhood who don't warrant a second look. Here in Hollywood, though, men and women in expensive clothes rub shoulders with hippies—there are blacks and Hispanics and even a woman in a bright red sari moving through the airy cream-colored, green-roofed buildings where nobody has to lean toward a fire for warmth. The network of passageways between the buildings leads to dozens of stalls for butchers and bakers, sellers of seafood, homemade peanut butter and freshly baked doughnuts, and most anything else you could imagine. The buyers could be tourists from anywhere in the world, Ted told him, or they might be movie stars. Ziggy looks around him: there are bright pyramids of oranges, glistening silver fish on beds of ice, dark sausages hanging from racks, dozens of different kinds of mushrooms. The smell of freshly ground coffee and frying onions, of cheese and baking bread fills the air. You couldn't spend much time wandering through the place before you'd get hungry. Fortunately, as Ted told him, you can get anything from an ice cream cone to a full course meal under those green roofs. In fact, lots of people are walking around eating.

It isn't long before Ziggy succumbs and gets himself a hot dog, which he takes with him as he continues his rambling inspection of the Farmer's Market. He's standing near an open-air restaurant, chewing on his hot dog, not thinking of anything in particular, when he hears a woman's laugh that he could swear he's heard before. Who could it be, though, out here? He looks into the restaurant area and sees a couple embracing no more than fifty feet away. The woman, who's obviously just come in, is wearing a green pants suit but he can't see her face. When she and the man sit down at the table she isn't looking at Ziggy—in fact, the man and woman are looking at each other with the kind of hunger that only belongs to lovers; but he sees enough to make it clear that he's seeing his daughter-in-law, Gloria. And the man she's with is certainly not Charlie.

The sight jolts Ziggy, and he steps back, wary now of being spotted. He puts on his dark glasses though the unlikelihood of his being here would probably make him invisible to Gloria even if she looked right at him. Nevertheless, he's determined to keep his distance and stay out of sight. Meanwhile, he's trying to determine whether this is what it looks like—a cheating wife meeting her boyfriend—and what it all might mean. Gloria has apparently just arrived, so they're likely to stay a while. It gives him time to think and to try to get things straight in his head.

For one thing, he doesn't know how he feels about this discovery, if it is what he thinks it is. Gloria's nowhere near his favorite person, and he and Charlie don't get along all that well either. Still, it doesn't please Ziggy to think there's trouble in his son's marriage. He's got to try to be sure about this. But he has to be careful, to stay out of sight. To that end, he buys an *LA Times* and a cup of coffee and seats himself at a small metal table within sight of the restaurant. He holds the paper up before him like a screen. He has a sudden thought of Linda, who worked for a private eye. She could probably give him some advice about tailing people. Well, he'll just have to count on common sense. The first thing, his target is pretty stable at the moment and, given that she's in an open-air restaurant, she can be visible from a distance.

Also, he's in a perfect place. Large numbers of people are passing this spot so he's not likely to stand out. And, based on his further observation of the couple, they only have eyes for each other.

By now he has no doubt about the identity of the woman: it's Gloria, all right. And every indication suggests this isn't just a casual lunch. Still, Ziggy feels the need to acquire more evidence before coming to any conclusion. Covertly, he tries to size up the man. He's in his forties, for sure, maybe his fifties. Though he's a little beefy, it looks as if he tries to keep himself in reasonable shape. He's expensively dressed and his haircut probably cost him a bundle as well. "Smooth" is the word that comes to his mind, maybe "sleek." Even from this distance, the way he gestures to the waitress convinces Ziggy that he's somebody who knows his own importance.

Jesus, Ziggy thinks, trying to deal with this thunderbolt, I've even forgotten about Przybylski. And yet, spying on Gloria this way, trying to collect information, seems somehow part of his quest. Already, though, he's dealing with complicated questions. If this should turn out to be what it looks like, he's going to have to keep it to himself. There's no reason for Ted to know, of course. A tougher call, though, is what to say to Maggie. Maggie's always been kinder about Gloria than Ziggy's been, though she's well aware of her daughter-in-law's pushiness and her inclination to think she's the smartest member of the family. But still, this is a development that would cause Maggie a lot of pain. At the moment he's sure it's best to keep this thing, if it turns out to be a thing, to himself.

It isn't just Maggie whose feelings he has to be careful about. Ziggy's screwed up enough things in his own life; to think that it passes on to the next generation is a depressing thought. But for the moment he has to stay on the alert. He glances occasionally at the paper, but his eyes keep returning to the couple at the table. Their meal is punctuated by hand-holding, long, soulful glances and, Ziggy would bet, a certain amount of action under the table. At last, with a sense of haste, they finish their lunch and the man signals the waitress. Ziggy gets ready.

As they leave the restaurant, he follows them from a distance. What he's looking for, he doesn't know, but he feels that in a situation like this you can't have too much information.

The man escorts Gloria to her powder blue Buick convertible. She works as a realtor, Ziggy knows, and the snazzy car is probably required for her business. The two of them clinch for a long time before she gets into the car and drives off. Ziggy watches the man cross the street to a parking lot and he follows him, less careful now about being seen. He hopes to learn more about this Romeo when he sees his car. That turns out to be a silver Mercedes. Well, Gloria's not shopping the bargain basement. Still feeling like a private eye, Ziggy could kick himself for not bringing a pencil and paper. Now he's going to have to try to memorize the guy's license. To his immense relief, when he pulls out of the lot, his license plate reads ROGER W.

Ziggy watches the mystery man pull away. He's excited, a hunter caught up in the pursuit of his prey, but his feelings are confused. He stands there beside a smooth-barked eucalyptus tree, inhaling its strong menthol scent. Like the palms and the cactus, Ted told him, the eucalyptus is an import, from Australia. Everyone, Ted laughed, and most everything that's here, comes from somewhere else.

Yeah, Ziggy thinks. Like me and Ted and Gloria, maybe even Roger W. And Przybylski, if he's here.

He's on time to pick up Ted at the bookstore. Ted, looking a little distracted, asks him about his day.

"I saw a lot," Ziggy says. "I even got lost for a while in the hills. I guess I drove a little too far north before turning back inland."

"Oh," Ted says. "You were in one of the canyons. Wasn't that something? They can be pretty wild. And then, that's where they have so many fires, and mudslides. You wonder about why people would even build there, except that it's so beautiful."

"One thing was strange," Ziggy says, remembering that drive. "There were a couple of places there that looked very familiar to me."

"Familiar?" Ted, who's at the wheel, turns toward him. "What kind of places?"

"It happened once or twice when I was driving past a field that had long grass and some of those twisted trees."

"Live oaks, you mean?" Ted suggests.

"Yeah, I guess." Ziggy shakes his head. "I looked at that and I said to myself, 'I swear I've been here before.' But that's impossible."

Ted's brow wrinkles. "You know," he says after a moment, "they used to film a lot of old westerns in those canyons. It's possible . . ."

"That's it," Ziggy says. "That's exactly where I saw those places before: the movies." To think of it: coming all the way here and returning to a scene he first laid eyes on as a kid in the Ritz Theater. Once again, his first thought is that he's got to tell this to Maggie.

"Where else did you go?" Ted asks.

Ziggy tells him about the Santa Monica pier and the Hollywood Farmer's Market, though he says nothing about what he discovered there.

Ted nods, obviously preoccupied about something, and Ziggy can sense bad news coming. When they've returned to the place in Venice, Ted says with a sigh, "Look, Ziggy, I have to go out tonight. There's something Linda and I have to work out. There's plenty of food, so if you don't mind . . ."

"No, no," Ziggy says, figuring that his days here are numbered. "Look," he tells Ted, "I don't want to be in your way."

"No, no," Ted protests. "It's just . . ."

"I know the two of you want to get back together here."

"Well, that's certainly true," Ted says, "but Linda still has to stay with Sarah a bit longer. She won't be coming back tonight, but I have to tell you it could be as early as tomorrow night. It depends on a few things. But she'll be back here in a couple of days at most."

"I understand," Ziggy says. "You don't know if she's managed to find out anything about Przybylski?" he can't keep from asking.

Ted's face wrinkles into a frown. "Don't worry about that. If anyone can find him, she will."

Here Ziggy is at the Santa Monica pier again. Ted dropped him off on the way to see Linda and gave him all the information he needs about the bus that will take him back to Venice. Ziggy was the one who suggested the pier rather than a quiet night at home, and he's pleased to be walking here amid the larger evening crowds, the air filled with calliope music and the smell of popcorn. In the murmur of voices around him he senses an undercurrent of excitement, the kind that comes with the recognition that the day is soon going to give way to night. The carousel turns, the big-eyed horses bob, there's a laugh somewhere behind him, a teenaged voice: "No, Bobby, don't." A giggle. "Not here."

As Ziggy leaves the amusement section and walks to the end of the pier with a cup of coffee in his hand, he can feel the coolness in the air. The colors out here have changed since the afternoon: the blue Pacific is becoming silver; on the shore, pinpricks of light have appeared around the curve of the coast and the mountains are dark purple now, they look like cardboard cutouts. The sky behind them, for a time a soft peach, is suddenly a chilly blue and all at once the mountains go black. Under the distant sound of the calliope music, Ziggy hears the insistent whisper of the surf beneath his feet, and he feels a shiver.

What is it, this sudden wash of sadness that's come over him? Whatever it is, it's something familiar, it has nothing to do with the scene he's looking at. As unseen waves boom under the pier, it doesn't take him long to identify the source of this melancholy. It's his older sister Terry, long dead—he remembers thinking about her this morning when he was talking to Ted about what he believed. Yes, he knows his sister isn't alive, but he's never been able to accept the fact that she's really gone.

Terry was the one who always made the world clear to the young Ziggy when he was ambushed by childish terrors brought on by the nuns at school, or his mother's highly charged brand of religion. Terry grew up to be a rebel and Ziggy always remembers her with a cigarette in her mouth, making wisecracks about things others took seriously. "Oh, those sisters," she'd say when he'd tell her about some dire prophecy one of the nuns at school had made. "Their problem is that they don't get out very much, they stay in the convent and pray all the time. They don't ever go to the movies, I'll bet they don't even listen to the radio. They need something to make their world a little exciting, that's all. That's why they make up those scary stories."

When Terry left for Chicago to live with a man named Lyle (nobody ever knew if they got married), their mother went into mourning and declared that her daughter could never set foot in her house again. She kept to her word when Terry moved back to Detroit without a mention of Lyle, and got an apartment near Seven Mile Road. In the numbers now, Ziggy would visit her there from time to time and talk to her about his rapid rise. Whenever he had a chance to move up in the business, he went to Terry for advice, knowing what she'd tell him. She was thin and wiry with short blonde hair, so nervous in her movements that she never seemed to be still, nodding her head as she listened, grabbing herself by the elbows and rocking back and forth as if she were remembering dance music from some place she'd been to that was a lot more exciting than it was here.

"So, what do you think?" he'd ask her. "Think I should accept J.J.'s offer?"

"Listen," she'd say with a tight little smile, "nobody gives you anything free in this life. Take whatever they give you, and what they don't give you, just grab." She looked at him hard. "Not doing something you want to do, Ziggy, and then spending the rest of your life wondering whether or not you should have done it, that's the worst thing that can happen to you."

He got the call in the middle of the night: his sister had been killed in a one-car crash. Somebody had to identify the body. The cops said she was going at least eighty when she hit the tree near New Baltimore on Lake St. Clair. One thing they found odd: the car's headlights were turned off. The cop who said that was obviously trying to imply she might have committed suicide, but Ziggy wasn't buying that. Wasn't it possible she might have been thrown against the light switch? The cops had to concede that was a possibility.

The next night he couldn't sleep, he had to look at the place where she'd crashed. It was the time of year when the fish flies suddenly appeared like snow in places like New Baltimore that were near the water, covering whole stretches of the highway in a slush of bugs so that cars sometimes skidded on their soft bodies. Ziggy wondered about that, but the cops said that particular stretch of road was clear.

When he went out there that night the marks of the impact were still on the tree, there were fragments of glass all around. He got out of his car and felt the cool night air on his face. He moved his hand over the shredded bark of the tree, he knelt to the pavement, picked up a piece of glass and ran it harshly between his fingers. He stood at the site of the crash a moment and began walking without any plan or destination. There was a little grocery store at the edge of town. For all he knew, it was one of the last things his sister had seen before she crashed. The place was closed but the streetlight beside it made it an island in the darkness, and before he realized it he was walking toward the light. How strange to be here, after everything that had happened. He was on his way up in the numbers, he already knew he was going to be a big success, but now Terry wasn't going to see that. Here he was at the edge of this little town, in a place that was alive with bugs. Fish flies kept striking the glass of the streetlight above him, they jittered and zigged through the night air, they brushed his face. Beneath him a brown carpet of insects covered the sidewalk as well as the grass, their bodies crackling under his feet.

He stopped before the store. In the darkened window were signs advertising Silvercup bread and Red Man tobacco. Nobody was in sight. Everyone else was asleep, it seemed, and the only living things in the Michigan night were himself and these creatures. What was he doing here? Where was he going? What did any of it mean? He crouched to get a closer look at the wriggling, pulsing things below him; on an impulse he dipped his fingers into the mass and scooped up a handful of fish flies—they were like penny candy, but lighter. They crawled and buzzed in his hands, a soft, damp weight. He held them for a while, then tossed them into the air; they fell with a faint beating of wings. All around him bugs flew and flitted, their long V-shaped tails moved in slow swimming motions, translucent wings glistened palely in the glow of the streetlight. The fishy smell was suddenly over-powering, and all at once, for all that he could see his success taking shape, Ziggy realized he didn't understand where anything was going. The bugs wriggled and buzzed all around him as he crouched there, somewhere near where his sister had died.

He feels that same scalding mass in his throat here, on the edge of the continent. Jesus, some things never end, do they?

"Terry," he says quietly, as if confessing a secret to the heaving ocean. What happens to people after they die, though? As Ted said, it's an important question. He knows that Terry is still alive for him as long as he can keep remembering her.

But what about me? Who's going to remember me after I'm gone? Who's going to know I stood here at the edge of the Pacific remembering my sister? Who's going to know I came all the way here on the bus looking for Przybylski, that just this morning I lost my way and drove into a canyon where I saw places I hadn't seen since I was a kid, soft hills with long grass and dark, twisted trees where masked men on horseback waited for a stagecoach?

He had no idea there was so much sadness in the briny smell of this ocean.

The next day Ziggy awakens under a cloud, feeling the full weight of his years. It ought to be damp and gloomy outside but, this being California, the sun is reliably shining. He knows it's just a matter of time before he's going to be booted out of Ted's place, and it looks as if he's going to be no closer to finding Przybylski. What the hell, he thinks, I should just go to Charlie's for a couple of days and get that over with, then go home. He has the use of Ted's car again but he isn't tempted to drive it today. Even the Santa Monica pier, which is close by, isn't an attraction after his spell of melancholy there last night.

He's smoking on the outdoor sofa when he hears the phone. It's Ted. "Linda says she has some news for you," Ted informs him. "She'll tell you tonight. She's coming over."

"About Przybylski?" Ziggy asks.

"Who else?"

That evening Linda is eager to share her news. "Artie came through for us," she says. "He solved the puzzle."

"I'm all ears," Ziggy says.

"OK," Linda tells him, "Art figured if we couldn't find the guy, maybe it was because he'd changed his name. Most people when they change their names keep the initial. That was a start. Then too, Art assumed your undertaker wouldn't have changed his profession. So he looked around in his usual way and what he found is that the answer was here all along, right under our noses."

"What do you mean?" Ziggy asks.

"There's a chain of undertakers in Southern California called Prince Funeral Homes. Art did a little digging around and found out that they've been here about as long as your Mr. P. has. He checked it out and, sure enough, Prince used to be . . . well, you know who. It makes sense, doesn't it, to change the name out here?"

Ziggy snorts. "He wouldn't be the first Polack that changed his name." He runs his hand through his hair. "But, OK, he was doing fine in Detroit. Well, fine for a neighborhood undertaker. A chain out here? How could he get so big so quick?"

Linda beams. "You could work for Art. He asked the same question and he got an interesting answer. It seems that a couple of years ago one of the alternative newspapers ran a story about Mr. Prince's funeral business. It was written by someone named Sal Russo who unfortunately drank himself to death not long after that. But he wrote a hell of an article. He called it 'The Prince of Darkness.'"

"It sounds like he wasn't exactly recommending the guy," Ziggy ventures.

Linda nods. "I'll say. This Russo guy said Prince started out with just one funeral home, but that there was a big expansion a few years ago. The guy seems to be making tons of money. Russo implies that there's something shady behind it, but he can't exactly put his finger on what. There's a history of charges of various kinds of abuses in the Prince chain, like the selling of body parts of the deceased. A lot of it is speculation, including the possibility that the business has been funded by money from organized crime."

"I can't believe that," Ziggy says, remembering the image of the prissy undertaker trying to keep his distance from the numbers in the parish. Was he a wolf in sheep's clothing all the while?

"Russo apparently confronted him about those allegations and Prince just brushed him off. Those were only stories, he said, started by jealous competitors. Russo said this guy was very slick, flashy but elusive."

Ziggy shakes his head. "Flashy is the last word I'd use to describe Przybylski."

"Haughty is another word he used. He said 'Edward Prince sometimes acts as if he thinks his name is Prince Edward.'"

"Wait a second," Ziggy says. "Did you say Edward Prince?"

"Yeah," Linda assures him.

Ziggy has to collect himself a moment before he can assimilate what he's just heard. "The guy I'm looking for is named Cyril Przybylski. Edward is his son, little Eddie."

"I remember Eddie," Ted says.

"I guess little Eddie's grown up now," Linda says. "But he'd certainly know where you could find his father."

Little Eddie, Ziggy thinks. He has a hard time reconciling the glamorous figure described by that Russo guy with the Eddie Przybylski he remembers from Detroit. Eddie was more sociable than his father, but he showed no signs of being anything more than the dutiful son, waiting his turn to inherit his father's business. What happened, how did this drab caterpillar turn into the splashy butterfly of the article? And, interesting as all this is, how did he get control of the company? What happened to the old man? Did he die out here? The fact is, Ziggy has just had one mystery solved, only to be confronted with another. But at least he has a lead, he has a name and it should be easy enough to get an address. He knows what his next step is, but he suspects he's going to have to launch it from somewhere else, since Linda's moving back soon and Ted's going to be in no mood to play detective.

Time is running out on Ziggy, at least his time here in Venice, where he's got only one more night. While Ted and Linda are out shopping, he tries to take stock of things. First, he's going to have to call Charlie and move his base of operations to Burbank, unappealing as that prospect may be. He's actually got used to being here in Venice, knows his way around a little, and is comfortable in the neighborhood, but he has little choice in the matter. Burbank it's going to have to be. But then there's the business of the apparent conflict in Charlie's marriage, which is likely to poison the atmosphere there all the more. Ziggy isn't looking forward to this.

Still, after what he's recently learned about little Eddie, he's more determined than ever to fulfill his original intentions and get in touch with old man Przybylski, or at least to find out what happened to him. But he's going to need wheels to do what he has to, especially here in LA. He has to play the cards he's got, and one of them has the phone number of Lennie's agent on it.

Sam Bluestone is wary. "Who did you say you were?"

"I was on the bus with Lennie," Ziggy tells him. "From Chicago."

"And you want . . . ?"

"Well, I wanted to see how he was doing, for one thing."

"Hey," Sam's voice is raspy and Ziggy imagines a bobbing cigar in his mouth, "like I keep telling Lennie, these things take time."

"He said he was going to be at some motel in Hollywood."

Sam snorts. "The Tropicana. That place is a zoo. How anyone can get an hour's sleep there with all those rock musicians I don't know. But I got Lennie a nice deal. I got him a sublet, really a house-sit for an actor who's in rehab."

"Is Lennie working?" Ziggy says. "I mean, I know he probably isn't doing his comedy stuff, but he said he'd be working at something else like maybe waiting on tables at a restaurant."

"Waiting tables is shit," Sam declares. "No, Lennie's driving people around. People who might be helpful to him some day."

"Do you have a number where I can reach him?" Ziggy asks.

There's a silence on the other end of the phone. "How do I know you're not a bill collector?" the agent asks at last.

"I know one of Lennie's jokes," Ziggy says. "He told it to me." He then repeats the line about the roaches with flea collars.

Another sigh. "He's going to have to do better than that, but that sounds like Lennie, all right." He gives Ziggy a phone number, which he immediately calls.

"I talked to your agent," Ziggy says.

"Sam Blood-Out-of-a-Stone?" Lennie answers.

"That's the guy. He says you're doing OK."

"He does, huh?" He doesn't sound convinced.

"He says it takes a while to make it."

"Don't I know that," Lennie says.

"Hey, buck up," Ziggy tells him. "You told me that yourself."

"I guess." After a while, Lennie says, "Did you find your undertaker?"

"Not yet," Ziggy says. "But I'm getting close. The problem is, I had the use of a car but now I'm not going to. I wondered if you could help."

"Well, I do have a certain amount of free time," Lennie says.

"I've got your number," Ziggy says. "Take this one down. This is where I'm going to be staying for a while. Maybe I'll call you from there. I'm not going to be out here for long."

When that call is over, he dials Charlie's number. Gloria answers.

"Hi, Gloria," he says. "I've been staying with a friend but now I'm ready to come to your place for a couple of days."

"Do you have transportation?" she asks. Ziggy listens for traces of guilt or betrayal in her voice, but it's just Gloria.

"I'll find my way there," he says. He'd thought about taking a bus but Ted has volunteered to drive him to Burbank tomorrow.

Linda, who's in the process of moving back into the house, gives him a big hug as she leaves for the night. "Keep us posted on your quest for Mr. P."

"I will," he assures her.

"Sorry about the suddenness of the last couple of days," Ted says when they're together in the car the next day. "The business between Linda and Sarah is complicated."

"Sure," Ziggy says.

"You see," Ted goes on, "Sarah is an ex-lover of Linda's from her days of sexual experimentation. They still had a lot of things they had to work out between them."

Ziggy's uncomfortable listening to this and nods without saying anything.

"Linda's a very complicated person," Ted says. "As I said, she needs her space."

"Well," Ziggy says, "you seem to be giving her that."

"She's worth it," Ted says, his voice catching, and Ziggy wonders if all the business between Linda and her ex-lover has been resolved.

"I can see that," he says.

"Well, good luck," the ex-priest says as they shake hands in front of Charlie's house in Burbank.

"You too," Ziggy says. And then he adds, "You know, to be honest, I never really liked you much when you were a priest, but I think you've turned into one hell of a guy. Give yourself credit: you've improved."

"That's what I keep telling myself," Ted says. "Sometimes it's hard, though."

"It's going to work out," Ziggy tells him. He hopes he's right.

CHAPTER EIGHT

"So finally you're at Charlie's?" Maggie says. "What's it like?"

"It's big," Ziggy answers guardedly. "Nice." He's in a room by himself but he still speaks quietly, not convinced he can't be heard. "They have three bathrooms," he adds.

"And how are Charlie and Gloria? The kids?"

"Oh, fine," Ziggy says.

"Well, good," Maggie says. "I'm glad you finally got there."

After a silence, Ziggy asks, "What's the weather like back there?"

"Warm," she says. "It's getting to be spring at last. The buds are out. Maybe we'll have a nice Easter." She sounds tired.

"Easter?" That surprises him. "When is Easter this year?"

"Next Sunday," she says.

"That's early, isn't it?"

"Not all that early," she answers. "Look, Ziggy, do you think you'll be able to be back by Sunday?"

Seven days to find Przybylski and travel back across the country. That would give him four more days at best out here, since he'd need three for the bus trip. His first response is to feel pressured. But there's no need for that: if he actually gets to see Przybylski tomorrow, then stays an extra day here in Burbank just to be sociable, he can leave on Wednesday and be in Detroit by the weekend. But he has to act fast. "Sure," he promises her. "I'll be back by Easter." Once he says it aloud he feels committed to it. Hell, if it comes to that, he can fly back, even if it means swallowing the cost of the return bus ticket. He wonders how much the plane will cost. "I'll be there," he says again, acknowledging all he owes this woman who's seen him at his worst and stuck by him through it all. He was just a young punk when they started dating, he had no way of knowing what was in store for him. He had no future beyond working at the Chrysler factory, if he was lucky, but he wanted more, he told her on one of their first dates. It was spring and there was a smell of lilacs in the night air that came from the priests' yard. "Maggie, I don't want to be like my old man," he confessed to her as they stood beside the brick wall that surrounded the yard, "I don't want to be just another Polack." He wasn't, she assured him, not to her he wasn't. And now, that's exactly what he is, and Maggie is still there.

"Look," he says, "I have so much to tell you about this place. Some of it you're not going to believe. But I'm going to take you out here someday, show you for yourself." There he goes again, talking big like the old Ziggy.

"You just find Przybylski," she tells him, "say what you have to say to him, and come back." There's no missing the urgency behind her words.

"I will," he assures her. "And in time for Easter." At the moment he wishes he were already back in Detroit—could the lilacs be out already? He's going to fly back, he decides on the spot, but he'll keep it as a surprise from Maggie until the day he leaves.

Meanwhile, he has to get this Przybylski business over with. He'll go to see Eddie tomorrow and find out what happened to the old man. It's possible he might even get a chance to see the old guy at the same time. Wouldn't that be convenient? Will he actually ask his former nemesis if he ratted on him? Right now, he isn't even sure of that. But after all the effort of getting here, seeing Przybylski has become a kind of solemn obligation, like one of those religious acts you had to perform, like going to communion on the nine First Fridays in order to get an indulgence. He can't not do it.

"I miss you, Ziggy," Maggie says.

"Me, too," he answers in almost a whisper.

Charlie has decided to welcome his father to Burbank with a family barbeque in his big backyard. Decked out in an apron that says "Griller-in-Chief," he's already pointed out the snowcapped peaks on the horizon a couple of times as if they're part of his property. "The San Gabriel Mountains," he says again. "Imagine: here we are in our shirtsleeves and we can see all that snow up there. There's no place like southern California." Like the house with three bathrooms, the spacious yard with the view of the mountains, even southern California itself is being offered up to the old man as proof of his son's success.

Ziggy and his oldest child have never been close and he isn't really sure why. Some of it no doubt has to do with his being caught up in the numbers, which didn't leave him much time to be a family man. Charlie certainly wasn't inclined to follow in his old man's footsteps, and the more schooling he got the less of a Polack he seemed to be. For sure, marrying Gloria, who has her own ideas about how the world should be run, didn't help. But Ziggy can't deny that the kid's made the most of his chances, especially since his father lost the numbers in the middle of Charlie's lengthy education, which cut off the flow of easy money—so his son can claim to be at least partially a self-made man. Here in his backyard, he's clearly proud of not only his accomplishments but those of his children, Alyssa and Paul. "Allie just loves horses," Charlie's told him, showing off her riding trophies; and Paul is apparently some kind of scientific genius.

The kids don't seem especially thrilled to have to spend time with their grandfather, and Ziggy can understand that. They're teenagers, for one thing, and they've lived out here now for a few years and have lives of their own.

"How come you still live in Detroit?" Paul asked him, looking genuinely puzzled. "It's really dangerous, isn't it, and pretty dirty."

It was a hard question to answer. "It used to be quite a place," he told the kid. "America couldn't have won the Second World War without Detroit," to which his grandson nodded politely, though obviously not particularly impressed. That was the war against Hitler, he wanted to tell the kid, but would he even know who Hitler was? No, maybe you had to have lived through those days, you had to actually have been there like he was, stopped at a railroad crossing near the Packard plant during the war.

He was at the head of the line, and as red lights flashed and a bell rang he watched flatbed cars rumble past carrying Sherman tanks, two to a car. It was summer and the heat rose, intensifying the smell of the tall, bee- and cricket-filled grass beside the tracks that mixed with the tang of oil from the tracks themselves and the exhaust from the cars behind him as the armored vehicles moved by, their drab silhouettes and long guns repeated endlessly. The bell clanged, lights flashed red and the tanks continued to slide by, a line of lumbering blind mastodons, their sheer number dizzying, the gleaming tracks bending under their weight. Behind him were other drivers, their cars, like his, with ration stickers on their windshields, the drivers' hands resting loosely on the steering wheels as this solemn procession of weapons moved past. The radios in the cars would have been playing, the different songs blending—paper dolls, moonlight and stardust, the same old story—until the music became inaudible beneath the rumble of the passing tanks that were bound for distant, dangerous places. Ziggy looked at his watch from time to time: five minutes passed, then ten, fifteen; and still the tanks continued to move by, their powerful treads still, their guns silent. The smell of all that metal seemed to envelop him in an invisible cloud. It wouldn't have been hard to convince himself that the train was literally endless. Then, just when it seemed that the monotonous procession of weaponry would go on forever, the caboose came into view at last. All at once the track was clear and he was facing the long line of oncoming traffic, horns from behind urged him on his way. But, Christ, what power! And how sad that memory makes him feel today.

You couldn't explain any of that, though. And the kid was right: Detroit is dangerous and dirty, and that Packard plant that used to run three shifts a day closed long ago.

Ziggy has to admit that the hamburger is damned good, and he tells that to Charlie, who smiles to himself at the compliment. He obviously enjoys cooking and just as obviously enjoys eating, having put on a few pounds since coming out here. Ziggy has a sudden flash of Roger W., no toothpick but looking firm rather than soft, and the momentary tranquility he's been feeling deserts him. Here in this sunny backyard where a family that's to all appearances happy and comfortable is celebrating their well-being with an American ritual, Ziggy feels the chilling presence of a looming cloud.

"Do you need anything?" Gloria is beside him. Wearing white pants and a black sleeveless blouse, she looks smooth and self-possessed, with none of her husband's obvious need to please. And it's clear she hasn't gained an ounce since coming out here.

"I'm doing fine, thanks," he says.

Gloria smiles coolly, her thin gold necklace flashing in the sun. "Well, anything you want, you know . . ."

Ziggy is wary around her, as if he's convinced she knows that he knows about her meeting with Roger W. And the fact is, underneath her outward calm, she does seem to be studying him intently, as if she's waiting for him to slip and blow his cover. Could she really guess I've got something on her, he wonders. "How's the real estate business?" he asks, trying to find a safe topic.

Gloria's smile widens. "Fabulous, actually." Then she pulls down her mouth with obvious irony. "It keeps me running, though. Sometimes I think I need more vitamins."

Vitamins, Ziggy feels, are the last thing she needs. Even in the green backyard, where she's supposedly relaxing, he can feel her restless energy. He supposes that selling real estate around here might in fact keep her pretty busy, given the vast spaces of LA. It's even possible, he thinks, that Roger W. might be a legitimate client, but that thought lasts only a second: not the way they were acting. Ziggy shakes his head. "I'll bet you love it," he says.

She extends her index finger and touches him gently on the upper arm. "You're pretty shrewd," she says playfully, but once she starts talking about her work there's no doubting her seriousness. "It's great to be able to do something," she says, "and know that I'm good at it." She folds her arms and smiles as if suddenly remembering something that pleases her. "You know," she continues, "when I decided to give it a try a couple of years ago I almost chickened out at the last minute, but Charlie knew I'd just be kicking myself for not trying, and he pushed me. I owe him a lot. I eventually learned the business and I made myself good at it, but I needed Charlie to back me, and he did."

And now you're going behind his back and fooling around, Ziggy wants to say. But he sticks to neutral territory. "So you must know the area pretty well by now."

Gloria nods, a quiet confidence on her face. "There are people who've been out here twenty years who don't know what I know. You want to find something out about a neighborhood, about who lives where and who used to live someplace, I know where to find out." Then, as if she's just realized that she's let her father-in-law see too deeply into what drives her, she pulls up short and continues in a voice more appropriate to the conscientious hostess, "Well, that's why it's disappointing that you're not staying longer, that you said you don't want to see Disneyland or some of the other tourist attractions."

"No," Ziggy says, impressed by her ability to convey the illusion of sincerity, "I don't really have much time. I promised Maggie I'd get home by Easter and I still have this business I have to get done."

"Well," she says, the dutiful daughter-in-law who already knows the old guy will be leaving in a couple of days, "if you need any help, you know you can count on me."

"So," Charlie says a few minutes later, "what is this mysterious business you have with Mr. Przybyslki?" The appetizing smell of cooking meat and frying onions is all around them.

Ziggy takes a swallow of beer. "Oh, it's just a couple of old-timers getting together and reminiscing." What else can he tell him? At this point that explanation comes pretty close to what he'd tell himself. The fact is, though, he set out on this trip because he wanted to see Przybylski and he's determined to do it. "But you say you didn't know that Prince was Eddie Przybylski."

Charlie shakes his head. "Everybody around here's seen those Prince ads but I still can't believe it's Eddie." He smiles. "Eddie wasn't exactly one of my buddies back in Detroit, you know."

Just then Gloria returns. "Is your dad telling you all about his wild times in Venice?" she says, putting her hand against her husband's lower back.

"He's not talking," Charlie says. "He's afraid I'll tell Mom what he's been up to."

"Venice is a pretty artsy place." Gloria says, "if you know what I mean."

Charlie turns to the grill to look at his burgers and for a moment he has to search for the spatula, but Gloria is already there to hand it to him before he has a chance to ask for it. For a couple who might be having trouble, Ziggy thinks, they put on a pretty good show of cooperating. But then, relationships, as he learned at Ted's, can be pretty complicated.

When he's flipped his burgers, Charlie says, "I don't know what kind of wild times you can have with a priest, though."

Ziggy wants to tell him that some of the priests at Connie's were quite capable of handling wild times, but contents himself with saying, "Ted's not a priest anymore. Anyway," he goes on, "I wasn't in Venice the whole time. Ted gave me his car and I drove around a bit in Santa Monica, then I got lost for a while in one of the canyons, but I managed to find my way out and get a look at Hollywood." He glances toward Gloria for some kind of reaction but she simply nods.

"Well," she says, "I feel better about not being able to show you around the area knowing you've done a bit of tourism on your own. Remember, though, if you should change your mind." She turns toward the house.

"So," Charlie says, "you're going to see Przybylski tomorrow?"

"Yeah," Ziggy tells him, "there's this guy I met on the bus who's going to give me a ride to the main Prince funeral home in Pasadena. I ought to be able to talk to Eddie and find out from him where his father is. With luck, he'll be somewhere close-by."

"Are you sure he's even alive?" Charlie asks.

Ziggy shakes his head. "I don't know that."

"And if he's dead?"

Ziggy's become more aware of that possibility lately. It certainly might turn out that way. That would be a huge disappointment, though. "Well," he says, "in that case I guess I'd just have to start getting ready for the return trip."

"But, Pa," Charlie says, "you know you don't have to take the bus. We can pay for the plane ticket. It's the least we can do."

Ziggy takes another swallow of beer. "Yeah," he says, "I've already decided I'm going to fly back. But I was going to pay for it myself."

"No way," says Charlie. "Like I said, it's the least we can do."

Ziggy can see how much this means to his son. "Well," he says, "If you keep pushing me I might just take you up on that." He raises the bottle in Charlie's direction before taking another swallow of beer. "Nice place you have here," he says, and sees his son smile. "You're right about those mountains. I'm going to tell your mother about that." It doesn't take much, Ziggy observes, to make Charlie happy. Then he remembers Roger W. and his mood sinks.

He drifts off by himself to a corner of the yard and glances up again at the mountains topped with snow. How close and yet how far away those white peaks seem. So this is where his family has come to, that line of Polish peasants who, almost a hundred years ago, left what was then part of Prussia, where they weren't even allowed to learn Polish in the schools, and came to Pennsylvania because they'd heard there was plenty of work in the coal mines. Fortunately, they didn't stay underground and eventually found their way to Michigan. Now Charlie, the most successful of his kids, has brought this branch of the Czarneckis all the way to the western edge of the continent.

In spite of Ziggy's ups and downs, his children have done all right, for the most part. Steve, unlike Charlie, never liked school and joined the army as soon as he could. But once he got out he married Ellie, started selling cars and pretty soon they moved to Warren, where they seem OK. Steve's sister Alice got married right out of high school to Wally, a boring but dependable guy who sells insurance. He's a Polack too but they live out near Pontiac, which Maggie thinks is too far away. It's only Jack who's never really found himself. The baby of the family who's almost thirty-five now, he's always been his mother's favorite. Everybody likes Jack, which is his problem: he's never had to work for anything. Women love him, men like to shoot the shit with him, he's a great buddy on fishing trips, he knows a million stories. He just can't keep a steady job. He's always available to tend bar, he can usually find himself a situation where he's leeching off someone. "Give him time," Maggie keeps saying. Ziggy's knows that when Jack's had a bit to drink he isn't shy about blaming all his troubles on his father and what happened to the numbers. You can't win 'em all.

"Were you really a big man in the underworld in Detroit?" He looks up to see his granddaughter looking at him ironically. "My father says you were."

Ziggy shakes his head. "He gives me too much credit. It was just the numbers. It wasn't like the movies." He can see her disappointment. "But you can kind of stretch things when you tell your friends about it."

She smiles. She's a pretty kid, tall and thin like her mother, with the mischievous look of someone who doesn't sit around waiting for things to happen.

"Actually," he tells her, "one of the guys I worked with was on TV before the Kefauver Committee."

Allie wrinkles her nose. "What's that?"

"Estes Kefauver was a senator who wanted to be president and went around the country holding hearings on TV to investigate organized crime." The would-be president from Tennessee is dead now, as is J.J., who had his own few minutes of TV celebrity. Even the big mobster Frank Costello, who only allowed the cameras to show his hands while he testified, which made him seem all the more sinister—he's dead too.

"That sounds like pretty big stuff," Allie says.

"It was," Ziggy tells her. "Those hearings were so popular they knocked *Howdy Doody* off the air for a while. You can look it up."

"*Howdy Doody*?" She wrinkles her nose.

Ziggy searches for something she can relate to and settles for, "I guess you could say it was like *Sesame Street*." But that's enough about the past. "Anyway," he says, "I'm impressed that you're a horse rider. You'd never get me on one of those animals."

She laughs. "I'll bet you wouldn't say that once you were in the saddle. Actually, I used to feel the same way," she says. "Then I heard this girl I know, Gayle, bragging about riding and I said to myself, if she can do it, so can I. Once I got on a horse it seemed as if I'd been doing it forever."

"Good for you," Ziggy says, thinking that if his grand-daughter had been around a hundred years ago in the old country, she'd probably have been one of those who pushed the idea of leaving for America. "Well, I'm impressed," he tells her. "What about your brother? Does he ride?"

"Are you kidding?" She shakes her head. "He can tell you all about the horse's prehistoric ancestors, but riding a live one doesn't interest him at all." Then she quickly rushes to her brother's defense. "He's smart, though, really smart."

"Yeah, I know," Ziggy says. "When I told him about my trip through the desert, he explained to me how the animals, cactus and other plants out there survive with almost no water. You could see how interested he was in that kind of stuff. To tell the truth, I think he'd have got a lot more out of that trip than I did," he says.

"Paul can seem like a bit of a geek," Allie declares, "but he's OK."

After she's left, Ziggy ponders the mystery of his grand-children's heritage. Where did the little intellectual get his brains, where did his horse-riding sister get her courage? He can't help wondering how those two are going to turn out; although even as he thinks it, he recognizes that there's a good chance he isn't going to be able to find out. The fact is, he realizes, all of us are caught up in the middle of a whole lot of stories and nobody gets a chance to see how all of them turn out. Hell, for that matter, who knows what Detroit's going to be like fifty years from now?

But, closer to home, he wonders about what's in store for his son's marriage. The Griller-in-Chief acts like a man who thinks he's landed in heaven. He obviously loves his work, his family and most likely his wife as well. What's going to happen to him if he has to face disruption in his household? But will he, necessarily? Is it possible that he and Gloria have worked out some sort of arrangement that goes beyond what was acceptable to Ziggy and his generation? Not for the first time, he feels a tug toward home, where things are simpler.

When Lennie shows up in Burbank the next morning, he's driving a shiny black Cadillac. Ziggy whistles. "I was expecting a boxy Checker with a roof light," he says. "This is a pretty high class cab." In fact, there's no indication that the car's for hire: not only is there no roof light, there's no lettering on the door, no meter.

"It's really a special livery service for show business people," Lennie explains. "We don't just pick up anybody." He's wearing a dark suit that's a little roomy on him and Ziggy can see a chauffeur's cap on the front seat. "Most of my work is later in the day," Lennie says. It strikes Ziggy that, even though Lennie no doubt has the papers to prove his legitimacy, he still looks like someone who's impersonating a chauffeur.

"How do you like your job?" Ziggy asks.

Lennie shrugs. "It's a job. At least I'm not likely to run into my cousin Morris out here."

"Is it OK if I sit in front?" Ziggy asks a moment later. "Or is that againt the rules?"

"Be my guest," Lennie says.

Well, I'm traveling in style again, Ziggy thinks. He remembers how proud J.J. was of his Caddy, though J.J. would never have had a black one. White, he said, was a classy color, black was for hearses. So maybe this is exactly the car Ziggy should be going in to see Przybylski.

"I'm still learning my way around the streets here," Lennie says when he's behind the wheel. "I was glad when you said you only wanted to go to Pasadena. It's pretty easy to get to."

"Good." Ziggy takes a long drag on the cigarette he's just lit. He's surprisingly nervous about this venture, but then, he can't help remembering Linda's description of Edward Prince's lucrative empire of the dead. He's glad Lennie has a dark suit on, since his presence might be able to lend him a little borrowed elevation. The best he's been able to come up with from his own traveling wardrobe is a clean white shirt and a pair of pressed brown pants. "Your agent says he got you a place to live," he says. "How is it?"

Lennie keeps his eyes on the road. "It's true that motel where I spent a couple of nights was a zoo," he says. "In the space of a few hours I got opportunities to become a drug runner, a roadie and part of a threesome, none of which were particularly appealing. Given the weight of the other two participants, I guess you'd more accurately call it a fivesome. I mean, Meat Loaf and Mama Cass would have been more than welcome there. I know Mama Cass is dead but I'm not sure that would have been a problem with that particular ensemble. Anyway, when Sam tells me about this place he's found for me, I'm ecstatic. Sure, he says it's in a canyon. I figure out here that's just a fancy name for a street but no, this is a real canyon with hills and trees and empty spaces, coyotes even, and, for all I know, packs of ravenous wolves roaming the wilds—you've got to believe that was my first thought after Charlie Manson. When I lock the door at night, I'm sure not opening it until the sun comes up. I mean, I never heard of the guy who's in rehab who lived there before me, but I wouldn't be surprised if he's someone from the cast of *Grizzly Adams*. Then of course, there are all kinds of signs warning about fires, so I'm lying awake at night thinking the choice might come down to staying inside and getting roasted or running outside and taking my chances with the wolves. As my uncle Bernie used to say, "*Oy vey*, for this I left Russia?"

While Lennie rattles on Ziggy tries to get himself mentally ready for his meeting with little Eddie Przybylski. Like his father, Eddie kept his distance from the numbers, so there's not a lot of small talk that Ziggy has available to break the ice. Still, you'd think the man would have to be cordial to a visitor from the old neighborhood. It irritates Ziggy that he should be so concerned about holding up his end of this encounter. After all, he reminds himself, he's just paying a call on an undertaker, not an actual prince. Still, he wishes he had his favorite houndstooth jacket from the old days, maybe a Hathaway shirt with the ruby cuff links and a silk tie, the whole outfit topped by his pearl gray Dobbs hat.

"This has got to be it," Lennie says after a while. "Didn't I see this place in *Gone With the Wind*?" Ziggy looks up to see a stately building with tall white columns set on a slight rise amid a handsome array of shrubs and small trees. A curving driveway leads to a portcullis, but a sign directs the visitor to a parking lot in the rear. The sign, like the one that identifies the place as "Prince Funeral Homes," is discreet and tasteful, even a little intimidating.

"OK," Ziggy takes a last puff on his cigarette, "let's do this thing."

Lennie pulls the car into the parking lot and once again Ziggy's grateful he's arriving in a Cadillac. "Why don't you come along with me?" he says, more than ever banking on the status that Lennie's dark suit might convey.

When he pushes open the heavy door, Ziggy's greeted by refrigerated air that's faintly flavored with a floral scent. The expensive spaces before them, bathed in muted light, convey a sense of hush, as if he and Lennie are entering a church. They haven't taken a dozen steps across the thick plum-colored carpeting, though, before they're greeted by a thin blond young man dressed in gray.

"Can I help you?" he asks softly.

"We'd like to see Mr. . . ." Ziggy almost says "Przybylski" but catches himself, "Prince."

"Is this something I can help you with?" the man smiles thinly. "As you might imagine, Mr. Prince is very busy." Cordial as his tone may be, he's giving the two of them the intense scrutiny of somebody who's ready to call Security the instant he sees something that strikes him as fishy. That's not surprising, Ziggy thinks, given the allegations made about Prince in the press. How does he know his visitors aren't reporters?

The silence that follows the man's offer is filled with the soft sweep of stringed instruments coming from hidden speakers.

"Actually," Ziggy says, "this is a social call. I'm here from Detroit for a very brief visit and I used to know Mr. Prince there. I understand that he's a very busy man but I'd just like to say hello. And what did you say your name was?" he asks.

"I'm Peter Crane," the man obliges. "Mr. Prince's personal assistant."

"It's a pleasure to meet you, Mr. Crane." He gives the man his name. "I'd really appreciate five minutes with Mr. Prince," he says.

When Crane moves off, Lennie glances toward what looks like an antique table holding a tasteful and undoubtedly costly arrangement of flowers. "This is like a country club for the dead," he says. "I wouldn't be surprised if I popped into one of those chapels and saw somebody laid out in tennis whites. I bet they even frown on noisy mourning here."

"It's pretty spiffy, all right." Ziggy's trying to take in what seem like acres of softly lit corridors. How many chapels does this place have? he wonders. The old man's parlor back in Detroit was nothing like this. Whether or not little Eddie's being bankrolled by the mob, it certainly has to take a lot of money to run this kind of operation. And if there are branches, that would just multiply the expenses.

Peter Crane is with them again, smiling less guardedly now. "Fortunately, Mr. Prince just does happen to have a few minutes," he says. "Follow me."

"I'll wait here," Lennie says, which gets Crane's attention.

"OK," Ziggy says, "I'll be back soon."

"Please make yourself at home," Crane tells Lennie. "There's coffee in the hospitality room." He nods slightly, indicating the direction. "I'll be right out to help you if you need anything more."

Ziggy follows the man down a corridor past a half-dozen chapels. He hears some murmurs from within, but elegant oriental screens keep the deceased as well as their mourners discreetly out of sight. From what he manages to see, the funeral home is quite ecumenical, with none of the crucifixes and pictures of the Virgin Mary or the Sacred Heart you'd find in the place in Detroit. At the end of the corridor Crane gives a soft rap on a paneled wooden door and steps back. "Just walk in," he motions with his hand.

The first thing that bugs Ziggy is that Eddie Przybylski hasn't bothered to come out to greet him. Instead, he's sitting behind an imposing desk of dark, polished wood that's big enough for a helicopter to land on, set so far back in the room that his visitor has to cross twenty feet of carpeting to reach him. It's only when Ziggy's arrived within a pace or two of the desk that Eddie gets up and throws out both hands, like some tuxedoed crooner on TV who's finishing his number on a high note.

"Ziggy," he says, standing there with his head to one side. "What a pleasant surprise."

The performance is totally fake, since nothing in their past relationship would justify that much enthusiasm, but Ziggy assumes that in his line of work Eddie must have had a lot of practice being insincere. Then too, everything about this encounter seems staged. It's obvious that Mr. Prince wants his visitors to spend a few seconds making their way to him so they'll have time to take in the expensive furnishings and the art on the walls. Little Eddie certainly isn't trying to create the impression that he's just plain folks. Ziggy has no idea how Przybylski's son has been able to pay for all this, but he can't believe it's just the result of smart business practices.

After holding his pose for a couple of seconds, Eddie comes out from behind the desk and extends his hand. When Ziggy takes it, Eddie puts an arm on his visitor's shoulder and directs him to a chair. "Sit, sit," he urges. "Please." What he thinks of Ziggy's bargain basement outfit he doesn't say, but when he settles back into his own chair behind the desk, he fusses a bit with his cuffs, bringing the gold links forward, then he leans back with a smile. "How's the old neighborhood?" he asks.

"Pretty much gone to hell, to tell the truth," Ziggy says. As if you didn't know, he thinks. The man seated across from him is Eddie Przybylski, all right, a bit older but a lot smoother-looking. Tall, thin and tan, in his tailored gray suit, he reminds Ziggy of a lizard, a very self-satisfied lizard. Every move he makes shows how much he enjoys playing the role of Edward Prince.

Having heard the news about his old neighborhood, Eddie observes a few seconds of respectful silence, nodding his head solemnly. "It's tragic," he says at last, his voice dropping, "what's happened to that city." After a couple more beats, though, his frown unwrinkles and he brightens. "By the way, can I get you anything? A cigar?" He brings his hand forward again, sneaking a look at his watch. He has his father's small mouth and when it's closed it resembles a coin slot—for dimes, nothing bigger.

This is one smug asshole, Ziggy thinks. "No, thanks," he says. "Mind if I have a cigarette?"

"Not at all," Eddie says, though the ashtray on the desk, a gigantic piece of what looks like crystal, is immaculate.

Ziggy lights up and sends a cloud of smoke in Eddie's direction. For a moment he just watches the smoke; the tobacco has relaxed him. "I had a hard time finding you," he says. "I didn't know about the name change."

Eddie sighs. "A business necessity pure and simple," he declares. "You can imagine how well 'Pr-, Prz-, Pryzybylski' would play out here." He draws the word out with a comic stammer, as if it were being pronounced by someone unfamiliar with Polish. Eddie's eyes are a soft blue, and for an instant you could almost believe he regrets having dropped those extra syllables from his name, just as it's possible that someone who didn't know him might believe Eddie actually gives a shit about what happened to Detroit. At the same time, though, the faintest flicker of irony shows itself in those eyes, as if it wouldn't displease him at all for you to know that he's bullshitting, just as long as you acknowledge that it's pretty high quality bullshitting.

"You seem to be doing well," Ziggy tells him. "The name change must have worked."

"Yes, we've had some success." Eddie raps on the table. "Some of that's luck, good timing, I suppose. Yeah, I'm a lucky man."

"Don't be so modest," Ziggy insists. "It's impressive, coming into an area like this where there must be plenty of established businesses. It's got to be hard for an outsider to make a dent." He flicks some ash into the clean ashtray.

Eddie's made his hands into a steeple on the desk. He nods thoughtfully, basking in the celebration of his triumph.

"It's even more impressive," Ziggy says, "that you seem to have made a lot more than just a dent. I mean, I understand you have a string of places like this." He takes another drag. "I suppose that, like every business, you've got to have a talent for getting to know the right people. And that is a talent."

Once more Eddie beams, his small mouth curved into a smirk.

That smirk gets to Ziggy. It has a sharp edge, like one of those small, curved knives used for cutting linoleum, and he draws hard on the cigarette, pulls the smoke in deeply before exhaling, then crushes the several remaining inches in the ashtray. He came in here determined to keep his cool, at least till he'd got the information he wants, but he's already had all he can take of this guy. "It's too bad," he says, "that some people might get the wrong idea about your success. I understand some of them have even gone so far as to call you the Prince of Darkness."

For a second or two Eddie's at a loss for words. He sits there a few feet from Ziggy, motionless, his eyes unguarded, like someone caught in a compromising act by a photographer, frozen, blinded for a moment by the surprise of the flashbulb; and in that instant Ziggy can glimpse an unmistakable animal fear. Then all at once Eddie's face turns hard, his mouth tightens and his eyes go ice-cold. Jesus, Ziggy realizes, that was stupid of me. Across from him, Eddie has become composed now. He sinks back slowly against his padded chair, his frown shading toward a sneer.

"Success breeds envy," he says at last. Then, after a pause, "Envy breeds lies." He laughs out loud. "Nobody's proved a thing about me." A couple of seconds later, he adds, "I'd imagine that you, of all people, would be able to appreciate that."

Ziggy's blood is boiling; he wishes he hadn't put out that smoke and looks longingly at the bent cigarette lying amid the ashes in the gigantic ashtray. The thought strikes him that, for all his shortcomings, the elder Przybylski had a hell of a lot more class than his son. What's happened to little Eddie out here? Back in Detroit he was a nobody. People had to pay him attention because he stood to inherit his father's business. Otherwise, he was just somebody else in a dark suit who spoke softly as he led you toward the most expensive casket. But who could guess that under that bland exterior there lurked the smug egotist who's sitting a few feet away? Still, even though the man is insufferable, Ziggy realizes that his own temper has got him into trouble, and not for the first time. He reminds himself that he didn't come here to pass judgment on Eddie Przybylski; his business, whatever it is, is with his father. He's going to have to backtrack pretty quickly.

"Yeah," he says, "don't I know. People want their stories."

That apparently isn't enough to mollify Eddie. He inhales deeply, lets out his breath and looks pointedly at his watch. "Well, Ziggy," he says, all business, "this has been fun, but I have a lot on my plate this morning."

"I was actually hoping to talk to your dad," Ziggy says.

Eddie isn't wasting any energy trying to be charming. It's obvious he's already decided that Ziggy isn't worth the time. "Well, I'm sorry to disappoint you," he says without a trace of visible regret, "but you can't see my dad. You came here too late for that."

"Is he dead?" Ziggy asks.

Not a muscle on Eddie's face moves. He looks even more like a lizard. "No," he says flatly. "Shortly after we came out here, he had a stroke. He's been in a nursing home ever since then."

The news stuns Ziggy. A stroke—you wouldn't want to wish that on your worst enemy. "I'd like to pay him a visit," Ziggy says, still trying to grapple with this colossal piece of information.

"There wouldn't be much point to that," Eddie says. "He's pretty much a vegetable. He wouldn't understand a word you said, he wouldn't even recognize you." In his description of his father's condition there's no trace of concern or compassion. In fact, Ziggy could almost convince himself he hears a tinge of satisfaction in the man's voice. Jesus, Ziggy thinks, this guy's turned into a real monster.

Ziggy doesn't know what he's feeling at the moment. Even his hatred of Eddie has faded before his recognition that his old nemesis has been lying in a vegetative state in some bed in California all these years. "I . . ." he gropes, "I guess I'd like to see him if I could."

"That won't be possible," Eddie says.

"Why not?" Ziggy asks.

Eddie's voice is level. "My father's condition is unchanged. There's no reason to disturb him."

"But . . ." Ziggy wants to say that if the old man's so out of it that he wouldn't recognize his former neighbor, what chance would there be of his being disturbed by a visit? But he knows that isn't the reason for Eddie's opposition to a visit: the younger Przybylski's been crossed and he doesn't like it. He understands this is something Ziggy wants and it must give him a real jolt of satisfaction to withhold it from him. So when Ziggy asks the next question, he already expects the answer. "I don't suppose then that you'd be willing to tell me where he is?"

Eddie shakes his head slowly. "I'm not obliged to tell you," he says.

Ziggy sits there a few seconds waiting for more, watching Eddie try to hide the faintest trace of a smile.

"Well," Eddie says after a while, straightening in his chair, "as I said, I have a lot to do this morning. If you want to look around the place, I'm sure Peter will be more than glad to oblige."

"Thanks," Ziggy says, "but I have to get somewhere too. Say hi to your father from me next time you see him." Though, he thinks, I sure as hell wouldn't want to be the old guy waiting for a visit from this prick.

Back outside the funeral home, Lennie says, "That guy Crane followed me around like a shadow. He was awfully pleasant but you could see he was very suspicious. Maybe he thought I had a hidden camera or something. Anyway, once he was called away for a couple of minutes by this gorilla in a brown suit who either had muscles in strange places or was packing heat. Crane was very deferential to the guy, but then, so would I be. So, did you find out what you wanted?"

"I found out little Eddie Przybylski is an asshole. Back in Detroit he was a nobody. Now he's a somebody and that somebody has turned out to be a shit. Going west didn't improve him."

"But what did you find out about the old guy?"

Ziggy tells him what he learned from Eddie.

"Wow," Lennie says, "what a letdown that has to be: to come all the way out here to find out that the guy you're looking for is a vegetable."

"Yeah," Ziggy says, "and a vegetable that his son doesn't want me to see."

After a moment, Lennie says, "If he won't tell you where the guy is, it does seem to be a dead end, doesn't it?"

But Ziggy's still fuming. "I'm not going to let that little prick keep me from seeing his old man," he says. "I didn't come all this distance to find my way blocked by that . . . that lizard." He lights up a cigarette. "I'm still going to find Przybylski, one way or the other." As he inhales the tobacco in the shadow of Prince's opulent parlor, he remembers the naked fear he glimpsed on little Eddie's face when he made a reference to the article that called him the Prince of Darkness. The guy's afraid, Ziggy knows, he realizes that this palace of his is standing on very shaky ground. If he's really taking dirty money, between the guys who own him and the people who are trying to bring him down, little Eddie may realize that he's in over his head, and the chapters to come are likely to bring him anything but a fairy tale ending.

"But how are you going to find the guy?" Lennie asks.

"I don't know," Ziggy answers. "But while I'm here I'm sure as hell going to try."

CHAPTER NINE

꧁꧂

On the gloomy ride back to Burbank, Ziggy keeps thinking, he stiffed me, the little shit stiffed me. He looks down at his clenched fists, disappointed in himself. The rage that's overcome him is something he thought he'd learned to control. There were all those years of feeling sorry for himself, after all, looking for sympathy in the bottle, when what was in front of his face was a blur, while he kept trying to call up those days when he was somebody—when he might be in his little office on a warm summer afternoon studying the figures on the roll of paper coming from the adding machine, his white sports jacket draped over the chair as he leaned back and took a drag on his cigarette, wondering when the monsignor was going to call and offer him the presidency of the East Side Homeowners' Association.

It took him a while to accept that none of that would be coming back. He almost killed himself with his grieving over what he'd lost; but when things cleared up at last, he came round to realizing it was a hell of a lot better to be alive than dead, even if you no longer had flunkies who'd cheerfully run errands for you, you weren't getting visits from big-shots who wanted everyone to know they knew you, people who were trying hard not to look too obvious when they were desperately hoping to get some favor from you. Even when all that was gone, it was still a pretty damned good thing to wake up in the morning, make yourself a cup of coffee and, while the refrigerator hummed dependably in the background, read the paper in your kitchen, watching the world go by while you were still a part of it. All that other stuff didn't seem to matter much anymore. The secret, he'd learned, was to do like the people in AA and take one day at a time. One hour at a time, actually. But back in that palace of a funeral home this morning, in less than a minute he blew it.

Still, he's not going to apologize for the way he feels. Even when he should know better, it makes his stomach churn to think that the little punk just brushed him off and wouldn't pay him the courtesy of telling him where his old man was. It's all well and good to have left that place convinced that little Eddie Prince is headed for a big fall someday soon when either the good guys or the bad guys catch up with him. Still, it rankles Ziggy that Przybylski's son showed him so little respect.

It would be nice if he could put all the blame on that smug bastard who reminded him of a lizard, but the truth is that's not what he's feeling now. Sure, he's mad at Eddie for his stonewalling, but he's madder at himself. Because he knows there's a very good chance that Eddie might have handed Ziggy the information he wanted—after all, what threat would a visit be to him if his father really is the vegetable he described? All Ziggy had to do was hold his tongue while little Eddie sat there smirking and basking. But something snapped for him, and what happened is his own fault.

"What are you going to do now?" Lennie asks as he directs the big car smoothly along the sunny streets of Pasadena.

Ziggy shakes his head. "I don't really know." He won't say it out loud, but, in spite of his frustrations to this point, he can't really let go of the idea of somehow getting to see Przybylski, in spite of everything. "I don't know," he repeats.

"That sure was a tough break," Lennie says, "after coming all that way."

Ziggy says nothing. Lennie, taking his cue, responds in kind.

In front of Charlie's place, the former bus passengers take leave of each other, possibly for the last time. "Good luck with your career," Ziggy says, "and surviving in that canyon. I'll be watching the news more carefully now for stories of wolf attacks in Los Angeles."

Lennie snickers. "Thanks, it'll be a comfort to know somebody's paying attention. I've got your address," he says. "I'll let you know if anything happens to the Prince funeral home business."

"Who knows?" Ziggy says wistfully, "maybe I'll have to call on you yet again before I leave. My son's offered to pick up the cost of my flight back to Detroit, so if I should happen to need your services I can pay you this time."

Lennie shakes his head. "You got me out of jail back there in the wild west. Your money's no good with me."

Back inside the expensive, air-conditioned spaces of his son's house, Ziggy feels empty. For a while on the silent ride here he had a momentary surge of hope, thinking that, after all, Linda's friend was able to track down Prince. There's a way to find anyone, isn't there? But then he remembered that the last time he talked to Ted and Linda they were planning some kind of a camping trip in the mountains, so he isn't going to be able to use Linda's services to find the old undertaker's whereabouts. He's on his own now and once more he's boxed into a corner. Damn.

He goes out into the backyard to smoke and look at the snowcapped San Gabriels. He wasn't happy to learn that Gloria is at home—it's one of the reasons he's fled to the yard. Her proximity is enough to remind him of the possibility of trouble in his son's marriage and, given his present state of mind, that's the last thing he wants to have to deal with.

But it looks like he's going to have to deal with Gloria, who's come out into the yard and approaches him with her quick steps. "Did you see Przybylski?" she asks brightly, and

Ziggy can't help thinking that she's genuinely eager for this meeting to take place since she knows that her guest is committed to leaving once he's seen the old undertaker.

"No," he has to admit. "I got to talk to his son, that's all." Having to mention Eddie brings up the anger he thought he'd been able to bury. "There's a guy who's . . ." He backs off. "He's full of himself." He remembers Eddie sitting there like an honest-to-God prince waiting for Ziggy to cross the carpet to him before he even stood up. "He told me that his father had a stroke and has been in a nursing home for years. The only thing is, he didn't want to tell me where he was."

Gloria frowns. "Why did he do that?"

Ziggy takes a drag on his cigarette. Because he's a petty little prick, he wants to tell her. He settles for, "Just plain meanness, I'd say."

"So what are you going to do?" she asks after a while.

The trees rustle in the breeze and Ziggy picks up the sharp smell of eucalyptus. "I still have a couple of days," he says. "I might still be able to find him on my own."

Gloria looks at him skeptically. "How are you going to manage that?"

"I thought I'd look in the Yellow Pages and just call up nursing homes and ask if they have anyone there named either Przybylski or Prince."

"Hmm," she says. "There are plenty of nursing homes around the area and I'm not sure all of them are listed in the Yellow Pages. Some places may not want to give out that information, either. I don't know. It could be tough trying to do it that way."

Good old Gloria. That's just the kind of encouragement he needs. "Well," he says, irritated, "I don't have a lot of choice, do I?" Already, though, the prospect makes him feel as if he's just signed on for a hike through ankle-deep mud.

In the silence that follows, Gloria stands a couple of feet away, her head lowered, an unreadable expression on her face. She seems preternaturally alert, like a runner waiting for the starter's gun.

"Look," she says abruptly, "you can't spend all your time searching for Mr. Przybylski. I have a couple of free hours. I can show you a little of the area, as long as it's someplace close by. Come on," she urges, "you can't be serious all the time. This is southern California, after all."

It's true that Ziggy has no stomach just now for beginning the task of plowing through the Yellow Pages and phoning all those nursing homes, especially if Gloria's going to be around here. But what's he going to do while she's here? It might be easier to be somewhere else looking at things, which would at least give them something to talk about. After his visit to Pasadena, he's not all that keen on seeing the sights, but all at once he has an inspiration. "Actually," he says, "there is one place Ted told me about that I'd like to go to: the Farmer's Market in Hollywood."

Did she just flinch? He can't be sure. "I thought you went to Hollywood the other day," she says.

"I just kind of passed through," he says. "Got a look at some of the houses there." He isn't sure why he suggested this trip, but the prospect of returning to the scene of Gloria's lunch with the mysterious Roger W. excites him; it lifts him out of the funk caused by his failure with Eddie, it gives him the sense that he isn't just somebody to whom things happen, that he has a say in things.

After her momentary surprise, Gloria resumes the role of tour guide. "Sure," she says, "the Farmer's Market is a good choice. Yeah, we can do that."

Ziggy learns quickly that his daughter-in-law is a skillful, confident driver who knows where she wants to go and moves decisively toward her goal; she drives like someone who's really at home out here. Buzzing down the streets with the top down on her powder blue Buick convertible, they're in Hollywood in a flash—Ziggy didn't realize how close it is. Sitting beside her in the front seat, he keeps his eyes open for some sign that she's nervous about going to the Farmer's Market. It's true that there's a kind of edginess to her but it's hard to tell what's at the source, since she's so hyper in general. When they arrive at their destination, Ziggy can't help noticing that she parks in pretty much the same place where she parted company with Roger W.

"The market is only a short walk from here," she says after inserting the Buick into a tight space with a couple of efficient moves.

"We're lucky to find something so close on the street," Ziggy says.

Gloria smiles. "I never use the parking lots," she says. "I can always get something in the street. So, of course," she gives a little laugh, "I don't consider it luck at all. I like to think it's knowledge and persistence."

"You didn't need to be very persistent this time," he says. "You found it on the first pass."

"True enough, but you should see me when things are tough. I don't give up easily."

Ziggy can believe that. "I'll bet that's something you need in the real estate business," he offers.

She cocks her head in his direction. "You don't know the half of it."

So far she's keeping up a good façade of finding her father-in-law tolerable, but he can't help feeling it's only because she hears a ticking clock. She knows Ziggy will be gone soon and then she can return to her own life, a life, he's come to realize since he came out here, that she clearly likes to think she's created.

It's cool and refreshing under the roofs of the market. Plants have recently been watered and there's a smell of wet earth around them. As was the case on his earlier visit, there are plenty of other people who've come to this place. Once more Ziggy finds himself responding to the liveliness of the scene, the sights and smells, and he's glad he suggested this visit. "Nice," he says, trying to act as if he's never been here.

"Ted says that one of the reasons to come here is that you might see movie stars. Ever see any?"

Gloria laughs. "The trick is to be able to tell the real ones from the people who want to look like them. Oh, yeah," she says, "I did see Ernest Borgnine once. Does he count?"

"Oh, sure." Ziggy and Maggie used to watch him on TV. "I remember him from *McHale's Navy*. Was he shopping?"

She shakes her head. "He was having lunch."

"I'll bet the food's good here," he says. "It should be fresh, anyway."

"Oh, yes," Gloria says. "There's quite a variety too. You can get all sorts of meals, from casual to gourmet."

"What about you?" he asks. "Do you ever have lunch here?"

For a moment Gloria doesn't answer and Ziggy senses some hesitation, a slight crack in her cool exterior. He'd swear their being here has rattled her just a little. "Yeah," she says at last, "I've had lunch here occasionally."

In fact, to Ziggy's surprise, they've come into the vicinity of the restaurant where he saw her the other day, and he stops so that Gloria has to stop as well. "This place looks expensive," he says. "I'll bet only the bigwigs eat here."

"Oh, no," she says, "it's a mixed crowd." It's clear she wants to move on. Standing beside him, she opens her purse and searches for something, then snaps it closed, her head still bent to the purse as if she can't bring herself to look at the scene of the crime.

Ziggy is facing the spot where he saw her, the exact table, in fact. "Have you ever gone there?" he asks with an attempt at nonchalance.

She looks up and gives a quick nod. "Yeah, it's OK," she says, turning away immediately. "But, really, you don't have to come here to eat," she adds. "Actually, being in this place is like being in an art museum: you can stop by and just stroll around, looking at the food." It's hard for him to imagine Gloria strolling around anywhere in a leisurely way, taking her time. Just now she makes a sweeping gesture with her arm. "I mean, the seafood by itself is incredible." She starts walking in the direction of a stall where creatures who recently inhabited the ocean are displayed on beds of ice, and he follows her. "The fresh fish here is marvelous," she says. "Do you like red snapper?"

"I can't say that I know if I've ever had it," Ziggy answers. "I'd be willing to give it a try, though." He can see that Gloria isn't very comfortable being so close to the scene of her recent tryst. But this observation doesn't bring much satisfaction. Where can he take this, after all? He doesn't have any intention of confronting her openly about her meeting with Roger W., which would just raise more questions than answers. In fact, he's not sure what he wants, and then, this is really none of his business, is it? They look at the fish for a moment and then move on, with Gloria pointing out cheeses and meats and Ziggy keeping in step, occasionally nodding.

When they're in the next building and she suggests they have a coffee, he agrees. So, what has he proved, what's he got out of it, bringing her here? He realizes once more that he doesn't know this woman very well. He feels more relaxed at the little metal table, a cigarette in his hand. Gloria takes a sip of her coffee.

"It's pretty clear you like living out here," he observes.

"I love it," she concedes. She still seems tense, and answers as if she feels he's challenging her in some way. "Actually, the whole family likes it out here," she insists. "We're all happy we came." After a moment, she asks, "What about you? What do you think about all this?" She gestures with her hand.

"It's different," he says. "It's a big change for me." Admitting it makes him feel his age. He shakes his head. "I guess it's hard to teach an old dog new tricks." In fact, here among these passing strangers in sunglasses, he suddenly wishes he were back in Connie's, telling Turk and some of his regulars about his adventures on the coast. Hell, even being stiffed by Prince Eddie would make a good story.

Gloria looks off into the distance. "I'm sure it's different for you," she says. "I know a lot of things changed for you. The thing is, you always had your place back there, even after you lost the numbers." She turns back to him. "But I wish you could try to imagine for a minute what it was like for me in that environment. Yes, there were colorful traditions but everything was so cramped, there were limits everywhere. Whenever the family got together for a holiday or a birthday I had a role to play, Charlie's wife, and I could never get out of it." Her voice is strong and passionate. "Here, I can try new things, I can be who I want to be. It's my life, after all, and it's the only one I've got."

Ziggy checks his first impulse to comment on the kind of things she might be trying out here, like having a secret meeting with a man who drives a silver Mercedes. "Look," he says, "I know you don't particularly like me, and the truth is, it's been hard for me to get used to you." She looks at him without blinking, her mouth set. "Still," he goes on, "I can appreciate what you just said. I'm not going to tell you how to run your life because you wouldn't listen anyway," he says. "And I don't suppose the way I've lived my life is any kind of example anyone would want to follow. But I just want to say that trying things out is fine, finding out about yourself is fine, but you have to be careful about . . . about losing what you have. I mean, it could end up being awfully dangerous."

Gloria has stiffened noticeably, she's on the alert. "What's that supposed to mean?" she asks quietly, aware, he's sure, that they're not talking about abstractions, nervous, maybe, about being here where she recently was with the man Ziggy can only think of as her boyfriend. For an instant Ziggy thinks one or the other of them is going to make a reference to her lunch here a couple of days ago, but the moment passes. Gloria looks at him steadily but says no more.

"I don't know," Ziggy tries to make himself clear. "I guess I can understand you wanting to get as much as you can out of life—believe me, I know the feeling. It's just . . . well, you can lose things too, things you never can get back."

She laughs harshly. "God, that's a gloomy way of looking at the world."

For a moment the two of them listen to a couple of passing tourists arguing about where to go to dinner tonight.

"Well," Ziggy says, "I sure as hell know about losing." He sighs. "I know Charlie blames me for letting the numbers dribble away with my drinking. He's right too. Me, I'm just glad I came out the other side." That, he knows wasn't guaranteed, and there were times when the odds that he'd make it would have been very long. "You're right, though," he says. "I suppose I'm being gloomy. Maybe that's just who I am."

The fact is, in the last couple of minutes he's felt a gradual loosening. It's as if, without spelling anything out, he and Gloria have actually got something settled. He lifts his eyes to the clock nearby and catches sight of the minute hand jerking forward. "Look," he says, moved by a sudden urgency, "the fact is, I'm going to have to get back to Detroit soon and I could use your help. I came out here wanting to see Przybylski. Maybe the reasons behind it were stupid, but now it looks like that business might wind up in a blind alley. You said you know LA, you said you know the people to ask about things. Would you know anyone who could find out where Przybylski is? I mean, I'm running out of time and I want to get to see this guy."

Gloria looks at him for a few seconds. "Why exactly do you want to see him?" she asks.

He hesitates, knowing that nothing he says will make much sense. "Beats me," he confesses at last. "He's part of my story, I guess, and I wanted to know how he fits in, what role he played in that story." It's been a long time since he had that feeling in the basement of Connie's, the unquenchable need to find the undertaker. "Now," he says, "I don't know. But I still want to see him."

Gloria is silent for a while. Her eyes are clear, though, she seems less clenched than she was just moments ago. There's even the faintest trace of a smile on her lips. "Let me think about this for a while," she says. "It's possible I do know people who know people who could get their hands on that information."

Ziggy can't help thinking about Roger W. "I promise," Ziggy says, "as soon as I get to see Przybylski, I'm out of here, I'm on the first flight I can find."

Gloria doesn't seem to be listening, though. He'd bet she's already calculating possibilities, running through a list of names. "I just might be able to do something," she says.

Back in Burbank, Ziggy calls Maggie. "I saw Eddie Przybylski," he says. "He calls himself Edward Prince now. He's changed: he's very smooth and sleazy. He's got a real fancy operation here but there's something fishy about the whole thing."

"What about his father?" she asks. "Did you see him?"

"No, according to Eddie, he had a stroke a little while after they came here and he's been in a nursing home ever since."

Maggie waits a few seconds before asking, "Are you going to be seeing him?"

"I want to," he tells her. "But I don't know where he is. If you can believe it, Eddie wouldn't tell me."

"Why would he do that?" she asks.

"Because he's an asshole," Ziggy says. "The prince of assholes."

Again, Maggie doesn't respond right away. "Well," she says, "did you ever think that maybe you weren't meant to see him?"

No, he says to himself. He tells Maggie, "I still have a couple of days here."

Faced with his insistence, Maggie gets quiet again for a while. When she speaks again, her voice is distant, as though she's trying to catch hold of the memory. "Do you know what I was thinking about when I got up this morning?"

"What?" he asks.

"I was remembering that story you told me about when you were a kid and the guy from Chicago had a flat that you fixed. The guy with the fur coat."

"Oh, yeah," he says, feeling a momentary disorientation as he touches that distant area of his past. The stranger with the big Packard looked like an Indian, he probably worked for Al Capone. You're going to go far, kid, he told Ziggy when he'd given him the money after he'd replaced the tire. Ziggy always treasured the statement as a prophecy of his future success. "Yeah," he says. "That's strange, though. That you'd be thinking of that."

"Well," she laughs, "he said you'd go far and now you have, haven't you?" In a moment, she adds, "But isn't it time to be getting back?"

"I'll be back," he tells her. "Before Easter. I promise." Przybylski or no Przybylski, he's going to keep that promise.

All next day he seems to spend smoking and looking out at the San Gabriel Mountains, waiting to hear something from Gloria. At last she calls in the afternoon. "He's in Palmdale, at the Oasis Nursing Home," she says. "He's there under his old name."

"Great, Gloria, thanks," he says. His heart bangs against his ribs. "How the hell did you find that out?"

"I told you I know this area," she says. "If I don't know something myself, I know who to ask."

How did she find that out? he wonders. Hell, he wouldn't care if the information came from the devil himself. He's going to see Przybylski at last.

He calls Lennie right away. "Can you get the car tomorrow morning?" he asks. "Hell, I'll pay. I need a ride to Palmdale."

"Palmdale. Where's that?" Lennie says.

"From what my daughter-in-law told me, it's in the desert, but pretty close, only about fifty miles away."

It's a while before Lennie answers. "I don't know, that could be tough. I'll see what I can do."

Chapter Ten

Ziggy can hardly believe it: at last he knows for certain where Przybylski is, and it's only about fifty miles from this spot where he's standing in Charlie's backyard, as close to here as the place on the island was from his own house in Detroit. His heart is racing, but it isn't just anticipation he feels: when he tries to pull a cigarette from the pack he has trouble controlling his hands. It's as if he's afraid. But of what? Finally, after the long and not very comfortable trip across a big stretch of the country, after all his searching with the help of Linda and the private eye she worked for, after the runaround he got from Eddie, Ziggy's within reach of what he came out here to do. So there's nothing to be afraid of; instead, he should give himself credit, he has a right to be pleased with himself, doesn't he? When he's fished out the cigarette at last and lighted it, he pulls down the smoke and feels the calm settling over him. Yeah, Przybylski's out there, close by, he has the man in his sights, and he sure as hell isn't going anywhere soon, at least nowhere in this world. Everything slows down for Ziggy. The nearby eucalyptus trees rustle dryly, releasing their now-familiar scent; the snow on the distant mountains gives them an air of silent repose.

What can he expect from a meeting with Przybylski when he gets there, though, if the old guy is in as bad shape as Eddie said? At no point in his life has Ziggy had any great desire to visit a nursing home. The thought occurs to him that just finding out about Przybylski could be considered enough. Why take the trouble of driving that fifty miles into the desert anyway? Why not just accept that the undertaker has been located and is obviously in no condition to respond to any of Ziggy's questions. In fact, given that prospect, it's kind of stupid to actually go out there, isn't it? Why not just declare the game over? Couldn't he still consider himself in some sense the winner?

But of course he's going to Palmdale. By now he isn't even asking himself for any kind of reasons that would make sense to anybody else. This is his trip and nobody else's. Something in the breeze reminds him of his time on the bus, which seems to have taken place in the last century. It was something, wasn't it, traveling through those midwestern storms, into the immense sand-colored spaces where the eye was always being carried to the horizon, his fellow passengers leaving him, one by one: the man who made golf balls, Roy Spears on his busman's holiday, Sharlene with her pool cue, the woman who said she was traveling to the graves of presidents, not to mention the different drivers who'd brought him here. If nothing else, he owes it to them to complete what he set out to do.

Most of all, he has to see Przybylski with his own eyes.

But he certainly doesn't relish the idea of spending more than a couple of minutes in the presence of someone so frighteningly reduced as Przybylski is likely to be. That prospect isn't particularly appealing, he knows, but it's the last part of the pilgrimage. Once he sees Przybylski he'll be free to get back to Detroit, and quickly, above the clouds this time, not crawling across every hill and valley of the land.

It's odd, the nervous excitement he feels, a sense of expectation, though it's hardly joyful, more like what he felt as a very young kid when he was about to go to confession. There was a secret burden of sin he'd been carrying around and he didn't look forward to those few minutes in the musty confessional, his knees pressed against the hard kneeler as he waited for the slat to slide open, making visible the blurred image behind the grille, the priest to whom he'd have to name his offenses, bringing them out into the open; but he knew that when he left the church his step would be lighter, a Get-Out-of-Jail card in his pocket that worked at least for a while.

He isn't going to confession, though, he's going to Palmdale, and that means he still has to work out the mechanics of getting himself from here to there. Lennie said he'd know within the hour whether he'd be free tomorrow and Ziggy impatiently endures that hour before calling him.

"Sorry," Lennie says, "no can do. Not tomorrow anyway. I've got a couple of jobs. Thursday's fine, though."

Ziggy's more disappointed than he'd expected to be. Since it was Lennie who drove him to the Prince Funeral Home, he must have imagined that if there was going to be any follow-up, it was going to be Lennie who'd be taking him there; and for a couple of seconds he entertains the notion of putting off the visit to Palmdale by a day. But he knows he isn't going to be able to wait that long, not the way he feels. And a delay wouldn't be fair to Maggie. He has to get this thing over with, and as soon as possible.

"Look," he tells Lennie, "I'm going to have to try to find other arrangements to get me to Palmdale." Still, he doesn't want to end his contact with his fellow bus-rider yet. "I'm going to be able to use you Thursday, though," he says. "When I wrap things up with Przybylski, I'll be ready to go home. You know your way to the airport, don't you?"

Lennie laughs. "Don't I ever. That's where I have to go today. Twice."

"I'll call you about it tomorrow," Ziggy says. The airport, he thinks. It's really ending then.

"I can't wait to hear how that meeting turns out," Lennie says.

Ziggy laughs. "I don't expect to be swapping funny stories with the guy, but I think I have to do this."

"I understand," Lennie says. "Give me a call after."

It turns out not to be very hard to work out arrangements in the end. Gloria can't take him to Palmdale, which isn't surprising, since she needs her car for work. But, ever resourceful, she's quick to come up with a Plan B.

"Why not ride to work with Charlie and take Charlie's car to Palmdale?" she suggests. "I don't imagine your visit is likely to be too long, so that you should be back at Charlie's office in plenty of time for me to swing by and ferry you back to Burbank. Unless, that is, you want to hang around the office and watch your son do a root canal."

"Hey, she's right, Pa," Charlie is quick to agree. "I don't need my car when I'm working." He's obviously enthusiastic about having an opportunity to show his father the place where he practices his profession. It wouldn't surprise Ziggy if he took his wife's suggestion about the root canal seriously.

"Good, then," Ziggy says. He still wishes he weren't going out to the desert alone.

The next morning, father and son set off together. Charlie is in a talkative mood, reporting on his children's successes in the classroom and in the saddle. And then there's Gloria. Ziggy isn't surprised to learn that she's been honored by the real estate company for her salesmanship.

"What about you?" Ziggy asks.

"I can't complain," Charlie says. "You'll see when we get there that I've got a very satisfactory work situation. We cater to a pretty high-end clientele."

"Sounds good," Ziggy says, remembering Dr. Zemba's cramped quarters on Chene Street that smelled unpleasantly of some kind of medicine, or possibly booze, where the shrill whine of the drill could be heard in the waiting room by the squirming unfortunates nervously skimming through old magazines.

The Tall Trees Dental Center is on a quiet street in Glendale on the fringe of a residential neighborhood. The unobtrusive two-story building faced with light brown brick looks as if it might house insurance offices and a travel agency, which it in fact does. Charlie takes Ziggy on a tour of the suite of offices on the second floor that he shares with his partner, one Edward Hagopian, a tall, dark man in blue hospital scrubs whose smooth diplomatic manner doesn't quite hide something intense in his eyes that makes Ziggy think of Dracula—he looks as if he could drill a hole in your teeth just by staring at them for a few seconds. "It's delightful to meet you," the man says with a voice that could be used to sell caviar, "but I must rush off to a patient now." As he moves away in a brisk but unhurried glide, Ziggy figures that Charlie is the affable, outgoing member of the duo, his bouncy cheerfulness countered by his partner's air of quiet assurance. He also has no doubt about who runs the show.

Soothing string music emanates from an excellent sound system in the waiting room, where muted lighting softens the already gentle colors. On the pale blue walls pictures of sunny beaches devoid of swimmers hang beside photos of smiling celebrities or people who want to be taken for smiling celebrities offering handwritten tributes to "my favorite dentist." Behind the desk in the registration area sits a receptionist with big hair who could easily pass for a starlet. The two trim, well-tanned women on leather and chrome chairs who are leafing through the glossy magazines look as though they're anticipating a pleasant experience, say a gentle massage or a session of tanning. There's a scent like incense vaguely wafting through the corridors and the entire enterprise is totally without the sense of dread and dinginess Ziggy remembers from Dr. Zemba's parlor. Even in the spacious, carpeted rooms themselves where the instruments of the trade are presumably employed, the same soft music plays and the aqua dental chair looks more like a Barcalounger.

"Nice place," Ziggy tells his son. "And it sure looks like you're doing well." Charlie beams and Ziggy can't help thinking of Roger W.

As he gives Ziggy the keys to his car, Charlie turns serious for a moment. "You clear about how to get to Palmdale?" he asks.

Ziggy nods.

"Well," Charlie mumbles, "tell Mr. Przybylski hi from me. That is, if you think it would do any good."

"You never can tell," Ziggy says.

In a couple of minutes he's adjusting the seat and the mirrors in Charlie's dark blue Buick Estate Wagon, a far less sporty machine than Gloria's, but a big battleship of a car with plenty of horses to get it where it has to go. He's pretty much memorized the directions to the nursing home, but he starts out carefully as he makes his way along the Glendale streets to I-5 North—the last thing he wants is to get on the freeway headed in the wrong direction. The signs are clear, though, and soon he's on the ramp, merging with the traffic, and within seconds he's part of the rushing current on this wide bright concrete river. It's a beauty of a road. Out here, he's very much aware of the physical features of the land, the mountains on each side that wall off the valley through which he's traveling. He can't let himself get caught up in the scenery, though: remembering Ted's caution about how easy it is to lose oneself on the complex tangle of roads, he keeps alert, his eye out for the exit that he expects to come to in about fifteen miles for 14 North, which will actually take him northeast.

To his satisfaction, he manages the maneuver without a hitch. That was the hard part, as far as he was concerned, and now he can breathe more easily. He can see clearly that he's leaving one valley, as Gloria has told him, the populous San Fernando Valley, and passing through the San Gabriel Mountains into Antelope Valley. It's different here: the thickly clumped houses of LA are behind him and there are more open spaces. For a few moments he's even driving by a field of brilliant poppies, but soon the landscape takes on the features of the desert. "While you're in the vicinity you really should see the Vasquez Rocks," Gloria said. "They're like something from another planet, shapes sticking out of the earth, tilted at weird angles—it's almost as if some other race buried them there. In fact, that place has been used as the setting for science fiction movies and TV shows." When she told him that, Ziggy couldn't help remembering the Cadillacs planted in the earth in Texas. Give Gloria her due, she made those rocks sound like something he'd like to see, but he isn't going that far today. Still, it's strange enough-looking out here, without all the color of LA and perceptibly hotter once he's come down out of the mountains. It looks like the desert he passed through on the bus, with cacti and Joshua trees, a little scary, in fact. He can't help wondering why Eddie would put his father this far away from where he lives. He'd guess that the son doesn't visit the old man very much. Jesus, he thinks, what a fate: to be turned into a vegetable and stuck out in the desert far away from anyone you know. Maybe that's what hell is really like. That could be scarier in its way than eternal fire.

The Oasis isn't in Palmdale itself but on the outskirts, and it isn't as easy to locate as Ziggy had hoped it would be. In fact, he passes it twice before realizing that the nursing home is hidden behind a wall of green at what seems like the edge of the desert itself. After noticing the discreet sign at last, he makes his way through an opening in the screen of palm trees into a large open area dominated by a two-story building that looks like a freshly baked loaf of bread, its brown stucco exterior blending in with the colors of the desert behind it. As Ziggy comes closer, he can see that there are a pair of wings jutting out from the trunk of the building back toward the sandy wastes. He parks in the near-empty lot, and feels the sting of the hot dry wind for the few seconds it takes him to reach the entrance, where, once inside, he's greeted by a blast of refrigerated air. The door closes behind him with a click that seems to suck all the sound out of the room. Not many steps from the door a muscular young man in a dark suit sits behind glass in what looks like the ticket booth of a movie house and lifts his head at the visitor inquiringly. When Ziggy tells him his business, the man gives him a once-over before soberly directing him to a set of doors with frosted glass panels onto which a geometrical pattern has been painted.

Once past this barrier, Ziggy enters a bright cool high-ceilinged space where the filtered daylight coming from sheets of tinted glass is augmented by pools of illumination from strategically placed domed lamps. At one end of the large room a fire is burning in a stone fireplace. When he hears a shrill cry that comes from the opposite direction, he turns his head and catches sight of a flash of scarlet. It takes him a second or so to make out about a half-dozen tropical birds in a cage spacious enough to allow them to fly. This is some place, he thinks. Colorful plants are arranged around the room and there's an actual lemon tree with real lemons in a wooden tub on the pale brown carpeting. Though he can't see anyone yet, Ziggy picks up an ambient buzz of voices from somewhere nearby. Following the man's instructions, he makes his way to the formidable registration desk, where he presents himself as a visitor. "Would you like to sign in?" a white-haired woman in a checked suit asks him. "Whom do you wish to see?"

He gives the woman Przybylski's name and she repeats it, pronouncing it "Pryz-bylski."

"Are you a relative?" she asks pleasantly.

"A friend," he answers and watches her flip through the pages of a bound tablet.

"Would you please sign here," she directs him.

"Has he had many people come to see him recently?" Ziggy asks, surreptitiously taking in the surroundings. This has got to be costing Eddie a pretty penny.

"I wouldn't know that kind of thing, sir," the woman smiles at him. "Here, Caroline will take you to his room."

An attractive light-skinned black woman in a gray dress glides toward him and indicates that he should follow her. As they pass through another door, Ziggy glimpses a nondenominational chapel and a reception room where a TV is playing while a couple of people in wheelchairs silently watch. In spite of those amenities, he's struck by the sense of emptiness here. He and Caroline continue down the corridor, Ziggy bracing himself for the harsh smell of urine and disinfectant, but somehow the people who run the Oasis have managed to keep both of those odors hidden under a faint, vaguely flowery scent. He hears an occasional cough and once what sounds like a muffled scream, but the place is for the most part eerily quiet.

Near the end of the corridor he and Caroline enter a large, wide elevator that travels so slowly that there's no sensation of ascent before the doors open, presumably putting them on another floor. Here the quality of light is subtly different, dimmer, and Ziggy assumes the tough cases have been deposited upstairs. A couple of women in hospital scrubs are talking quietly in the corridor as Caroline leads him briskly along so that he doesn't have an opportunity to peek into any of the rooms. At last they've come to room 230.

"There you are, sir," she says. "I'll leave you now."

"Thank you," he says.

Inside the room, a large black woman in the same kind of outfit Ziggy saw in the corridor introduces herself as Amanda. "He'll be ready for you in a second," she says. It's only then that he notices the man strapped into the wheelchair. "We like to have them sit up part of the day," the woman explains. "For their lungs."

Ziggy's first thought is that's it's not Przybylski. They sent me to the wrong place, he thinks. But as he continues to look, he gradually accepts that he might indeed be standing before the former undertaker, now a shrunken, mummified figure, absolutely inert. It's unsettling that the man's lifeless eyes, directed toward some corner of the floor, have made no acknowledgment of Ziggy's presence, no acknowledgment of anything.

Amanda fusses a little with the green blanket that covers the patient's legs and lifts herself heavily. "I'll leave you with him for a couple of minutes but I'll be close by," she says.

"Can he . . ." Ziggy whispers. "Does he understand anything?"

The woman's mouth turns down sadly. "I been with him about a year and I ain't seen nothing. But you never can tell." She adds more confidingly, "I always think there's more going on there than you think. You got to believe that. There's a chair, by the way. Let me wheel him over near the window and you two can have a visit."

When she's gone, Ziggy slowly lets himself down into the chair beside the window a few feet away from Przybylski. "Jesus," he says under his breath.

The man's head lolls, his eyes still directed downward, though Ziggy can't be sure that he's seeing anything. His claw-like hands are limp on the arm of the chair where Amanda put them. I wouldn't wish this on my worst enemy, Ziggy thinks, and at the moment it's hard to think of the man in the wheelchair as anybody's enemy. He's simply vacant, there's no one there. His empty eyes show no signs of recognizing that someone else, let alone someone he once knew and might once have considered a rival, is nearby, and Ziggy takes advantage of his apparent invisibility to study Przybylski carefully. The undertaker used to be tall, he had blond hair, he carried himself stiff as a ramrod. The man across from Ziggy looks shrunken, a few lank strands of dirty gray hair do little to hide the shape of his skull. His eyes are glazed and everything about him sags, pulled earthward. And to think he's been this way for years. It seems a shame the poor wretch can't be released from this state. In the last few moments, Ziggy has become aware of the humming of the air-conditioner, of other faint noises involved with the running of machines, and the labored rhythm of Przybylski's breathing. When he hears another kind of sound, he turns toward the window, where he glimpses a fly buzzing against the glass that looks onto the desert outside. How the hell did that fly manage to survive in a place as carefully managed as this, he wonders. He returns his attention to Przybylski, who's exactly as he left him.

What if hell is like this, Ziggy thinks again, just this forever? The idea sends a chill up his spine.

"Przybylski," he ventures, speaking quietly. There's no reaction: not a blink, a twitch, a change in the rhythm of his breathing. No, he thinks, there's no point in trying to start up a conversation. They say, though, that you never can tell. He listens to the hum of the machines, to Przybylski's reedy inhalation and exhalation. How much time has he had alone with the man? Seconds? It seems like hours.

Well, at least I'm here, he thinks. I got here where I said I was going to go.

Get out of here.

Ziggy starts. Did the man in the wheelchair really say something? No, he's exactly as he was moments ago. I'm going batty, he thinks.

Who are you and what are you doing here? There it goes again. But how can it be Przybylski? *Nobody comes to see me. Nobody.*

Ziggy's trying to get a grip on himself, to calm the rising terror he feels. This is like Eddie's wake, he thinks. There's got to be some reasonable explanation. He can see that the man in front of him hasn't moved a muscle. Still, is it somehow possible to talk to a person without actually talking? *Przybylski, is that really you?*

Who else did you think it might be?

This is crazy. Ziggy knows he can't really be talking to Przybylski. Still, maybe something's going on, maybe that wreck of a creature a few feet away can actually communicate, by ESP or something like that. Anyway, what's he got to lose by going along with this for a while? *Przybylski, do you know how long you've been here? Do you have any sense of time?*

Was that a groan? *I've been here forever, I'm going to be here for all of eternity.*

What a terrible thought. Once again Ziggy feels a shiver of dread. This isn't what he came all this way to hear. *No, Przybylski, that's not right. You've been in this place a while, yeah. But you'll only be here until . . .* Actually, it's probably not such a good idea to go any further in that direction. And as the seconds pass, it occurs to Ziggy that the undertaker may have conveyed to him all he wants to say.

This is my punishment.

OK, it isn't stopping yet. *Punishment? For what?*

I don't know, but believe me, I've had time to think about things. What else is this if it's not punishment?

The air conditioner hums, the fly resumes its futile buzzing against the glass, obviously perplexed to find the usually friendly medium of air suddenly turned hard and resistant. *You can't think that way, Przybylski. Actually, you're here because you got sick, that's all.*

Hah! If you're sick you either get better or you die. Not this.

He's got Ziggy there. *I don't know what to tell you. Things end, though, eventually.* This is too creepy. It certainly wouldn't break his heart if this encounter were to end, and soon.

Przybylski's apparently not done, though. *This is all I know. There's nothing but this. Nothing.*

No, Ziggy wants to tell him, you're wrong about that. He can't help feeling that, as terrible as the man's condition might be, it would be even worse to be robbed of all sense of the past. *But, Przybylski, there was something before this, don't you remember?*

Something before this, you're saying? He sounds challenging, wary. But interested.

Sure. Do you remember Detroit at all? St. Connie's, the priests, the numbers? Do you remember the war, when Detroit was booming?

There's nothing for a while, as if he's thinking over this new idea. And then: *De-troit*. It comes slowly, in two parts, it sounds like a foreign word. *Yeah, maybe*. Another pause. *Maybe there's something. A long time ago. I might remember something.*

It's a start anyway. *That's right, St. Connie's parish on the east side of Detroit. Remember? Przybylski, you and I were the big cheeses in the neighborhood back then, we were in competition. Remember the scoreboard the monsignor got us to go halves on?*

Ziggy doesn't have to wait so long for a response this time. *Oh, yeah, I remember you now: the big shot, the numbers guy. Strutting around in your flashy clothes, giving away a handful of tickets to a Tigers game. Like you were some kind of, what? A duke or a lord or something like that? As if you'd actually earned your money and not got it from other people's gambling.*

Wait a minute, Ziggy wants to say, bristling at the accusation. It's the same old Przybylski, isn't it? Still, even as he feels the sting of being misunderstood, he takes some satisfaction in having jogged the man's memory. *Przybylski, that's water under the bridge, isn't it? Hell, we did cooperate on that scoreboard, after all. We might not have liked each other but we pitched in to help the school.*

The man is utterly still. It scarcely seems possible that he's even breathing. And yet Ziggy listens for more. *That scoreboard, I do remember it. I think my share was over nine hundred and so was yours. The monsignor. Yes, a tall, dignified man. Victor Baran. Quite an impressive figure, our monsignor. Crafty too.*

For all his craftiness, Baran couldn't save the neighborhood, Ziggy thinks. He couldn't save the parish. *I hate to tell you this, Przybylski, but that scoreboard is gone now. They closed the school down a couple of years ago. The grade school and the high school both.*

Gone, you say? The grade school and the high school too? The nuns? The football team that never was any good? Ziggy could swear he just heard something that sounded like a sigh. *That's very sad, but I'm starting to remember more now. I remember how the neighborhood was changing, a whole generation moving out to the suburbs. Well, you could see where that was going to end up. It's a shame, though.*

That's not all, Przybylski. It's even worse than that. You wouldn't believe how even the church has run down. St. Conrad's. There's some talk that the archdiocese is going to try to close the parish down some day pretty soon.

St. Connie's, no. Would they really shut it down? The air conditioner coughs and then resumes its regular hum. *That was one magnificent church. It was like a cathedral for us Polacks.*

That's true enough. Ziggy can remember the celebration of the monsignor's twenty-fifth anniversary as a priest, when the cardinal said mass at St. Connie's—'48, as best as he can remember. And now . . . *They say it's very empty during Sunday masses. I wouldn't know. I don't go except on Christmas and Easter, and you can even see the decline there.*

St. Conrad's. Yes, I can see it clearly now. Ziggy, that church was built in 1911, the year I was born. My grandmother told me about those days when the Polish-American population was growing so fast they couldn't put up enough churches, however big they might be. And St. Conrad's wasn't only big. There was a majesty to the place. All those weddings, all those funerals, the processions that would spill out of the church and into the street, the priest under his canopy, an army of altar boys, the old ladies with their candles singing in Polish, the flags of the religious societies flashing in the sun . . .

During the long silence that follows, Ziggy wonders whether memories like this can be any help to someone like Przybylski. Under the circumstances, maybe complete oblivion would be better. But they've started down this road; they might as well continue. *The city's changed, Przybylski, the neighborhood's*

*changed. Hell, the only ones desperate enough to move in any-
more are the Yugoslavs.*

Another long silence. *How did that happen, Ziggy? Why?*

*Beats me. Growing up, you'd think those things were going
to last forever. That's how much we knew.* His attention is
momentarily captured by the fly. It's silent just now as he
watches its tiny legs moving quickly along the glass. But
Ziggy's thoughts have abruptly taken him somewhere else.
*You want to hear something funny, Przybylski? This just popped
into my head. Maybe it's all those memories, I don't know, but
I haven't thought of this for a long time and now it's like it
happened yesterday.* He drifts off, his mind filled with images
from the past.

Well, get on with it, then.

*OK, you know, even after the cops raided all the Polish num-
bers places on the east side, there was a time when everything
looked like it was back to normal. The day after the raids people
were playing the numbers like always. We knew there'd be trials
coming up, but nobody wanted to think about that. I had my big
party out on the island that summer and it was the best one I
ever had. You should have come to those parties, Przybylski,
they were something. Anyway, the festivities were just getting
started, you could smell all that great food Mrs. Rowinska had
made—ham and kielbasa, homemade horseradish, both white
and red, pierogi, kapusta and potato salad. There was the clink
of metal coming from where some guys were already playing
horseshoes, a couple of the priests were there early. Gabby Sendlik
even got the monsignor to give us an imaginary indulgence for
any small transgressions we might commit that day like drinking
too much. I walked out by myself to the end of the property. It
was a great day, with a blue sky, the river was bright with its
own kind of greenish blue, there were a couple of boats tied
to the dock already—the monsignor's was one of them—and I
looked down the river knowing that in a little while Big Al was
going to come cruising up in his big white Chris-Craft, and I*

realized I was about as happy as I'd ever been in my life and I just wanted one thing more.

What was that?

I wanted it to last forever.

Forever?

Yeah.

That wasn't very smart, was it? Don't you know nothing lasts forever? For a while there's no more, just the fly's restless buzzing. *So where did all that flash get you, Ziggy? Those parties on the island, the tickets to the Tigers games? In the end, where did they get you?*

Ziggy has neither the energy nor the will to tackle that question seriously. He laughs to himself. *I guess it got me here, to this place on the edge of the desert. Talking about old times with you.*

After a few moments' silence, Przybylski's whistling breath sounds like a sigh. *Well, I should talk. I suppose I used to think the same thing about my funeral business. We did a good job, we provided a service, we were doing well. It should have gone on forever. I used to worry, though.*

That surprises me. If you worried, you never used to show it. I always thought you were kind of smug, looking down on us numbers guys.

There's another silence. Then: *Did you ever think I might envy you your flash just a little, that I might be jealous of the risks you took, the freedom not to be careful all the time? In the end being careful didn't seem to work for me, did it?*

It's Ziggy's turn to sigh. *I guess neither of us turned out to be much of a success story, did we? But, hell, we weren't the only ones. Not in that city. Still, when all is said and done, I guess we're all responsible for our own stories. I'm not going to try to wriggle out of that. I imagine you could see even before you left town what kind of a mess I was making of things.*

Anybody could see that, yes.

Well, I guess I had my time. I should be thankful.

And me? Should I be thankful?

Oh, I don't know, Przybylski. But I'm still wondering, how did this happen to you? You were smart enough to get out of town early, and still . . .

This, you mean? Being left alone like this, on the edge of the desert, as you put it a minute ago? Being deposited here between life and death, without anyone in the world giving a fuck?

Would the real Przybylski actually say "fuck?" Under these conditions, maybe. *Yeah, how did all that happen?*

It was Eddie who kept pushing me to leave. I was nervous about what I saw happening in Detroit, but Eddie had big plans. I was too stodgy and old-fashioned, he kept saying. Out west we could not only save the business, we could really make money.

Ziggy remembers smug little Eddie sitting behind that enormous desk of his. *Looks like he was right about that.*

I guess so. I'm not sure it was money I wanted, though. I should never have listened to him. But he was smart, he had a plan. I let myself believe him. There's a brief silence. *Well, what happened, happened. I know what my mother would say: that stroke was God's punishment.* Mine too, Ziggy thinks.

There's a cough from the door. It's Amanda. "I'm going to have to attend to him soon," she says.

"Yeah, sure," Ziggy tells her. "One more minute, OK?"

She nods and steps back into the corridor.

Thank God, Ziggy thinks, at least he's got her to look in on him every now and then. *I'll bet Eddie never comes to visit, does he?*

What do you think?

Ziggy's trying to look for the bright side. *At least he's got you a pretty nice place here. It must have cost him a bundle.*

Conscience money, that's all. It's cheaper than having me around.

Ziggy never thought Przybylski was dumb. *Well, I'm sorry about how this turned out. I really am.*

Did you have anything more to ask me? I'm getting a little tired.

OK, Ziggy thinks, here's your chance to find out if he had anything to do with tipping off the cops. When he was sitting there at the bar at Connie's, sipping his Vernors, was he just hoping Ziggy would fall on his face, or was he remembering a phone number where people were eager to hear what he had to say? Really, though, at this point, what difference would it make, however Przybylski answered that question? *No, I don't really have anything more to ask. Nothing important. Again, I'm sorry.*

Don't waste your pity. We all wind up here sooner or later. I just got here a little quicker than you, that's all.

When Amanda returns, Ziggy is more than ready to leave. "You never know," she says. "Sometimes you might just sit there and say nothing, and they still appreciate that. It all helps, I think."

Ziggy makes his way down the dim corridor, his steps heavy, as if the clothes he's wearing are made of lead. So he managed to see Przybylski at last, and where did that get him? He passes a couple of women in hospital scrubs and gives them a vague nod but he doesn't slow down. He doesn't belong here, he wants them to know. Alone in the elevator that seems not to move, he raps his fingers against its cool, smooth metal wall, impatient to get to the first floor, to leave the Oasis. He takes a deep breath, assuring himself that the elevator is actually descending. A couple of minutes later he's sitting in Charlie's Buick, gratefully breathing in the car's smell. He turns the key and soon the Oasis is in his rearview mirror, then it's gone entirely. Already as the car follows the curves of the desert road, his mind is on the route to Glendale, where Gloria will pick him up and drive him back to Burbank, his last stop before the plane that's going to take him back to Detroit tomorrow.

He's said his goodbyes to everyone and Lennie has come for him in an extremely long black limo. He's dressed a little differently today: in jodhpurs and chauffeur's cap, the black leather gloves he's wearing, he looks like the Green Hornet's driver Kato. He doesn't have a mask, of course, but his big sunglasses do as much to conceal his face. He must have a really fancy job later today, Ziggy thinks, because he seems unusually quiet. Without a word, he opens the door for his passenger and deposits his bag in the car's spacious trunk. Ziggy's getting a kick out of this royal treatment, figuring that Lennie's probably practicing for the big shot he's going to be taking around after he leaves Ziggy at the airport. It's super quiet in the luxurious interior of the limo, but the backseat is a long way from the driver's part of the car and Ziggy can't help feeling all alone. He'd welcome a few of Lennie's wise-cracks just now but his driver remains quiet, which doesn't help Ziggy's mood. Something has started to bother him, though he can't put his finger on exactly what that might be. He hasn't flown on a jet before, but that isn't it, there's something else. It can't be the fear that he's going to miss his plane. As far as he knows, they have plenty of time to get to the airport. Relax, he tells himself, there's nothing you can do about anything now.

When he looks out the window he's surprised to see that Lennie has pulled off the freeway and is traveling along a familiar-looking street.

"Where are we going?" he asks.

Lennie says something without turning around, but Ziggy can't catch it.

Where the hell are we? he thinks, I know this place: palm trees, canals and bridges. Then all at once he realizes where he is: they're on their way to Ted's, to say goodbye. That's a nice gesture, he thinks. Lennie must feel they have plenty of time, and he ought to know.

They've drawn up before the little house and, almost before the car has stopped, Lennie comes round to the door, quietly pulls it open, then brings himself gravely to attention. There's the yard, the brown palm fronds on the grass, the sofa—Ziggy experiences a surprising rush of love for the place where he spent his first couple of days in LA. He's happy that Lennie has brought him here. He'll have a chance to tell Ted that he ought to feel good about what's happened to him since he left St. Connie's, that in the long run he turned out OK. Linda too. "You're lucky to have her," he'll tell him. When he steps out of the limo, though, his feet seem encased in cement. Could they have fallen asleep during the drive? If he can only make it to the sofa he'll be halfway to the house, and maybe he can rest there. He tries to push himself forward but it's as if he's walking through water until Lennie gently takes him by the elbow and gives him an assist.

"Thanks," Ziggy says. "Let me get to the sofa where I can sit down for a while."

When they get there he lowers himself onto the sofa's sagging contours. In fact, so glad is he to have reached his destination that he stretches out and lies full-length, his head propped against one of the armrests, his hands crossed on his chest. Ah, that's better.

But he's very tired all of a sudden, and he remembers the episode he had a couple of days earlier right here when he blacked out on this same sofa for a moment. The fear that rises sharply is countered by a wave of calm, and he's bathed in a sense of peace. It's OK, he tells himself. It's a nice day, after all. Things around him shine with a pearly light, sounds—birds, people's voices, the drone of a motorbike— seem to be coming from very far away, and then he notices Ted standing before the sofa, dressed in the solemn black robes of a priest. A sweet plume of smoke issues from the censer he's swinging, the silver chain clicking softly as the incense-bearing vessel falls back at regular intervals, striking the chain. In a soothing voice, he's muttering something in Latin. Just behind him is Linda, dressed as an altar boy, a black book in her hands. Oh, my God, Ziggy thinks, this is it, and I'm not ready.

He wakes with a start. His heart is pounding, but he's already savoring the slow ebb of the terror and he lets out a long breath, as if exhaling after a deep drag on a cigarette. He's here, after all, at Charlie's, just a few hours away from leaving for Detroit. He remembers what Przybylski told him, if you could call that telling, that we all wind up where he is, only he's got there quicker. Ziggy pulls himself up in bed, the contours of the room gradually taking shape in the dark. This is real, he reminds himself, this bedroom in Charlie's house in Burbank, and that dream has nothing to do with him, it's even less substantial than the Oasis and that fly in Przybylski's room, which exist only in his memory.

He swings out of bed and brings himself to his feet. This isn't where he belongs, though. He can't get back to Detroit soon enough. God, he thinks, I'm still alive, that's the important thing. Who knows for how long, but he's alive. And he's done enough traveling for now. What a bunch of stories he has for Maggie. Some he's not going to tell her, like what he learned about Gloria. That situation is just going to have to work itself out between Charlie and his wife. But the other stories, ah, the others. He can see himself at the kitchen table with a cup of coffee and maybe a piece of cake. Why don't you sit down, he'll tell her, and then he'll fill her in on his adventures, one by one.

His nervousness escalates as the plane makes its bumpy run up the tarmac. He clutches the seat through the ear-splitting shriek of the engines that lift the heavy machine off the runway and thrust it upward at a startling tilt. The plane shudders as it continues its climb, and he keeps himself clenched, his lips moving in some wordless prayer. Only after what seems like a lifetime does the long metal cylinder gradually level off. Shortly thereafter, the seat belt bell tolls softly, accompanied by a calm voice and, little by little, Ziggy begins to feel easier. I'm miles above the ground, on a jet, he tells himself, I'm OK. When the stewardess offers him a drink, he accepts gladly. He runs his lips across the rim of the plastic glass, the first sip of bourbon already warming him, expanding his newfound sense of well-being. No longer a terrified peasant cringing before the angry streaks of lightning and explosions of thunder, he's now a voyager returning home with wondrous tales of strange places and remarkable creatures. I've come from above the clouds, he'll be able to say. And the first person who'll hear those tales is Maggie.

Maggie's always been the one who's listened and made those stories real for him, ever since they were both teenagers, when he told her about the time he first started to believe he was going places. It was odd her mentioning that very story when he'd talked to her on the phone yesterday, the one about his fixing the flat for the guy from Chicago.

By the time he'd told it to Maggie, he'd already replayed that sequence of events over and over in his own head, what happened that November day. The sky was gray, no snow had fallen yet but pedestrians hurrying along Chene Street were remembering winter once again. Twelve-year-old Ziggy was one of them, on his way to get the evening paper for his father. As if it made any difference what was in the paper. "Oh, yeah," he knew his old man would say, "things have never been better. That's what they say. But any day they could cut back on my overtime and then where would we be?" He'd shake his head. "You know why they write this stuff? They're just trying to get you to spend money." His mother would be nodding approvingly as her husband went on. "You have to get ready for the bad times," he'd say, "because the bad times will always come."

But Ziggy didn't want to think about the bad times. It was the 1920's, after all, not the 1820's. Actually, he felt that his father would probably welcome bad times, the way he was always talking about the terrible things that had happened to his family, the uncles who were trapped in a coal mine in Pennsylvania, the aunt who died in a fire, the times, if you believed him, when he went without food for days. Even if, as he said, the only way they'd get him into a church is in a casket, in some ways he was just like the nuns with their stories of God's punishment.

Ziggy was telling all this to Maggie:

So I'm out on Chene getting the paper and this guy calls, "Hey, kid." I guess he had to say it twice before I realized he was talking to me. Then I look and I see this Packard pulled up to the curb, black, shiny, big as a battleship. "Hey, kid," the guy inside says again, "can you change a tire?" He wasn't from around here, I could tell right away—I never heard anyone who talked like that.

"Sure," I said. I'd already spotted the Illinois plates. "I can fix a flat." The car was one of those big four-door twelve-cylinder models that can go like the wind, with a long boxy hood with louvered ventilation panels, and that lady with wings on the grille that all Packards have.

"Can you work fast?" the guy asks. He was leaning across the front seat.

"Sure," I said, my eyes still on the car. I wanted to tell the guy they make Packards not far from here, over on Grand Boulevard.

"I'll give you a buck if you don't waste any time," he says. A buck! That's when I stopped looking over the car and started to pay attention to the guy. He had a wide face that made him look like an Indian and he was wearing a pale gray fedora pulled down close to his eyes. And he was big, like a bear in that fur coat he was wearing. When he stepped out, that Packard rocked a little. I couldn't help thinking, Where would you be going in a car like this?

"Here," the guy says, and he shows me the place in the back of the car where the jack and the spare were stored. "Ever work on a car like this before?"

"No," I told him the truth, "but I know about cars." I took out the spare, I leaned it against a light post, real gentle, and I put the tools on the sidewalk. Even though my eyes are on the

tools, I can't keep my mind off the guy's coat: it was fur, thick, dark and shiny. I'd never seen anything like it on a man. Well, I know how to change a tire, so I loosen the lugs on the flat, then set the jack under the car's frame. Still, out of the corner of my eye I keep looking at the big guy in the fur coat. He's on the sidewalk a few feet away. He lights a cigar and I can smell it as I'm lifting the car on the jack. I can see that people who are passing by get real quiet as they come close to him, and I tried to imagine what they're seeing: the shiny black Packard with the long hood, the man in the fur coat and fedora smoking his stogie, me at work on the car, like we were together. It made me feel proud to be part of the scene and for some reason I was reminded of the stories the nuns tell at school about the saints, who were always doing extraordinary things. That was the word Sister Rachel used, "extraordinary," and I remembered it. I always liked to collect unusual words, though I knew enough not to try to use them around the house when the old man was there.

"I thought Detroit was supposed to be a big town," the guy with the cigar says.

The idea that anyone would think Detroit wasn't a big town surprised me. The tablet I used for school had a drawing on the cover of the tall buildings rising along the Detroit River. There were a couple of big boats in the water and a plane was flying above those buildings. For a second or two I didn't know what to say. At last I told the guy, "I think they're talking about downtown."

He just grunted. "I been downtown," he says. Then he says, "I guess it's better than Canada, though, at least what I seen of it."

As I took off the flat I could hear the guy whistling to himself. "Are you from Chicago?" I ask him without taking my eyes off my work.

The guy laughed as if I'd just told him something funny. "Yeah," he says, "I never thought of it that way but you could say I come from Chicago. Chicago by way of Brooklyn."

I'm being real careful to keep working as I talk. "Chicago must be pretty big, huh?" I ask him.

"Yeah," the guy says. "It is. You should go there some day. It's some town, all right."

"I guess I will," I told him, and just saying it made me feel good. I was really working quick: I tightened the lugs and lowered the car, then gave the lugs a final turn before I put the flat where the spare was and replaced the tools. I knew I did a good job.

"Well," the guy says, "I guess I found a live one in this town. Thanks, kid, I'm giving you a bonus." He reaches into his pocket and hands me two silver dollars. I couldn't believe it—two dollars for that little work. What if I did that three or four times a day? I could make a lot of money. More than my old man, maybe. I was feeling pretty good but it was only up close, when the guy was giving me the money, that I really got a good look at his eyes. There was something hard there, not like what I'm used to seeing in my old man's eyes but something colder, and for a second or so I was actually scared. Still, it really felt good to have those two coins in my hand.

Then, this is where it gets funny, the guy says, "Go ahead, touch it." He could see that I'd been looking at his coat. "It's real, all right," he said. Well, I put my fingers to that sleeve real slow—as if the priest was letting me touch something in church that was old and expensive, like some golden altar cloth that came from Poland—and I ran my hand across that soft dark fur. I swear, I never felt anything like that before.

"Well," the guy says, "I got to get back to Chi-town." He turns toward the car. "You got what it takes, kid," he says. "You're going to go far."

Even after he was gone and the usual traffic was moving down Chene Street once more, ordinary people going by in cheap little cars, a streetcar full of Polacks on their way home with empty lunch boxes, I kept standing there wondering about that guy. He had to be part of the Chicago mob. So what did he come *to Detroit for? Could he have murdered someone? Did he bring in liquor from Canada? I kept squeezing the coins he gave me as if I thought they might disappear. I wondered where those coins had been. Over and over I kept remembering what he said: I was going to go far, I had what it takes.*

Well, it didn't take me long to remember that the old man sent me out to get the paper. Those silver coins weren't going to be any protection against him once he started his raging. And, yeah, sure enough, I can smell the booze when I get home and he's yelling, "Where the hell have you been, you little bastard? Didn't I tell you I wanted the paper now? Didn't I?" In a second the belt was out. Well, it doesn't do you any good to cry, you just kind of grit your teeth and try to harden yourself against the leather, you suck in your breath, and after a while it's over. I've got those silver dollars, I kept telling myself, they're mine, they're my secret. And what the guy said about me, that's my secret too. When the old man's had his fill and disappears with the paper, my mother comes in, quiet as a mouse. "Your father works so hard," she says, "you have to do what he says. Pray that God will forgive you for your disobedience."

"Yeah, ma, yeah," I tell her. But I don't say anything about the coins in my pocket. They belong to me.

It's what he told Maggie when he first began to think that she was the one, she was someone he could trust. There beside the priests' garden in the night that smelled of lilacs he told her, "I'm not going to be just another Polack like my old man."

"You're not just another Polack," she told him. "Not to me you aren't."

And here in the sky above the western United States, remembering his story, Ziggy's able to call up all the sensations of that November evening in the 1920's when he started to dream. He remembers the big Packard and the man who looked like an Indian, remembers the smell of his cigar, the way the gray fedora was pulled down close to his eyes, he remembers clutching the silver dollars, and most of all, he remembers reaching toward the sleeve of the man's coat.

"You wouldn't believe it," he told Maggie that night long ago, still able to touch the moment even earlier when he ran his fingers through that fur. "I never felt anything like it in my life."